A SECRET IN CONARD COUNTY

BY
RACHEL LEE

First Published in Great Britain 2016
By Mills & Boon, an imprint of HarperCollins*Publishers*
1 London Bridge Street, London, SE1 9GF

© 2016 Susan Civil Brown

ISBN: 978-0-263-91929-5

18-0216

"You want action," Lance answered simply.

"I get it. Well, I could take you to bed and make you forget it all for a while."

Everything inside Erin lurched sharply, as if from an earthquake. She'd been trying to bury it, but with those simple words he opened wide her growing hunger for him.

Irritated with herself, she snapped, "Think you're that good, huh?"

He amazed her by laughing. "I suspect we're both that desperate. You think I haven't noticed you eyeballing me?"

Oh, God. But she refused to be embarrassed. Far better to go on the attack. "You are a hunk," she said bluntly. "So? Does a swelled head go with that?"

"No, but another kind of swelling…"

"Stop it," she said sharply. "You can't jump my bones yet, and I don't want to jump yours."

Damn him, he caught the one word that gave her away. Arching a brow, he repeated, "Yet?"

* * *

Don't miss the next story in Rachel Lee's
Conard County: The Next Generation series,
coming to you Summer 2016.

Rachel Lee was hooked on writing by the age of twelve and practiced her craft as she moved from place to place all over the United States. This *New York Times* best-selling author now resides in Florida and has the joy of writing full-time.

Prologue

Two days had passed, but the bomber was still shaking. He hid out in the abandoned warehouse, in one tiny corner, and had built up an extra wall of empty crates to hide behind. He had plenty to fear.

Someone knew who he was. Someone had put him on a job that had caused him to shoot an FBI agent. Shooting people sickened him. Bombs were so much cleaner, and while he enjoyed reading about the aftermath, he didn't want to see it. One bomb, *poof*, the person was gone, turned into a red mist that left little enough behind. Shooting…not so clean. It was close, it was personal and he'd never forget that agent's face.

Plus, it was bad enough having the Feds after him even before he'd hurt one of their own.

Inevitably, his cell phone rang. Nobody should have his number, but someone had got it, and he knew what he'd hear on the other end: the mechanical voice that had given him this last job. Ordered him to complete it under threat of exposing him.

But he'd never dreamed he'd have to shoot that woman. Her face haunted him as no face ever had before. He needed to erase her, but was terrified of it. He needed to turn her into a red haze, and he didn't want to see it happen. What if she remembered *his* face?

His hand was still shaking as he answered the phone. As expected, it was the mechanical voice, calling from a number he couldn't locate or identify. Once the number had even changed.

"You fool," said the mechanically distorted voice. "You shot her, you blew up her house and she's still alive. I told you she was close to getting you."

"I know." His voice sounded thin to his own ears.

"You should never have called her to taunt her. You put her on guard. You made a mess of it. Now you're going to have to clean up your mess."

"I can't do anything in a hospital. Too many people." He never wanted to hurt a lot of people. Only his carefully chosen victims, women who had treated him badly. Not little kids. Not nurses and doctors. Not even FBI agents.

"Not now. She looks like she's going to survive. Later, when she's on leave, you're going to blow her up."

He could do that if he knew where to look. Some of his tremors faded. "Yes."

"I'll tell you when and where. And this time you'd better not screw it up, or I'll turn you in. You'll spend the rest of your life confined to a tiny cell. Maybe they'll even kill you."

Dealing death was one thing. Being killed was another. He said nothing.

"Do you understand me? You take her out and I won't turn you in."

"Yes," he said. A new mission, a new target. His heart rate steadied. He could do this.

"For now lay low. I'll tell you when it's time."

He looked at the bomb he'd been building, a pastime that soothed him, and felt a pang of disappointment. It would be ready soon, but now he couldn't use it.

"Harry," the voice said, reminding him it knew his name. "Do you understand?"

"Yes."

"Then wait for my call tomorrow, ten in the morning."

With a click, the line went dead, leaving only a hum. Slowly he turned off his own phone, removed the battery and turned back to the bomb. In some odd way the call had calmed him. He felt better now.

He went back to building his bomb.

Chapter 1

Erin Sanders opened her eyes. The flashing lights reflected from her rearview mirror straight into them. A cop was pulling up behind her in a tan SUV. She sighed, kissing off the hope of a brief nap, wondering why he was stopping. She'd pulled off the highway onto a dirt turnout just to take a little rest. Road hypnosis had begun to get to her, as well as fatigue, hardly surprising since she was still healing.

The day was bright and sunny, and being parked on the side of the road was hardly suspicious. As far as she could see, for miles around there wasn't another soul. Drying summer grasses, punctuated by brush, fences and mountains. Practically the middle of nowhere.

Then again, her job had taught her to be suspicious of even the apparently ordinary, like a cop pulling up behind her on a nearly deserted highway. In the fifteen minutes she'd been parked here, she'd watched several trucks tear by at top speed, and a few pickups and cars. Now there was nothing in sight except the vehicle pulling up behind her.

Instinctively she slipped her hand into her suit jacket and gripped the butt of her service pistol, thumb on the safety. A few minutes passed and she knew what he was doing: checking her out-of-state plates. At last she saw the door open and its occupant climb out. Watching in her side-view mirror she took in the khaki uniform, the tan cowboy hat, the gun belt. As he walked closer, she noted that he was tall and strongly built. He had an easy stride, a comfortable bearing. Okay, he wasn't looking for trouble.

She waited, not yet ready to remove her hand from her pistol. It was too soon to trust anyone, most especially someone in a uniform. The guy who had nearly killed her had been wearing a police uniform.

He reached the side of her car and bent down, giving her a full view of his rugged face. Late thirties, maybe? Sun and wind had taken a bit of toll. He looked at her from aquamarine eyes that reminded her of the waters around the Florida Keys. The punch of instant attraction she felt was unwelcome and unwanted.

"You okay, ma'am?" he asked through the three-inch opening she'd left in her window. His voice was pleasantly deep.

"Fine, just resting," she answered.

"Lonely place for a break," he remarked.

"Better than running off the road because I'm tired."

One corner of his mouth lifted. "True. You wanna tell me what you're holding under your jacket?"

Smart, too, she thought. And a stupid rookie mistake on her part to telegraph that she was holding something. Another sigh escaped her as she realized he wasn't just going to walk away. Now she'd have to explain and get out of the car despite the pain and deal with an alert county mountie. She could have stood on her rights, but he also had a court-granted right to protect himself. Time to cooperate.

"Deputy," she said, "I'm holding my sidearm. If you want to back up, I'll pull it out where you can see it and show you my ID."

He scanned her face quickly, nodded once and backed up to the rear of her vehicle. At the same time he released the snap on his own holster and drew his pistol.

He was good, Erin thought sourly. She hoped this didn't drag on for too long. On the other hand, at this point she was fairly certain he was exactly what he appeared to be. Now it was her turn to reassure him.

She pulled her pistol out of the holster, rolled down the window all the way and placed the pistol on the top of the car, grimacing as her ribs screamed. Dang, she felt naked now. And he was still watching from the back, his gun at the ready.

She pushed the door open, wincing with every movement. Getting away for a while had been a great idea. Sitting still for so long in a car hadn't been. Every single injury that had brought her to this point protested. Torn muscle and scarred skin cried out. She wondered if she'd be able to stand.

Moving cautiously, as much because of her body as anything, she climbed out, keeping her hands in plain view. Then, facing him, her hands up, she called, "FBI. I'm going to pull my ID out of my pocket, okay?"

"Go for it," he answered, keeping a bead on her.

She'd stuffed it in the pocket of her jacket. Now she jabbed her aching fingers in and fished it out. It took both her hands to flip it open and show it.

He scanned it, then holstered his pistol and walked up to her. She let him take the badge case and study it.

"Mind if I call this in?"

"Be my guest, as long as I can sit down again."

Those amazing eyes of his leaped from the case to her face. "What's wrong?"

"Two weeks out of the hospital. Not everything is up to par."

"Wanna sit in my car?"

"That's more moving than I want to do right now, Deputy." She scanned his name badge. Deputy Conroe. "I'll just perch here while you check me out."

She hated it when he took her pistol off the roof of her car and carried it with him. She understood, but hated it anyway. These days she couldn't stand having the thing out of her sight.

Five minutes passed while she sat with her feet on the dirt and her bottom on the edge of the driver's seat. Warm, dry prairie winds blew over her, and at last another burst of traffic arrived, sweeping past them and leaving even more heat in its wake. She watched them go by in both directions, hoping they were all feeling better than she was. On their way to exciting destinations. Not just on the run from themselves.

She heard crunching and looked over her left shoulder to see Deputy Conroe coming back. He carried her badge case and her gun, apparently satisfied.

She managed a faint smile as he passed them back to her. "Sorry for the hassle, Agent Sanders."

"No hassle," she admitted. "Once you knew I was armed we were going down this road, weren't we? Some things you have to do."

He surprised her then by squatting so their faces were

nearly level. "You're not all right. Even I can see it. You want a ride into town? We can pick up your car later."

She looked into that rugged face and read more than a professional concern. "I honestly don't know what I'd do in town. I'm just rambling."

"I heard. So let's get you and your gear to someplace where you can rest. If you're worried about your car, I can get it towed before we leave here."

She wondered what else he'd heard in those five minutes. She had the worst urge to tell him she didn't need any help, but a glance to the west warned her there wasn't much time left before the sun sank behind those mountains. Weariness had caught up with her and seemed to be deepening by the minute. What was she going to do? Sleep out here in her car? Messed up though she was, she retained a vestige or two of common sense.

"Thanks," she said finally.

"Give me your keys. Suitcases in the trunk, right? I'll help you get into my car, we'll wait for the tow and then I'll take you into town. You can sleep if you want."

For the first time in months, Erin felt peace wash over her, as if the universe had just sent a blessing her way. Maybe there was still some good left after all.

Lance Conroe figured Agent Erin Sanders had no idea how bad she appeared right now. Framed by short dark hair, her face displayed smooth, classic lines, but just then she looked as pale as white muslin, and awfully fragile. Her sherry-brown eyes were a bit sunken. Given what she did for a living, he didn't figure this was the former version of herself. Sure must have been some kind of hell that put her in a hospital and left her dragged out like this.

He had to walk slowly to stay beside her, but he didn't offer to steady her, suspecting that might offend her.

When it came time for her to climb in the passenger seat of his SUV, however, she didn't even try to argue against his assistance. He slipped his arm around her shoulders, his other beneath her knees and put her in the seat. Too easily. Light as a feather. Too light.

"Nap," he suggested. "I'll get a tow here in about twenty minutes."

She closed her eyes and didn't stir at all as he radioed for the tow truck and told them to step on it. While they waited, he unloaded two suitcases from the trunk of her vehicle. It must be her personal vehicle because he didn't find additional weapons but he did find a Kevlar vest and dark blue FBI operations jacket. He brought those, too, placing everything in the back end of his car, squeezing it in among his own collection of job tools, from shotguns and ammunition, to protective clothing and rain gear. A cop's trunk was his home away from home.

Then he checked her glove box, but all it contained were the owner's manual and her registration. Sure that everything was safe, he stood by, waiting for the truck.

He wondered if she'd be gone by tomorrow or if he'd get a chance to learn her story. Whatever it was, it was bad.

Thirty minutes later he was following the tow truck toward town. In all that time, Erin Sanders hadn't stirred. His radio crackled, he'd reported what he was doing, and as he drove he passed another deputy headed out to take over his section of the state highway.

Then he heard a cell phone ring. He half expected Erin to sleep right through it, but maybe some things ran deeper than sleep for a law enforcement officer. She popped her eyes open and felt around in her pocket, pulling out her cell. She lifted it to the side of her face and said, "Sanders."

He kept his gaze fixed on the truck and her car just ahead. He'd told them to put her car at the garage. Larry would keep it in his lot until she wanted it back.

"Fran, I'm fine," he heard Erin say. "I was dozing beside the road and a deputy picked me up. Of course he checked me out when he found out I was armed."

A long silence.

"I don't know exactly where I am. Somewhere in Wyoming. We're headed to some town where I can find a bed."

"Conard City," Lance interjected helpfully.

"Conard City," Erin repeated with a slight nod to him. "And if you're worried about it, you can check him out. Deputy Conroe."

"Lance Conroe, Conard County Sheriff's Office."

"Did you catch that, Fran? Okay. I'm fine, just tired."

Another long silence, then Erin spoke impatiently. "Why would I want to do that? I've got the whole kit and caboodle, all the wounds and scars, an ex who pesters me, a killer who got away, a body taking forever to heal and nightmares that won't quit. What more do I need? Another man? No, I will not call Tom, and I won't be returning his calls. I need this break."

Whoa, thought Lance, that was an entire mess in one succinct passage. He felt a bit of sympathy for her as he heard her wind up the call and put her phone away.

"Sorry," she said. "You didn't need to hear that."

"Too much information?" he asked lightly. "It's okay."

"No, it's not okay. I sounded whiny."

"You sounded fed up. Big difference."

She stirred at last, turning slowly in her seat, her cautious movements betraying her. Something still hurt, something was still healing and moving wasn't her favorite activity. At once his mind slipped into another gear. He'd planned to leave her at the La-Z-Rest Motel, which for all it was decrepit was at least clean, but right across the state highway was a truck stop. No silence, even at night.

"You're a nice man, Deputy," she said.

"Lance. Not doing anything special."

"I beg to differ." She fell silent for a few seconds. "I saw signs for a big resort on my way here. Is it open?"

"Not yet." Biggest joke around. Finally they were pulling everything together for the long-promised resort and it all had come to a huge halt last spring because of a landslide. It was as if the Fates conspired against the town. Not that everyone wanted the place, but it would have offered some jobs and put a little extra cash in the local economy. "All we have to offer these days is a flea-bag motel across the highway from a truck stop."

"It'll do. I've slept all kinds of places."

He imagined she had. He wished he could put her someplace better, but the few rooming houses rented by the week or month, not by the day. And asking a family to take her in would probably be miserable for her and everyone else. He thought briefly of his aunt but knew he couldn't make the offer without checking with Maria first. So the motel it was. She'd probably be there only one night anyway.

"You need to eat?" he asked.

"Why do you ask?"

"Because I can take you to a diner in town before I leave you at the motel. Considering you don't seem to be moving too well, that might be better than trying to cross the highway to the truck stop."

Silence. For some reason he expected her to get vocally annoyed by his interference. It really was none of his business. Yet the thought of dropping her off like that seemed hardly better than having left her in her car by the roadside.

"Knight-errant?" she asked.

"Who, me?" That surprised a laugh out of him. "Just a cop trying to help a fellow cop. The way you're moving, I'm not sure they should have let you out of the hospital."

"Apparently you don't have much experience with insurance. Anyway, I wouldn't have let them keep me."

He could well believe that. "Listen," he said presently. "The speed limit by the motel is supposed to be thirty. Well, we get all types coming along the state highway, and some don't read too well. The thought of you trying to cross that piece of road when some knucklehead comes barreling along at sixty…"

"Got you," she answered. "Thanks. The diner sounds good."

He reached for his radio, and called Larry who was driving just ahead of him. "Larry, change of plans. Take the lady's car to the La-Z-Rest. Thanks."

The woman beside him spoke. "That's the name of the motel?"

"Yup."

"Oh, God," she said. It was all he could do not to laugh again. Instead he just said, "Yup," once more.

Then she utterly astonished him by laughing quietly herself. "The La-Z-Rest," she said. "I can hardly wait."

She really had arrived at the ends of the earth, Erin thought as she eased into a booth at the nearly empty diner. Lance Conroe took a minute to let the dispatcher know where he was, then followed her inside.

Just as he settled across from her, a Gorgon of a woman slapped menus down in front of them. "Coffee or the fancy stuff?" she asked.

"Coffee," Lance replied, then looked at Erin. "Latte if you want it."

"I'd love a latte." She tried smiling at the Gorgon, who apparently went by the name of Maude, but after a flickering look, the woman dismissed her and walked away.

"Nice," she murmured.

"Just Maude." Lance smiled. "The food makes up for it unless you're a vegetarian."

"Not a chance," she replied, picking up the plastic-covered menu with a hand that trembled ever so slightly.

"You're not okay," Lance said bluntly.

"Just tired. Too many hours driving, too much sitting still. I shouldn't have pushed it so far today."

"I thought medical leave meant resting and relaxing."

She bridled. "So they told you about that, huh? Blabbermouths."

For the first time, he sighed. "It's written all over you. What happened?"

She'd learned long ago not to be open about much, certainly not about her job. Not with anyone except another agent. Something in his expression made her want to dump the whole story, but she resisted. "Bad outcome to a bad confrontation."

He compressed his lips a bit, simply nodding, then leaned back as the coffee was slammed down in front of them. The clatter seemed pointed.

"Give us a couple, Maude?" Lance said, looking up. "My guest hasn't had a chance to read the menu yet."

"I know what *you're* having," Maude grumped, then glared at Erin as if she were a clogged drain line before stomping away.

"What a piece of work," Erin whispered.

"Everyone's used to it. And like I said, the food more than makes up for it."

Erin reached for the coffee first, however. She needed the caffeine in hopes that it would stave off the fatigue that seemed to be overwhelming her, at least until she reached a bed. Not only did she hurt all over, but she had begun to feel light-headed. Food would probably help that, as would the milk in the latte. She drained half of it before she even picked up the menu again.

The words seemed to dance in front of her eyes. "Damn," she said. "I can't even focus. You pick for me."

"Carnivore?"

"Definitely."

"Hungry?"

"Famished." She seemed to remember having eaten last night. Oh, man, this was bad. She'd been warned not to push it too hard, but had she listened? Tom's voice came back to her, *Hardheaded, stubborn, idiotic...* Maybe he was right about her.

She put her chin in her hand and closed her eyes as she listened to Lance Conroe order two steak sandwiches. Tired though she was, the sound of it made her mouth water.

This deputy was being incredibly nice to her, she thought. Maybe it was just cop-to-cop courtesy, as he'd said, but it felt like more than that. Like he was genuinely concerned about her. More than willing to go out of his way to make sure she was looked after. Pretty special. From a friend she might expect it, but from a total stranger?

He let her be, too, as she sat there with her eyes closed, hovering at the edge of much-needed sleep. She couldn't believe how much her injuries had taken out of her. Surely she ought to be coming back faster. Nor did it feel good to know that the man who had done this to her was still out there somewhere. Oh, he was being hunted, but after the past months, she didn't have much faith that they'd find him. Anyone who stayed off the grid and kept moving was pretty much out of reach, even these days. Disposable cell phones, working under the table for cash, just enough to get by, skipping town every few days…yeah, you could hide forever until you slipped up. Her personal Moriarty didn't slip up often.

Their meals arrived with a pointed clatter and slam. Erin jumped, her eyes popping open, her hand instinctively sliding beneath her jacket again.

"Easy," said Lance Conroe. "That was the local version of the dinner bell."

Despite the surge of adrenaline that had just coursed through her, she had to smile faintly. The local dinner bell? Cute. But the adrenaline proved salutary, and she felt wide-awake. It wouldn't last, but it might get her through a meal.

In front of her sat a huge sandwich on thick slabs of bread with steak poking out all around. Juice ran from it onto her plate, sneaking up on the French fries. The aromas were heavenly, causing her mouth to water, and fatigue seemed to slip away as she reached for half the sandwich.

Lance let her eat without interruption as he ate his own sandwich. Her eyes wandered out the window, watching people strolling by, noting the age of the town with hints of the Wild West and hints of the Victorian and hints of the twenties and thirties. A mix that managed to be charming.

"Small town," she half asked.

"Five thousand in town, another four thousand or so scattered all over the county. There are smaller towns in Wyoming, but bigger ones, too. We're big enough to be on the map."

That description brought another faint smile to her face. "But small enough for some good gossip?"

"It fills a lot of hours," he admitted.

"It won't cause you any trouble to be seen having a meal here with a strange woman?"

He shrugged. "What are they going to say? This couldn't be any more public."

"True."

"And it's not as if I'm married."

Her smile widened a shade as the calories began to hit her system. "Well, that takes all the juice out of the gossip."

"Maybe. Or it could rev it up." He shrugged again and took another bite of his sandwich. "So, do you have any idea where you're going?"

"No," she admitted. "I just wanted to get away from Chicago, and figured I could wander through the West, take in the sights. What I didn't count on was the pull of the mountains. I wanted to reach them, once I started seeing them, and...I drove too long today."

"Well, you've reached them now. Hang around a few days and I'll be glad to take you for a drive to some really spectacular views."

Quite a nice offer, but it made her feel uneasy. Was she leaving one mess behind, however temporarily, to make another one? She didn't want to. Instead of answering, she looked out the window again and noticed how flattened everything looked. Apparently the sun had slipped behind the mountains, and while the sky remained bright overhead, the shadows that added dimension were gone. Curious. She liked it. It seemed to suit her rather unpleasant mood.

But then, weary or not, she realized she was being rude to a man who was only trying to help her out. He didn't deserve it, and while he might put it down to her being unwell, it still wasn't right.

She turned to him again. "It's a pretty little town," she offered.

"A bit worn about the edges. When the resort was getting ready to open, they started sprucing us up a bit. New sidewalks, new streetlights, maybe some paint…but it hardly got started before the landslide shut them down."

She managed another bite of the sandwich, knowing she needed the energy. "Are they going to try again?"

"I don't know. They were almost ready to open, but there was a lot of destruction. Nobody knows if they'll write it off now. Thing is, one of their people lives in town now. He said that landslide was a freak of some bad weather. The company hired him on again to recheck the geology up there. That landslide may have been a one-time thing, and if so…" He shrugged.

"So everything's on hold."

"It's been on hold more years than I can count. We've had at least five companies interested. This last one came closer than anyone has. They even finished building a new runway to handle more air traffic." He shrugged. "Still, who can say when a project becomes more trouble than it's worth?"

"Not being in the business, I couldn't venture a guess."

He nodded and pushed his plate aside. His sandwich was gone and he'd ignored the fries. Erin took another bite of hers, finally feeling the restorative effects of the food. "If you're in a hurry," she said tentatively.

That drew a broad smile from him. "We're rarely in a hurry around here. Oh, we get our share of problems, everything from toxic dumping to a serial killer, but it's not constant. Small-town policing is pretty laid-back usually."

"You like it?"

"After ten years in Denver, I love it."

"Did you grow up here?"

"I sure did. My dad was a schoolteacher."

"So you still have family here?"

"My aunt Maria, bless her heart." He leaned back as his coffee cup was refilled by the inimitable Maude, who then glared at Erin to ask, "Another latte?"

"Please."

The woman stomped off.

Erin pushed her own plate aside. "I guess I'm going to need a doggie bag."

Lance leaned forward, resting his elbows on the table. "No problem. You know what you said about a bad confrontation with a bad guy?"

She stiffened, barely nodding.

"I had something similar happen to me. Hence the small-town policing. Some things you never want to experience twice."

Wow, she thought. Instantly she liked him even more. He'd walked in her shoes and there was probably very little she had to tell him, because he understood.

Except maybe he didn't understand this running part. Well, it wasn't exactly running. She wasn't fit for duty yet, and the Bureau had wanted to put her in protection. Instead she'd chosen to clear out for a while, since the bad guy was still on the loose. No, not exactly running, she assured herself. Merely taking a wise evasive maneuver.

The fresh latte arrived along with a foam box for her leftovers. Apart from being a Gorgon, Maude seemed to read minds. Not a word passed, not a query about whether she wanted to take that half sandwich with her. Of course, maybe it never occurred to the woman that anyone would leave her cooking behind.

"You're looking tired again," Lance said suddenly. "Let's go. I'll help you move into the motel and get you registered."

"I need to pay."

"I run a tab with Maude, so forget it. As for the motel, no payment required until you leave."

Erin felt her brows rise. "That's a great way to get ripped off."

He smiled again. "It would be if they let everyone do that. FBI? I think they'll give you the same courtesy they'd give me."

She was beginning to feel as if she'd gone down the rabbit hole to a very different universe.

Chapter 2

Erin awoke early in the morning, and for a blessed few minutes nothing hurt. The TV ran quietly, creating background noise to mask the engine roars from the truck stop. The half-finished latte stood on the nightstand. The clock told her she'd slept fourteen hours. Fourteen. And without a pain pill.

She didn't want to move. As soon as she stirred, the pain would return, at least some of it. She needed to get on the road again. The guy who'd nearly killed her was off the grid, and she had to stay off it, too, as much as possible. Keep moving, use cash wherever possible and wait for the phone call to tell her he was caught, or until she felt well enough to resume duty. She'd chosen this over protective custody, and every single day asked herself why. But she knew why. She felt safer in the middle of nowhere, and she knew she couldn't stand being in protection, virtually locked up in a safe house under constant guard.

They were sure he still wanted to get her. After all, he'd apparently come for her after someone had leaked her identity and that she was getting close to finding him. A serial bomber. Great thing to have on her tail. A great reason not to feel safe in a safe house, even if cabin fever wouldn't have driven her crazy.

She should get up and get going again. No matter how much it hurt. But she could see no harm whatsoever in enjoying these few minutes of peace, where no threat hovered, where no pain touched her.

She'd left the lights on, and she dared to turn her head a little. For a supposed fleabag, the La-Z-Rest wasn't that bad. The decor was badly outdated Western, the kind that shrieked cheap and old, but everything she'd used so far had been spotlessly clean. It would never get five stars, or even two, but all she cared was that it was clean.

Finally, the time to move had come. Her damaged body began to ache again, to throb in a few places. Sleep was losing its grip on her brain.

Sighing, moving slowly, she sat up and swung her feet to the floor. No carpeting, just linoleum that had been scrubbed almost bare of its pattern. Somehow that was reassuring. Next, a hot shower, as hot as she could stand. That would loosen her up for dressing.

Then she had to decide. Move on again? Or stay put for a few days? Staying put and walking the streets of this town lost in time seemed amazingly appealing after all the driving. And walking would help keep her loosened up, keep the pain from reaching shrieking intensity as it did if she held still for too long. The way it probably would when she stood up after such a lengthy sleep.

Agony struck her the minute she rose. It froze her in place while she sucked air from the shock of it, then it eased enough for her to move. It would get better. The docs had promised. It was just that she had suffered so much injury.

Which was putting it mildly, she thought with a kind of bitter amusement as she eased her way into the bathroom and turned on the shower. One of them had even tried to joke about it. "Pain is your friend. It means you're still alive."

Well, that was debatable, she thought as she stood under the hot spray. There were times when surviving being shot and being blown up didn't seem like such a good thing. Ironic, though, that the gunshot that had brought her down just as she stumbled on the bomber had helped protect her when the bomb blew up her house. Very ironic. Maybe someday she could even tell the story with humor. Not yet, however. Definitely not yet.

A half hour later, she was dressed in a light beige slack suit—probably not the style for this place—and comfortable walking flats. She still hadn't made up her mind about moving on, but she figured she'd stick out on the streets dressed this way. So what? Only Fran knew where she was, and she couldn't face the restrictive waistband on jeans today. This slack suit had elastic gores in the waist, reducing the pressure on some of her scars.

Moving with care, she managed to get her shoulder holster on over the royal blue shell and put her pistol into it. Once she pulled on the lightweight matching jacket, only an experienced eye would be able to tell she was armed.

She put her credentials and her wallet in the slacks pockets and felt as ready as she would ever be to face this day.

Breakfast first, she decided. But when she stepped outside, she saw what Lance had meant about this stretch of highway. Crossing it on foot might be suicidal unless a person could move swiftly, and that was beyond her now.

Car keys in her hand, she debated whether to try to find that diner. And she still had to pay for the room.

As she was standing there in an unusual state of indecision, a sheriff's vehicle rolled up right in front of her. Lance sat in the driver's seat and he leaned his elbow on the open window as he smiled at her.

"Saw your car still here. You staying for a while?"

"Thinking about it," she admitted. "Mostly thinking about breakfast. I see what you mean about the highway."

"Like I said, some fools can't read and others don't care. Hop in and I'll take you to the diner."

She liked the way he suggested she hop in, especially since he'd practically had to pour her into his vehicle when he picked her up yesterday. "Don't you have to work?"

"You're my work now."

Thunderstruck, she narrowed her eyes. "What do you mean?"

"Well, after I checked you out yesterday, my boss got a call from the Bureau. Asked us to keep an eye on you as long as you wanted to stay. So here I am, your protection detail. Wanna tell me to go to hell?"

The way he asked the question and arched one eyebrow drew a reluctant laugh from her. "No, but I do want breakfast."

"And the sheriff wants to meet you. So if you want to climb in, we'll do the diner first."

So much for a low profile, she thought, scanning the highway as her nerves started to jump. Why had the sheriff been dragged in on this? Why did they feel she needed protection?

All of a sudden a lot of questions hammered at her. "Sheriff first," she said decisively.

"You got it."

Appearing more rested, and dressed in that quietly elegant pantsuit, Erin looked as if she ought to be strolling the streets of a much bigger, classier burg than this one, Lance thought as he drove them toward the sheriff's offices. Kinda pretty, too, now that her brown eyes didn't appear quite as sunken. But no one would mistake her yet for being in perfect health. She did resemble a Fed now, though.

"You're looking a whole lot better this morning," he said.

"Fourteen hours of sleep will do that."

"Fourteen?" He whistled. "My dogs wouldn't let me get away with that."

A quiet laugh reached him. "How many do you have?"

"Two. One's an English mastiff, the other a short-haired Saint Bernard. When they jump on the bed, I don't have much of a choice."

"I guess not. There wouldn't be any room left."

"And to think I considered getting an Irish wolfhound once upon a time."

"Uh… I've only seen one in my life but they're huge, aren't they?"

"Practically need a stable for one. My guys are good dogs, by the way, so if you ever come by my place, you don't need to be nervous. They'd give away the store, not guard it. Of course, the mastiff might not let you leave after you robbed me blind."

That drew a genuine laugh from her, a nice sound that he was glad to hear. "I think I'd like to meet them," she said.

"That can be arranged."

At least she was no longer looking haunted and inde-cisive as she had been while standing outside her room. There was an instant change, though, when they pulled up at the sheriff's offices, across the street from the court-house square. Maybe she was expecting memories to be brought up, things she didn't want to talk about.

Well, he couldn't do anything about that. The sher-iff was a good man, but she'd have to find that out on her own.

It hurt to watch her get out of his car, but he didn't try to help. He sensed a huge independence in this woman and figured he wouldn't be wise to offend it any more than he already had. She had clearly not been thrilled to find out the Bureau had requested protection.

When she walked into the front office, he watched heads turn. A woman dressed like this would get atten-tion anywhere in this town, but everything about her suggested that she was federal. Even so, as lovely as she was, she'd draw male attention anywhere.

Elderly Velma, at the dispatcher's desk, quickly stubbed out her illicit cigarette. A first. Lance could have laughed.

"Agent Sanders for the sheriff," Lance announced.

"He's waiting," Velma answered in her smoke-roughened voice. "Coffee?"

"No, thanks," Lance said swiftly. Velma's coffee was legendarily bad. He gestured to the hallway leading to the back offices and let Erin precede him. He could al-most feel the air going out of the front office as depu-ties relaxed.

Interesting effect, he thought as he rapped two knuck-les on Gage's closed door.

"Come," Gage called.

Gage Dalton, a dark-eyed man with dark hair dashed with gray and a face marred by a burn scar on one side, rose with a wince. As Lance made the introductions, he shook Erin's hand. "Have a seat, Agent. Thanks for stopping by."

"I had a choice?" she asked wryly as she eased herself into a wooden chair. Once certain she was settled, Lance sat nearby. "Did Tom bother to tell you why he's so all-fired worried about me?"

"Actually yes. You got a call just before you were attacked. The guy knows who you are. He may be afraid that you could identify him. Your ASAC said he knows the risk is small, but it's not one he wants to take." Then he changed direction, surprising Lance. "A bomb got me, too," he said, touching the scar on his face.

Erin had survived a bombing? Lance looked at her, shocked. Her face seemed to have frozen.

"I was DEA," Gage continued. "It was a car bomb. Unfortunately my family was in the vehicle and I had run back into the house to get a diaper bag. I survived, they didn't."

Erin paled and whispered, "I'm so sorry."

"A long time ago. We can make peace with almost anything, it seems. But I want you to understand why this department isn't going to take the Bureau's request lightly. I once ignored an instinct that my family was in danger, to my everlasting sorrow. Your office has a feeling and I'm not going to ignore it. Lance has volunteered for protection duty, and we can get another few on board before the day is out. Good ones. Men with the kind of experience that often took them to undisclosed locations overseas. That protection will continue until you decide to leave. All I ask is that you put up with it. We'll be as unobtrusive as possible."

"Isn't this overkill?" Erin asked after a moment. "No one knows where I am."

"Supposedly no one knew where I lived either. But the Bureau knows, and apparently someone had loose enough lips to let it be known you were working the case against the bomber."

She drew an audible breath. "They told you that? They believe it was someone on the inside?"

"Yes. Which gives me cause for concern. How many people at your field office now know where you are?"

Lance felt his gut tighten. He'd never imagined this. Never.

"I'll leave right away, then," Erin said immediately.

"If you want, you can. But I suggest you hang around here for at least a few days. Take a breather and know we'll be watching out for you. Looks to me like you need rest more than anything else right now."

She looked down at her hands, resting on her lap. "I don't get why they told you all this."

"I do," Gage answered. "They apparently feel that if anyone knows where you are, the wrong person might know. And moving on won't necessarily help."

At that she raised her head. "Why not?"

"Because from here there are only a few directions to go. Because your whereabouts have been known to the Bureau since midafternoon yesterday. That's a long time if someone is hunting you."

"You're telling me I drove myself into a kill box."

Lance drew a sharp breath. When he'd helped Erin, he'd never anticipated the possibility that he could be causing her bigger problems. Nor, apparently, had she.

"Well..." Gage drawled the word slowly. "Truth is, Agent, that there are a whole lot of little bottlenecks in these mountains. Any one of them could have been a bad place to stop if you let someone know where you were. Lance here verified your ID, normal precaution. Then I guess from what he said that you talked to a friend and told her exactly where you are."

Erin didn't respond for several long seconds. "In short, I was an idiot."

"Didn't say that," Gage answered. "Sooner or later, your ID would have been checked simply because you're carrying a concealed weapon. Sooner or later you'd have told a concerned friend where you were. Just a matter of time. Going off the grid isn't easy for someone with a lot of connections. It would have been easier to slip away if you'd reached Seattle or some other big city, but it happened here, a place the state highway runs through and very little else. You can head east, you can head west out of here. If you have time you could get to a bigger city. We don't know how much time there is, so we'll just keep a friendly eye out."

Erin slowly shook her head, and finally Lance spoke. "Maybe it's better it happened here."

She turned those brown eyes on him. "Why?"

"Because strangers stick out around here. Easy for us to keep an eye out for you."

"And we have a fairly good department," Gage added. "You could have wound up someplace where they couldn't have provided the coverage we can."

Lance felt his heart tug a bit as he watched Erin lower her head. From what little he knew, she'd been through a hell of a lot, and now she'd been sandbagged. But what she finally said surprised him.

"This isn't fair to you guys. I should just hit the road as fast as I can and disappear again. Besides, he's a bomber. That type usually hunkers down. Him following me across the country is so unlikely."

Gage looked at Lance. No doubt, the sheriff was leaving it to him since he'd volunteered to be on this woman's protection detail.

"No," he heard himself say. "Maybe he won't follow you. We can't know that with any certainty. It's enough for me that your boss is worried about it. Regardless, you need more rest, and we can make sure you get it. Providing protection is part of what we do."

"But to a single individual? That's expensive. Man, I should have just let them lock me in the safe house."

"We provide as much protection as any individual needs," Lance replied. "Sometimes that's a whole lot. As for the safe house…"

"As for the safe house," Gage said, "apart from going nuts, which I know I would have, I can tell you this. I was undercover DEA. Nobody was supposed to know who I was or where my family lived. We got found anyway. I personally don't have a whole lot of faith in safe houses."

Erin looked at the two of them, one after another, and he watched something change in her face. He tensed and waited, expecting to hear her announce she was hitting the road anyway. But then she knocked the wind from him.

"To hell with it," she said bluntly. "I'm sick of this creep. If he's crazy enough to follow me, if he wants a showdown at high noon, this is as good a place as any."

Outside, she stood on the sidewalk, breathing in the warm summer air, taking in her surroundings. Lance stood beside her but said nothing. He seemed to know when not to say anything—a rare quality.

"That's the diner?" she asked, gesturing at the sign she saw half a block away.

"Yup. City Diner, aka Maude's diner. Wanna walk or drive?"

"I need to walk. Otherwise everything tightens up and I'll never get my strength back."

One stoplight. The end of the earth. Only two ways out. A kill box. But a charming one. If she had to take a stand, this was indeed as good a place as any. She just hoped there would be no collateral damage.

She stepped into the street when it was clear and began crossing. With every step, some part of her protested but she ignored it. Nor was she unaware that the man beside her measured his pace to her much slower one. No comment, he just did it.

When they reached the diner, pain had caused a little perspiration to break out on her forehead. Not bad. Better than it had been. She just wished there was some way to speed her recovery.

He opened the diner door for her and let her choose where to sit. She preferred booths and headed for one, hoping she could ease into it without too much trouble. With her back to a wall and the street visible through the big plate glass window, she felt safer.

She winced a few times and had to bite back a groan, but she slid into the booth without too much ado. Lance sat across from her.

"Don't they give you something for that pain?" he asked.

"I've got enough prescription painkillers in my suitcase to raise eyebrows. I don't want to take them."

He nodded. "Latte?"

"Please."

So when the Gorgon's daughter, who looked like a younger clone of Maude, arrived to slap down the menus, he promptly ordered their coffee and asked for a few minutes. Erin barely glanced at her, just long enough to take in the name Mavis. "A whole family," she whispered.

Lance laughed quietly. "The parts I've seen anyway."

She tried to smile as she squirmed a bit, seeking that elusive position that would be more comfortable.

"Maybe," he suggested quietly, "you could trust me just a bit and take a little pain medicine. Not enough to make you loopy, but maybe enough to give you some ease."

She answered with the bald truth. "I'm afraid of it. When I was in the hospital they kept me pretty well doped. If I need a brain, I don't want it stuffed with cotton and rainbows."

He nodded understanding. "But maybe you could let us be your brains for a few hours. I doubt the guy could be here already. You can't get much farther from anywhere than here. You could give yourself a few hours to rest some more. You need rest as much as activity, you know."

"Speaking from experience?" she asked dubiously.

"Four gunshot wounds of experience," he answered flatly.

She felt small. He'd already alluded to a bad confrontation and hinted that he'd been wounded, too. She had just assumed…well, what had she assumed? That nobody had ever really walked in her shoes? No, she definitely was nowhere near par. "Sorry."

"For what? I get your worries. I also understand that part of what we're trying to do here is take some of this off your shoulders. Gage understood why you didn't like the idea of a safe house. I understand how much you must resent needing all this recovery time. Of course, I didn't have to wonder if I was being stalked by a killer either."

She met his amazing blue-green eyes just as the lattes dropped in front of them. A pulse of pure, hot desire hit her core—probably the only place that didn't hurt, and he was making it ache.

"You look at them menus yet?" Mavis demanded.

"Still trying to decide between breakfast and lunch," Lance answered, giving her a friendly smile. "Hey, Mavis, you're not that busy right now. You can spare the booth."

"Yeah, right," the woman grumped, but she moved on.

Lance turned back to Erin. "We'd better hurry or she'll order for us."

"Would she?" An honest laugh trickled out of Erin and she relaxed internally as she reached for the menu.

"She would," Lance answered. "Years ago, when the former sheriff was trying to lose some weight, it turned into an epic battle. He liked to come over here for coffee. Well, Maude was always slamming a piece of pie down in front of him. Got to be quite a thing."

"Did the old sheriff lose the weight?"

"Twenty pounds. But I think he must have been cutting out stuff elsewhere."

"He didn't have to eat it."

"He did if he wanted to keep coming in here. Never insult Maude's pie."

"I'll keep that in mind." She was also really starting to like this place. In a very short time, Lance had made her feel like she was an insider, not an outsider, an unusual way for her to feel. Generally speaking, Feds were about as well-loved as a fungus infection, even among law enforcement.

She finally settled on an omelet and some toast. Heavy food didn't sit well on her stomach. Maybe it never would again. She brushed the thought aside and sipped her latte. Time to be friendly. It seemed the least she could do. "I appreciate all you and your department are doing for me."

"No, you don't," he said, but his eyes twinkled a bit. "You hate it."

When had she become an open book? But she knew. She hadn't been concealing her thoughts and feelings too well since the incident. It seemed to require more energy than she wanted to invest. "Okay, I wish it wasn't necessary."

"That'll do." He smiled at her over his own coffee. "How much can you tell me about what happened? I got a little from what the sheriff said, but I don't imagine they told him a whole lot either. I don't have to tell you it would help to know what we're up against."

"A raving madman," she answered. Moving carefully, she leaned back against the stiff but padded cushion, felt scars twinge.

"Professional assessment?" he asked.

"No," she admitted. "Purely personal. You get any training at Quantico?"

"Some," he acknowledged.

"Then you've had a look into the minds of people who do this kind of thing. We'd like to think they're insane. They're usually not."

"No, they aren't." He waited, regarding her steadily. She sorted through her head, trying to decide what he really needed to know, and how much she could safely share. The Bureau liked to play close to the vest, revealing nothing until a case went to trial or a grand jury. But then, cops couldn't freely discuss any open investigation. He was right, though. They needed to know something about this guy.

She sighed. "Without getting into details…"

"I know. Just what you think you can."

"Okay. Serial bomber. Not a man who just likes to

see things go boom. He likes to kill women. Individual women."

Lance drew an audible breath. "Okay," he said after a moment.

She hesitated, then plunged in. "This is not for distribution. We can't find a link between his victims except for gender and approximate age. All his bombs are different. So for a while we weren't sure we didn't have some copycatting going on. Then I found...a piece of evidence that linked all the bombs. We knew we were after one guy."

"So you've got this guy who has it in for women."

"Apparently. Little did we guess I'd be his next target."

Lance swore quietly. "But why? Any ideas? I mean..." He paused. "I guess if you can't profile his victims, you can't know why he picked you."

"Yes, we can. Because his victims were all much younger than me. Early twenties. I'm outside the box. Then I got a phone call. I can't say much about it, but at that point we were pretty sure he'd somehow learned I was on the task force working the case, and that I'd found an important piece of evidence."

He gave a low whistle, a frown settling over his face. He didn't even give Mavis a halfhearted smile when she slammed the food down between them. "That should never have gotten out," he said when they were alone again.

"No." She looked down at her plate, appetite nearly gone, reminding herself that eating was as important as breathing. She forced herself to pick up a fork. "Long story short. Before we'd even begun to really work the angle, I was at home alone that night, uneasy as all getout, thinking about just going back to the office, when I heard something outside. Just a little sound, but I was jumpy. I went out, walked around to the side of my house and there he was. I lowered my gun because I saw a cop."

"Oh, hell," he murmured.

"He turned when I called out and shot me. I fell. The house blew up. And here we are."

She stared at her plate, at the fork in her hand, and tried to shove the shadows of memory away. For a long time Lance didn't make a sound. Absorbing what she had told him, she guessed. Purely out of willpower, she cut off a piece of omelet and put it in her mouth. It might have been sawdust.

"I'm surprised you didn't shoot me," he said finally.

"Well, my hand was on my sidearm," she reminded him.

"True."

She cut some more egg. "I didn't get a look at his face. It was dark, and frankly I don't remember anything except the muzzle flash as he fired at me. The irony is that I survived the bomb because I was lying flat on my face in the grass beside a tree and bleeding out when it went off. Bet he didn't expect that."

He finally cut into his own pancakes. "I'm surprised they didn't put it out that you were dead."

At that she lifted her head. "How did he know who I was, where I lived and how to reach me? Until we figure that out, no cover story would work, because someone on the inside might have loose lips."

"You're right, that's what Gage said your ASAC is worried about."

She went back to eating and to compartmentalizing what had happened to her. These were memories she kept safely locked away, memories that bubbled up usually only in her nightmares. She was having plenty of them these days.

"A safe house wouldn't work either, if you've got a leak," he remarked.

"That's why they didn't argue very hard when I said I wanted to hit the road," she agreed. She began to eat a little faster, trying to put a distasteful chore behind her. At some level she realized she was eating a great omelet, but most of her didn't want to eat at all. Just get it done. Like everything else. One foot in front of the other until she could take the guy on again. Or until someone else caught him. At this point she didn't much care who took him down.

"You know," she said slowly, "before this happened there was an ugly part of me that wanted to be the one who nailed this guy. Me personally. Now I don't care who gets him as long as he's caught."

"You're competitive, right?"

She looked up. "Yes."

"And it must be harder for a woman in the Bureau than a man. Oh, I know all about equal opportunity, but then there's reality."

"Maybe," she said cautiously.

"Of course you wanted to be the one to bring him down. That's not ugly unless it hinders your performance. Just human nature."

She already liked this guy, but she realized she could start to *really* like him. "Who made you so wise?"

He laughed, the sound instantly lightening the mood. It rolled out of him easily. "Street smarts," he finally said.

Her curiosity about him was growing fast. "So what's your story?" she asked.

"My wounding, you mean? I didn't duck fast enough."

In spite of everything, she felt her lips starting to curl into a smile. "That simple?"

"Especially when you're facing an AR-15 on full auto, yes."

Shock rippled through her. "Full auto? It's a wonder you weren't cut in half."

"You can thank body armor and the economy for that."

That surprised a small laugh out of her. "The economy?"

"Guy was unemployed. He couldn't afford armor-piercing bullets. Still, he got me four times, arms and legs."

She nodded and scooped up more egg. "You've recovered well."

"It was years ago. I've had longer than you. Take it easy on yourself, Erin. We're here, we're not half-bad even by the Bureau's standards and we'll look after you. Just work on healing. When the time comes, we'll need you in the best shape possible."

When the time comes. She thought about that as she finished her breakfast. He seemed awfully sure that they were going to face the guy here. Well, she'd said they might as well have the showdown in this small town. But he also seemed to think they might have time.

But time enough for her to get her strength back? The Fates should be so kind.

Chapter 3

"You can't stay at the motel," he told her as they walked back to his car.

She had to agree with that. If she was at risk, then a lot of other people would be at risk. "Where, then?"

"I was going to suggest you stay with my aunt Maria, but much as she'd love the company, no way am I exposing her to you."

She liked his honesty and answered with her own. "I seem to be deadly."

"Exactly. So… My place."

"Your place?"

"I've got plenty of room, and it's away from other houses, so if this guy gets a wild hair to bomb it, nobody else will get hurt. It'll also give us some nice clear sight lines."

She could appreciate the sight lines but had other concerns. She kept them to herself until she had climbed slowly back into his vehicle.

"Well?" he asked as he turned over the ignition.

"Your house would be at risk."

"I know. It's insured."

"Not against criminal acts, I bet. Most policies have an exception for that."

"Not mine. I'm a cop and I can read. Look, Erin, you can't hit the road. Frankly, you're in poor condition to protect yourself, and like the sheriff pointed out earlier, whichever way you go, it'd be easy to follow you. Not a whole lot else between here and there, is all. You don't want to be crossing the mountains by yourself in your condition. Do I need to keep on?"

She knew she was tired of running. She'd as much as said so in the sheriff's office. Besides, she was beginning to wonder why *she* should have to be the one hiding or running. It made her blood boil just thinking about it. Trying to keep one step ahead of a criminal hardly suited her nature.

But she didn't want to cost Lance Conroe a whole lot. Like his house. Like his life. It seemed so wrong.

"Can I get a flight out of here?"

"Only two commercial flights a week—a puddle jumper in and out of Denver on Friday and Sunday night," he answered. "There used to be a daily flight while they were building the resort, but that's all on hold. We have some folks who own small light planes, and one guy runs an executive jet service out of here, which is usually more out of here than here, if you get me. I think he's in Mexico right now. Anyway, none of those little twin-engine jobs could get you safely across the mountains and I'm not sure their owners would even want to try. They're ranchers, Erin, not pilots, if you get my drift."

She got it. Definitely this was a kill box. She might persuade the Bureau to send a flight for her, if she begged hard enough, but she might as well put another neon sign on her back.

"I've been stupid," she said finally.

"Why?"

"I should have just elected the safe house or caught a plane to the coast, rather than thinking I could drive myself there. And I surely shouldn't have told Fran exactly where I was. Of course she'd tell my boss."

"I kinda think that's *my* fault. I must have lit up the boards when I checked your ID."

It was true. Apparently her field office knew her whereabouts and was concerned about how many might know. Maybe Fran hadn't passed it along. If anyone understood Erin's position it was Fran.

"I don't know," she said slowly.

"I do. If you're not afraid of me, I've got enough room to tuck you into. Let's go back to the motel and get your car and other things. If you decide you want to take off, I won't stop you."

She gave in. What else could she do? Reviewing the decisions that had led her to this small town, she had an uneasy feeling that she wasn't thinking with as clear a head as she might imagine, even without taking the pain meds. She was better than this.

With that gloomy thought, she let Lance take over.

Lance made it easy for her, and she was past arguing. She put the remaining few items in her cases and didn't object when he took them out to her vehicle. She walked slowly to the motel office, and paid the bill in cash, but by the time she was hobbling back to her car, she was limping noticeably.

A burst of frustration and rage socked her. She was

used to being able to do a lot more than walk, and now even walking could defeat her.

But, she reminded herself, she *was* walking. She might be limping but she'd walked a goodly distance this morning, to and from the diner, and now the length of the motel and back. She *was* getting her strength back. A week ago she'd have been ready to collapse.

Lifting her chin, she limped the rest of the way to her car. Lance was sitting in his vehicle nearby, engine thrumming, waiting patiently. She was so glad he hadn't attempted to go pay the bill himself. Carrying her cases was one thing; pampering her to the extreme would be another.

He smiled and touched a finger to the brim of his hat as she reached the vehicles. She hated to think what she must have looked like, attempting to bend herself into her vehicle so cautiously. But she did it, and felt pretty good when she leaned forward, stuck the key in the ignition and started it up. The tow truck had left her nose-out, which meant she didn't have to twist a whole lot to back out.

She pulled up beside Lance's car. "Which way?"

"Toward the mountains," he said, pointing. "I got me a little piece of heaven just a few miles down the road."

A piece of heaven, and she might draw a bomber his way. Oh, great. For an instant she felt a wild urge to just leave town, but then reality slammed her hard. Her decision-making hadn't been the best, obviously, no-where near the top of her form. And the sheriff had been blunt about traveling through the mountains and about being followed. How could she trust her own thinking right now?

They traveled west on the state highway for a little over a mile, then turned onto a county road that needed some fresh paving. It was crumbling around the edges, but at least dozens of potholes had been filled in. And the mountains seemed to loom larger in her windshield.

She wished she had a map. It seemed this county was tucked into a wide mountain valley. Well, more than a valley. The eastern mountains were far enough away to make this feel like a plain. But the western ones loomed close, purple dashed with green in the midday light. Probably farther away than they looked, she decided. She had no perspective for judging that, but when she considered how long she'd driven while watching them slowly grow bigger in front of her, she imagined she was still far from reaching them.

But she was in the foothills for sure. The land here rolled, the road snaked around some curves, an occasional narrow bridge crossed a tumbling stream.

Another turn took them onto gravel and a small house appeared as if it had been dropped in the middle of nowhere. Some trees dotted the brushy, grassy landscape, and little else until woods appeared like a distant ring of tall sentinels.

Lance pulled a wide circle in front of the house and she followed suit, stopping behind him. When he climbed out, she turned off her ignition and sat waiting as he approached, moving only to roll her power window down.

He squatted by the car. "Home sweet home. Future plans not yet accomplished, but right now it's just what we need. We're not as far from town as it may seem but you don't have to worry about anyone getting caught in any cross fire."

"Thank you," she said, really meaning it. "I'll certainly be harder to find out here."

"Counting on it. But not entirely. The other guys

should stop by this evening so you can meet them and know who they are. Then the waiting game begins."

He opened her door, and she twisted gingerly on the seat, finally putting her feet on the ground and pausing a minute. "You won't count too much on not being found?"

"Of course not. Everyone can be found if they have an address. What we're hoping is that this might stall him a while if he shows up. Nobody knows you're staying with me except the sheriff and the other guys who'll be watching over you, okay? Your ASAC was clear about not revealing your whereabouts."

As the inevitable pain eased, she pushed out and stood. "So I'm in a safe house anyway."

"Kinda," he admitted. "But not exactly. I called in your ID, you told your friend about me. If this guy is halfway smart and actually comes here, sooner or later it's going to occur to him where you might be."

She couldn't deny that. "We have to be ready." Always plan for any eventuality. That had been drilled into her. The most remote possibility sometimes happened.

"We'll be as ready as we can."

She turned a little, looking from the snug little house to him. "Lance? Are you sure you want to take this risk?"

His blue-green eyes met hers steadily. "Isn't this what we do, Agent?"

Hesitantly she nodded, acknowledging the truth of it.

"One cop to another, I'd do this. But oddly…" He rubbed his chin, staring past her over the prairie to the mountains. "Oddly enough, I'm developing a real need to catch this SOB. So buckle your seat belt, Erin. You're not alone in this."

"I never was," she argued.

"Until you left home. But now you're with people who have just one ax to grind. Catching this guy."

What an odd way to phrase it, she thought. Ax to grind? Did he think someone at her field office had it in for her? That revealing her identity hadn't just been a slipup?

But as he carried her bags inside, leaving it to her to decide when she'd follow, she ran through everyone she knew back home, and couldn't think of a single one who might want to put her in harm's way.

That didn't mean there wasn't anyone, just that she couldn't imagine who.

Sighing, gathering herself, she headed for the porch. Two steps. She laid her hand on the rail and was relieved that she could climb without clinging to it. Getting better indeed.

Lance watched her ease into the house after he put her bags atop the dresser in his spare room. He felt an urge to wince for her, her caution and slowness giving away her discomfort even if she managed to avoid letting a grimace reach her face. He knew what a bullet could do, but clearly she had been injured by the bomb that destroyed her house, tree or no tree. Falling debris, maybe? The blast wave? He had no idea what kind of injuries she had survived and didn't know how to ask. Seeing her move was a painful experience unto itself.

He watched her step through the door straight into his small living room, and glance around. Hardly something out of an interior design magazine, but comfortable and marked by long years. A battered chintz-covered couch, a wooden rocker with pillows, a braided rug.

"Have a seat if you want," he suggested, "or explore. Single story, so your bedroom is in the back on the left. Kitchen is through there," he said, pointing. "And you get your own bathroom."

She glanced at him. "In a house this size?"

He flashed a smile. "I shared this house with my mother until she died. Two bathrooms were essential. Coffee? I can't make you a latte, I'm afraid."

"Coffee would be great. I need to stay awake."

She needed more than that, he thought, and was relieved to see her at last settle into a padded rocker. It was almost like watching someone who was just learning how to use a body. "How about a pain pill to go with it?"

"You a pusher?" she asked, and he was relieved to hear the teasing note in her voice.

"Hey, if there's any time it would be safe to stuff your brain with cotton, the next few hours are probably it."

She just shook her head. "I'll get some ibuprofen in a minute."

Well, he could provide that as well as the coffee. In his kitchen—a comfortable room because his mother had made it so over the years—he started the drip coffee-maker and got a glass of water and the bottle of ibuprofen. He carried both back to her immediately, and she accepted them with thanks.

"I'm gonna step outside for a few minutes. Give me your keys and I'll put your car in the garage. I'll be back by the time the coffee's ready."

She simply nodded as she tipped two pills into her hand.

He walked out the front door and stood without moving for a while, feeling a bit like an old goat. Not that he was all that old, but that woman was raising his flag-pole, as it were. He felt guilty as sin for even having such feelings when she was so clearly in recovery, but she appealed to him on the most basic level. He'd have bet the homestead that she wouldn't like that either.

Regardless, he needed a few minutes to clear his head

and get back on the real purpose of her being here. They had work to do, and no time for dalliances, even presuming she'd tolerate it.

The air held the musty, dusty, not-quite-green scent of midsummer. The world still hadn't completely dried out from winter and spring, but it was on the way. They badly needed some rain, but he knew better than to wish for it. At this time of year, ponds were starting to dry up and only the toughest, hardiest of plants could make it. In a few weeks, dang near everything would be brown. That the mountains were still somehow managing to dump water into the creeks was amazing, but most of them wouldn't be running for long.

But thinking about rain wasn't helping him either. He stepped off the porch, sank into her small car and put it in his aging detached garage. Then he walked around the outside of his house, trying to make a professional judgment about what needed doing to keep Erin as safe as possible. The guys coming tonight would probably have more ideas than he, because they had more experience at this kind of thing.

But for now he looked at the windows, which no longer seemed like such a good thing to have, and the three doors, which was two doors too many right now.

He needed more information about the kind of man who was coming after her, more than that he liked to blow up women. They must have been piecing together some kind of profile, and Lance needed to know what was in it. Impossible to guard against the complete unknown.

And he was just wasting time and he knew it. Whatever demons this woman unleashed in him, he needed to bury them.

Finally giving up his search for a way to ignore his response to her, he went back inside. She was still awake, sitting in the rocker, and from the way she jerked when he came in she hadn't quite left fear behind her. She covered quickly, however. He had to give her that.

But what kind of person wouldn't be afraid after what she'd been through?

"I'll get the coffee," he said. "You want anything in it?"

"Just enough milk to lighten it a bit, if that's okay."

"Not a problem." He hung his hat on the coat tree by the door, then hesitated only a moment before removing his gun belt. He doubted the guy could find the place this quickly unless he was a psychic, and Erin was armed anyway. She could probably draw fast enough if necessary, despite her wounds. He did lock the door, though, something he rarely did out here.

He filled two large mugs with coffee and carried them back to the living room. He found her sitting bolt upright in the rocker.

"Erin? What's wrong?"

She drew a shaky breath. "Just some twinges."

More than twinges, he suspected. Frustration nearly goaded him into going through her suitcases to find some of those pain meds. Instead he set the coffee on the side table, then took up position on the couch facing her. He thought he'd settled down until the words escaped him.

"What are you punishing yourself for?"

She drew a sharp breath and her gaze landed on him with almost physical force. The woman she had been before all this. Powerful. In control. And right now angry with him. "What the hell are you talking about?"

"Staying alert is just an excuse right now. You know why they give you pain meds? Not just to make you more comfortable. No, they give them to you because pain is exhausting and can delay your recovery. Plus if you can't move around easily enough you won't limber up. So take a dang pill, give yourself some rest and start using some of those parts that hurt too much to want to move."

Those sherry-brown eyes glared at him, but he kept his mouth shut and waited it out. Finally her expression relaxed.

"I shouldn't be doing this to you," she said.

"Doing what?"

"Moving in on you, taking over your life. And now there seems to be no way out."

"I know I'm irritating, but that bad?"

Her face relaxed the rest of the way. "You're not irritating. What's irritating is how long it's taking me to get back to normal. What's irritating is how poorly thought-out this whole trip of mine was. I figured that if I just got in a car and roamed aimlessly, I'd be as safe as any safe house. Maybe safer. But now I'm pinned down."

"In a kill box," he said, using her earlier description.

"Yeah, and I should have thought that through, shouldn't I? But I didn't. I'm angry with myself."

He reckoned he could understand that, but didn't see how it would help anything. "What's done is done, Erin. You've been through a lot. Some poor decision-making is to be expected and if that's the worst of it, you're doing good. None of us thinks well when we've been through a trauma. Besides, I don't think your decisions were all that bad. How were you to know you wouldn't just sail to wherever without being discovered?"

Her jaw tightened. "I should have thought. After all, somehow this guy found out about me to begin with. Somehow that didn't seem to enter my calculations."

Why would it? he wondered. Not very many serial bombers chased a target across country. The Unabomber had, but he'd done it by mail. "It could have been a slipup.

Yes, your bosses are concerned there might be another one, but truth is, they don't *know* that. Nobody knows that yet. So they're being hypercautious. So are we. Just in case."

At last she leaned back in the chair, wincing a bit. "Just in case," she repeated. "Yeah. And it's causing a whole bunch of trouble."

"Not really. Hey, you're giving me a break from prowling the roads, writing tickets and trying to convince couples I know that they really don't want to kill each other."

At last he drew a small laugh from her. Relief filled him. "It's still not fair to you," she said. "Me invading your house, possibly with a whole lot of trouble coming."

"I volunteered," he said quietly. "Nobody made me."

She let go of it at last, and edged herself forward in the chair. "Half a pain pill," she said.

He bit back an offer to get it for her. "Your bags are in your room."

"Thanks."

She grimaced a bit as she rose, then stood still as if mentally testing herself. He had some idea how maddening this had to be for her. He'd felt that way after his own wounding.

He had left the door to her bedroom wide open and figured she could find it without him hovering. She didn't want to be hovered over, he could tell. Events had taken her independence from her, and she was struggling to take back every bit she could. He listened to her slowly walk down the hall, and when she didn't call out, he guessed she'd found her room.

He picked up his coffee, found it had gone cold and headed out with both their mugs to get fresh. Along the way he opened a couple of windows to let the breeze in. He returned just in time to see her settling into the rocker again. She'd dispensed with her jacket, revealing a sleeveless top that bared her arms…and some scars. A few small burns, a few cuts that had been stitched. Still angry looking.

But she hadn't ditched her shoulder holster. Interesting. He set the fresh coffee beside her and saw her take the pill with the glass of water he'd brought her earlier.

"Okay, rainbows and unicorns," she said.

He laughed. "Maybe you should ditch the gun, then."

She shook her head slightly. "Half a pill doesn't make me woozy."

But it was what she didn't say that hit him. She didn't feel safe anymore without her weapon. Not even here. Not even now. And maybe she was right that half a pill wouldn't affect her too much. In which case it wouldn't do too much for her pain.

"God, you're a pain," he said finally, keeping his tone mild.

"Really?" she asked acidly. "Okay, I'll leave."

He stood. "Just looking for an excuse, aren't you? But where will you go? You really want to be out there alone with this guy?"

"He probably isn't anywhere near here yet. I don't have to go over the mountains. I can head north…"

"More mountains."

"Back to Denver, then."

"Some mountains." He felt a smile trying to be born, but stomped down on it. "Look, Erin, if you take so little pain medication that it doesn't help, why bother? If you have so little trust in my department…well, I guess we can't just make that happen, can we? So do you trust anyone?"

"Not really," she said baldly. "Not right now."

"Fair enough." And it was fair. She didn't know him

from Adam. They'd met less than twenty-four hours ago. What else did she have to judge them by?

"Oh, to heck with it," she said abruptly and reached for the pill bottle she'd brought out from her bedroom. It was surprisingly large for pain meds. "One more won't kill me. Is that trust enough for you?"

Shocked, he fell silent. What was she trying to prove? That she trusted a man she hardly knew? Why? "I can't figure you out," he said finally.

She smiled sourly. "Few can." After popping another pill—a half? He didn't know—she reached for her pistol and removed it from the holster, placing it on the table. "All better now?"

"Not if you don't feel safe," he admitted frankly.

"I haven't felt safe since the incident. Nothing new in that. Might as well get used to it. You're in charge now, Deputy."

That, he thought, might be the crux of all of this. A sense of control was important to cops. All cops. He'd just badgered her into giving it up. Smart move, he thought irritably. What now?

Fifteen minutes later the pills started hitting. He could see it in her softening posture, in the way her breathing grew more relaxed. That much was good.

"So you lived here with your mother?" she asked.

"Yeah. When I quit the force in Denver and came up here, she was living all alone. It made sense to move in with her. She needed some looking after since my dad died. Things were pretty generally going to hell, and she wasn't all that well. Diabetes was catching up with her."

"I'm sorry."

"Me, too. It was impossible to convince her that insulin shots and oral meds didn't make it possible to continue eating down-home cooking. Stubborn woman."

"Seems to run in the family."

At that he smiled. "Good experience for dealing with you."

She smiled, really smiled. Oh, yeah, those pills were kicking in. "I'm a handful, or so I've been reliably informed. My bosses keep telling me to color inside the lines."

"A bit of a rogue?"

"Not exactly. I don't do anything illegal. I just don't fit too well in the box."

A short sound of amusement escaped him. "The FBI seems like a strange place for someone who doesn't fit in the box."

And at last a laugh from her. "It's interesting, all right. They give me my head sometimes, because I'm good. Was good?" The verb seemed to perplex her for a moment. "Oh, man, the fog and unicorns are here."

"Try to rustle up a rainbow."

Giving another laugh, she settled into the chair as if it felt more comfortable now. The sight relieved him. She picked up her coffee and drained half of it, probably trying to keep her head clear. "The pain seems a long way away right now."

"Good."

She dragged her gaze back to him. "So no wife?"

"An ex. Years ago."

"Same here," she admitted.

"But you said something about him stalking you."

She lifted both eyebrows. "I did? When?"

"Your call from Fran," he reminded her.

"Ah. Well, he calls from time to time. Wants to put it back together. But he's not the kind of stalker I'd be worried about. Just a minor nuisance."

"And this Tom guy?"

"My ASAC. Trying to mix business with pleasure. Never a good thing."

"I suppose not."

"Definitely not. One bad marriage was enough. Mixing it up with a career would be stupid. I'm not always stupid."

He hid a smile. "Rarely, I would imagine. Maybe just since you were wounded."

"Oh, I've been stupid before, like when I got married the first time. I still can't remember why I thought that would ever work."

"Love overrode reason?" he suggested. He was beginning to enjoy this softer side of Erin.

"I can't even remember that. I just know I don't punch a time clock—I'm a bit obsessive when I get on a case and he couldn't handle the hours. So the complaining started, and the more he tried to squeeze me into his box of expectations, the more I rebelled."

"A lot of boxes out there," he remarked.

"Do you fit in any?"

He thought about it, deciding she deserved an honest answer. "I was happy with my marriage. She wasn't. So whether that box fit, I can't tell you. But I enjoy my work a whole lot, and piddling around this place taking care of things. So yeah, I guess I found a happy box."

"Good for you." Her eyelids had just started to look heavy when she snapped them open again. "Can I get some more coffee?"

"Sure. Want me to show you where?"

She got out of the rocker more easily, and walked with a more comfortable pace into the kitchen.

"Okay," she said, "you were right about the pills. But I can't keep taking them."

"Got it. Just remember, you're not alone. You've got a team again."

"When are those guys coming by?"

"Tonight. You'll like them. They have a very individual box of their own."

Back to the living room with the coffee, but this time she didn't settle. Now that she could move, she wanted to. He just hoped she didn't overdo it. He watched her pace the small room and figured she'd probably love to get out for a walk. He wouldn't trust her on the uneven ground out there, however. Not on those meds.

"I had a little house," she remarked. "About the size of this. I planted all kinds of flowers around it. All gone now."

"I'm sorry."

She shook her head a little. "That's the least of it." All of a sudden she faced him, feet planted firmly. "Do you know what it does to you when a guy in a police uniform shoots you?"

He nodded slowly, waiting for her to continue.

"He isn't really a cop, of course, but the fact that he could get a uniform and fool me for as long as it took? That's probably how he was getting these other women. Officer Friendly."

"Ugly," he answered.

"I've worked on cases where cops used excessive force. I've seen the attempts to cover it up, and seen the results when we get called in. So you'll excuse me if I don't trust the uniform easily. But I wasn't prepared for that, distrustful or not."

Those pills were sure making her chatty, not that he minded. He was actually enjoying it. "I've known some dirty cops. Cops who push the line. I don't like it."

She nodded. "I hate it. Just a few bad apples make it

harder for everyone. When you can't trust the uniform…"
She gave a little shrug. "How did I get off on this?"

"The guy who shot you."

"Oh. Yeah. So we've got a really minimal profile. Useless profile, actually. How much of a profile is it that the
guy likes to blow up women? But now we know he probably poses as a cop, which gets him places he couldn't go
otherwise, makes him fairly invisible and makes it easy
for him to get women to cooperate."

This was creating wrinkles. Already he could see the
potential for disaster here. "I'm going to introduce you to
four guys tonight. Those four will be utterly trustworthy.
Don't trust anyone else. Fair enough?"

"I didn't really trust you at first when you pulled me
over."

His answer was dry. "I gathered."

"Now you know why. Anybody could get a deputy's
uniform, and I don't know your department."

"But my whole department knows everyone. That's
important, Erin. I'm going to call Gage." In fact, it was
the first real useful information they'd got.

Erin settled back on the rocker and enjoyed the relative freedom from agony. The pills didn't kill it all, but
they made it duller, less inhibiting, further away. Which
meant her mind wasn't working at top speed, but evidently she'd just offered some useful information. Good.
Leaning her head back, she let her eyes close. Lance
was making the call from his kitchen, but she heard bits
and pieces of it. Apparently he was telling the sheriff
about the uniform thing, and she gathered all the deputies would now be on the lookout for a guy in uniform
that they didn't recognize.

That might be helpful, or it might not. Would the

UNSUB even try that out here? Who knew. This wasn't the kind of place where a uniform would provide sufficient protective coloration. But it was still good to know the deputies would be alert for someone trying to pass as one of them.

The pill not only softened the pain, it made her drowsy. Right now she feared drowsiness. It felt odd to her to be placing so much trust in a man she'd just met, and she wasn't yet prepared to trust him by sleeping. Not that she had any reason to be suspicious of him at this point.

In fact, maybe she was being unreasonably suspicious. Maybe there was no reason to be fearful at all. If the bomber wanted her out of the picture, he'd already succeeded. She might still be breathing, but she was no longer involved with the task force.

When Lance returned to the room carrying the coffeepot to freshen her mug, she floated the idea by him.

He stopped, tilting his head, looking at her from slightly narrowed eyes. "They were worried enough they wanted to put you in a safe house. Instead you left town. Where did this idea come from?"

"I'm no longer part of the task force. No threat to him. People like him tend to want to work in familiar geographical areas anyway."

He nodded slowly and poured more coffee into her cup. "I'll get the milk. And I want you to think that through again. Carefully."

She guessed she wasn't making sense—hardly surprising—but he wanted her to think about it again. Her thoughts had turned into wisps that floated away before she could grab them. She was no longer a threat to this guy. His type preferred to work in familiar geographical areas. So...

All of a sudden she sat bolt upright, then wished she

hadn't as the pain broke through the fuzz and drew an unusual groan from her.

"What?" Lance asked as he returned with the milk jug.

"I had a thought…" She leaned back and closed her eyes.

"What did you think?"

"That there's something I don't know. Something my field office evidently *does* know, because now that I'm out of the area, I'd be taking this perp out of his comfort zone, and profiling says he wouldn't do that. So what do they know? What did I miss? Why are they worried at all about me?"

As the pain began to ease, she opened her eyes and saw that her coffee was again milky. Lance stood there screwing the top back on the gallon container.

"Let me think about that," he said. "Be right back."

She watched him return to the kitchen and felt her hand itch to pull out the phone and call Fran. Fran would know everything about the case, about whether there was new information. But something stayed her. God, she was getting paranoid. Now she didn't even want to call her best friend?

When Lance returned, he sat on the couch across from her. "Seems to me," he said, "that this guy stopped fitting a profile when he came after you. First, you weren't his victim type. Second, he shot you, so he's not afraid to kill that way. Most bombers are cowards, aren't they?"

She nodded. "Well away from the death and destruction they cause. Murder at long distance."

"This guy tried one up close and personal. So maybe they're thinking he's a wild card and don't want to inadvertently leave you hanging in the breeze."

"Maybe."

"And shooting a Fed? That's far from risk-averse.

Much as you all wanted this guy before, I bet your colleagues want him even more now."

She had no doubt of that. She'd lost count of the times her fellow agents had visited her in the hospital and made solemn promises to bring this guy down for her. Oh, they'd always wanted him, but now it was personal in a new way.

"So okay," Lance said. "Maybe this guy won't come this far for you. Like you said, out of his comfort zone. But nobody wants to bet your life on it now."

It made sense, as much sense as anything could when her brain seemed foggy. She was nowhere near 100 percent, mentally or physically, and that irritated her beyond words. She should never have taken the pain medicine. But even as she scolded herself for it, she was glad of this respite. For a little while, pain was far away, at the distant edges of her awareness.

"Lance?"

"Yeah?"

"Who are these guys who are coming by tonight?"

"I can't say exactly."

The fog instantly receded. "How can you not know? You're going to let strangers in?"

"Not strangers. I know all the guys Gage will contact. They've been around awhile."

"Men who've been sent on classified missions to undisclosed locations."

"Exactly."

"And you have more than four of them in this county?" The thought boggled her mind. Men like that didn't exactly grow on trees, and this county was far from overpopulated. Coming up with four shouldn't be a lottery.

Lance smiled. "It started decades ago with our former sheriff. He was a Green Beret in Vietnam. He brought a

friend a few years later, and for some reason more followed over the years. One of them is his son, a retired
navy SEAL. Somehow we've gathered them."

"I guess so. Aren't they rusty?"

"They don't let themselves get rusty."

That was a comment she would have liked to pursue,
but it seemed like too much trouble at that moment. Instead she put her mind to finishing her coffee in the hopes
it would help keep her brain in gear.

"Let me go make another pot," Lance said as he
watched her drain her cup. "I hope you don't mind roast
chicken for dinner."

"Sounds good. Thanks."

Watching Lance walk away, her unguarded thoughts
insisted on reminding her that he was one attractive man.
Too bad she hurt so much. Too bad she would be returning to the road as soon as she could.

Because she sure would have liked to get him in the
sack for just one night.

The bomber answered the phone, hearing the long anticipated mechanical voice.

"I know where she might be," the voice said.

The bomber had been growing antsy. Two weeks of
sitting on his hands until the agent got out of the hospital, followed by two weeks when the voice didn't know
where she'd gone. He had two bombs waiting to be used,
and he was itching to get out and look for another woman
who needed a lesson.

"You stay where you are," the voice said. "Don't go
after another woman. Not yet. It's still too dangerous."

That caused him to settle, like it or not. He'd been so
close to going out hunting tonight.

"I have to verify the information," the voice said. "And you need to get ready to travel."

"Travel?" The bomber didn't like the idea. Leave the only safety he had?

"You heard me. She saw you. She's out of the area right now. When the time comes, you either go after her, or you're going to be sitting in court with her pointing a finger at you. Understand?"

He understood. "When?"

"I don't know yet. You're not the only one who needs to be careful."

So the voice had some worries, too? He liked that. He eyed the bombs, and figured he could build another while he waited. After he took out the agent, maybe he could use them on his way back from wherever he had to go. Yeah, he liked that idea.

"Wait for my call." The voice disconnected.

Anger began to sizzle in him. How the voice had found him, he didn't know. But he didn't like having his strings pulled like this. Didn't like the idea of traveling. Didn't like that he couldn't set another bomb.

He hated the voice. But he feared its threats even more.

Chapter 4

Lance did all the cooking and wouldn't let Erin help with the cleanup. "Rest yourself," he said.

High-handed men. She almost snorted, then caught herself. He was right. She was a mess, utterly useless for most things, if only temporarily, and right then she was replete with an excellent dinner of roast chicken, mashed potatoes and mixed vegetables. So the man could cook as well as provide eye candy.

The pain pills had begun to wear off, and while her mind was grateful, her body wasn't. She did her best to conceal her discomfort because she didn't want to be pushed into taking them again. She needed a clear head. It was the only thing she had left going for her.

Not that she'd been making all the best decisions since she'd taken off from Chicago. She had to keep reminding herself of that. Even without a medication-induced fog her mind still wasn't functioning at its best. When she had left the hospital two weeks ago, the doctor had warned her about the recovery time, had warned her that not only would she experience continued fatigue, but that between weariness and pain, it'd be a while before her brain fully reengaged. She should have listened.

Leaving Chicago had seemed like a smart move for so many reasons. Just stay off the grid, not waste resources on protecting her in a safe house that could be found—hell, her own residence had been found, and that was just about as secret as a safe house. You couldn't just call the Bureau and locate an agent. They were awfully careful about that.

But she'd been found. And maybe that was the biggest reason, even bigger than the fear of cabin fever, that had driven her to leave. Staying off the grid had seemed like the best solution for everyone.

Now she wondered if she could have made a more stupid choice. Instead of relying on law enforcement people she knew, she was relying on a big unknown: the Conard County Sheriff's Department. Instead of costing the FBI and the Marshals for her protection, she was costing someone else.

Which left her wondering why her decision to leave had seemed so imperative. Was she fleeing? Grimly, she considered the possibility and what it said about her. She didn't like the answers. She wasn't one to run from anything.

She sighed, settling again into the rocker, and wondered just how much the bomber had really changed for her. Her house was gone—devastating, but not the end of the world. She had survived, was recovering, however slowly. The idea that this event could have changed her personality, made her over into a different person, unnerved her. She didn't want to be a different person. She'd been happy with Erin before the blast. Now she had to wonder if she'd ever feel that way again.

Lance joined her, bearing more coffee. He set her cup on the side table and resumed position on the couch across from her. "The guys will be here in half an hour."

"Okay." She bit her lip. "Lance?"

He turned directly toward her. "Yeah?"

"After you were wounded…did you feel like something inside you had changed?"

"I'd have been a fool if I hadn't changed."

Well, that was frank. "How so?"

"Sometimes life slaps us with the stark reality that we're not invincible and death is always lurking. You can't ignore it anymore. Yeah, it changed me. Why?"

"Because I'm wondering if I'll ever be myself again."

He shook his head a little. "You won't."

She felt herself frown faintly. "That's encouraging."

"It's the truth. You had a guy try to kill you. First a bullet, then a bomb. How could you go back to the way you were before? You'd have to be a robot."

She didn't answer, still trying to deal with the possibility that she hadn't been smart but had been running like a rabbit. She didn't want to be a rabbit.

Of course, she had made the decision to stand here. Maybe she hadn't lost it all.

"Look," he said after a minute or so, "it changed you. Things like that change everyone. But you'll get a lot of the old you back with time. When you stop hurting so much, when you feel yourself starting to take control again. But it'll be different this time, because you'll never again forget the instant when you had no control at all. When you almost died. Mortality will accompany you. It won't rule you, but it'll be real and present from now on."

She nodded slowly, thinking about what he was saying.

"Then, of course, you probably also feel a lack of trust. That'll be hard to get over, too. Someone in your office leaked stuff about you. Maybe innocently, maybe not, but if you ask me that's the primary reason you refused the safe house. You can't trust those folks yet. That's normal, too."

"I think I was running," she admitted, facing it head-on.

"Of course you were. Who were you supposed to trust?"

That certainly put a different light on it. She felt the corners of her mouth tug up a little. "You're making me feel better."

"Hey, you were the lady who said she wanted to make her stand here. That's no rabbit."

"Bravado," she said almost dubiously.

"Is that what you think it was?"

Finally she sighed and eased back. "No," she admitted. "I'm tired of running. I shouldn't be the one running."

"I get it."

Somehow she thought he did.

He spoke again. "There's a reason they don't let you come back to duty until a psychologist checks you out, even if you're physically fine. Everyone knows this changes you. They don't want you to be out there on the streets if you'll get yourself into trouble by acting foolishly. So relax for now. When your body is done healing, they'll make sure you're mentally and emotionally ready to go back to work. In the meantime, take it a day at a time. It's all you can do."

She supposed it was, but she'd be a whole lot happier if they could take down this bomber.

She was working on yet another cup of coffee, trying to hold weariness at bay, when someone rapped on the door. Lance, still wearing his now-rumpled uniform, rose. "That'll be the guys."

But she noted he peeked out the window before opening the door.

It felt like an invasion. In just moments the room filled with four additional men, all of them large, all of them fit, all garbed in black T-shirts and black tactical pants. A veritable army. If she'd been feeling better, she might have laughed with surprise and even some delight.

She was given first names only. "Wade, Seth, Micah, and Jared." She wondered if she would sort them out, or ever get to know them any better than that.

They all shook her hand, calling her agent, then found places to perch around the room. A little joking here and there between all the men, but then all the attention focused on her.

She wasn't easily intimidated, but she felt intimidated then. Where had these men developed those stares? She didn't think she wanted to know.

"Okay," said the guy who looked Native American, and had some gray streaks in his long hair. "Let's get to it. You have an unidentified bomber who may be after you, who has already tried to kill you once. Right?"

She gave a little nod.

"And the Bureau is worried about you being unprotected out here in the back of beyond."

"Apparently so."

"And you're not up to snuff yet from your injuries."

At that she sighed. "As my body keeps reminding me."

Micah smiled faintly. "Well, hell, there isn't a man in this room who hasn't walked in those shoes."

She looked from face to face and saw all those powerful men nod. They made this room feel overfull.

"Are you prepared to trust us?" he asked.

Just then there was another knock on the door. Tension snapped through the room like a zap of electricity. Postures changed instantly. Immediately one of them put himself between her and the door.

Lance went to answer it. "Well, hello," she heard him say with pleasure. "Come on in."

A slightly portly man in his sixties passed through the door and looked around the room with a smile. He had graying dark hair, and wore jeans and chambray shirt. "Howdy, fellas. I see my county is about to go to hell in a handbasket again."

At that one of them laughed. "It does that surprisingly often, Dad."

Lance introduced the man to Erin. "Our former sheriff, Nate Tate. Seth's his son. So, Nate, you volunteered?"

"I got tapped." Lance brought him a kitchen chair and he settled on it near Erin as the tension fled the room. "I'm your communications center. Gage didn't want all this going through Dispatch. We'll be on a different frequency, a closed loop unless we need to reach out. Best way to stay under the radar."

Erin approved, although she didn't feel she had the right to say so. Looking around the room, she wondered why she had ever objected to a safe house. Trust. Lance had been right. She didn't really trust her colleagues right now.

But these guys looked like someone's worst nightmare. Oh, they were all handsome enough, but there was something in their eyes… Of course, they considered themselves to be on a mission right now. Hardly surprising they appeared faintly murderous and hard.

"Gage briefed us all," Micah said. "We know what the FBI told him. What we'd like to know before we get started is what else you might know."

"Very little," she admitted. "I saw the guy but all I remember was the muzzle flash when he shot me, and the fact he was wearing a city cop's uniform. It was dark, of course. He was on the side of my house, so light from the street didn't reach him."

"Profile?" Nate asked.

"Sketchy. He likes to blow up young women who are in their early twenties. We haven't found a link between the victims, or hadn't before I was hit. Every bomb he makes is different, so at first we weren't sure we didn't have some copycats."

"But then?" Nate prodded.

She hesitated. "I found something that connected them all. I can't say what."

To her relief, nobody argued with her.

"Anyway, after I was shot I was out of the loop. My guess is he uses police uniforms to gain trust, and to be pretty much invisible. Bombers usually work at a distance, so him shooting me doesn't fit the profile. Killers generally like to work in a familiar geographical area but not always. The likelihood that he'd follow me this far…well, all bets are off, evidently. If the Bureau found something to worry them, I don't know about it. I just know they went into hyperdrive." She paused. "One other thing. The guy might like to hang at bars frequented by cops. How else could he have figured out who I was? He called me at work, taunting me. And that night he blew up my house and shot me. You can probably figure it out as well as anyone."

"Among these men," Nate said, "you don't have to worry about loose lips giving you away."

She could well believe it. But that was supposed to be true of the Bureau, as well. Except she'd already sensed how tightly knit these men were, and they'd offered their protection. They weren't the kind to fail unless they died. That was written all over them.

"I'm sorry you have to do all this for me."

"We're not," the one she had identified as Seth said. He flashed a charming smile. "We all like to be useful or we wouldn't be here. This one's an interesting challenge, though. One advantage we have is that strangers who hang around here for very long get noticed. If they just pass through, no one cares. If they stay, everyone wants to know who they are."

She caught her breath. "Like me?"

"As far as anyone knows, you left," Lance answered. "You spent one night at the motel. And now you've vanished."

"So no one should be able to find me."

"Except the Bureau knows you're in town," Lance reminded her. "And that seems to trouble them quite a bit."

Micah stood and the others, except for Nate Tate, followed suit. "We know how to do this," Micah said. "Just leave the details to us. If he gets through us, you'll have Lance. He's good."

"But not as good as you," Lance remarked. The rest of the men laughed.

"Good enough if you get an intruder," Micah retorted.

They filed out, leaving Erin to wonder if this wasn't overkill. She had her own private SWAT team? With experience that most SWAT teams would never have? She could have almost pitied anyone who stumbled on this place. Except she felt no pity at all for that bomber.

"Coffee, Nate?" Lance asked. "The two of us have been drinking it by the gallon today."

"When have you ever known me to turn down coffee?" Nate asked, arching a brow. Then he turned to Erin. "Well, I do occasionally. There have been times when

I've popped antacids like they were candy." He flashed a warm smile.

"This job can do that to you," she agreed. A wave of fatigue washed through her, but she tried to fight it down.

"I have six daughters," Nate said. "One is right about your age. Somehow that makes this personal."

She nodded. She understood how that could happen. "But aren't you retired? What does your wife think?"

"She likes it when I'm doing something that makes me feel useful. Otherwise, according to her, I can get underfoot." He winked. "Gage knows I like to keep my finger in things around here."

"How long were you sheriff?"

"Almost since I got home from Vietnam. Poor Gage, he took over from me years ago and they still call him the new sheriff."

She laughed quietly at that.

"Some things change slow around here," he continued. "And some things change too fast. Time just keeps slipping away. But I've still got some useful years in me, and handling communications with this crew is right up my alley. The kind of thing I used to do all the time. You're going to be safe, Erin."

She wished she truly believed that. But even as she sat there chatting with Nate, she could feel her skin crawling with awareness. The UNSUB could know her whereabouts by now. He could be on his way. He'd already proven he was slick and the one time he'd almost been caught, he'd used a gun.

A man like that was unpredictable. A man like that could be very dangerous indeed.

Nate left a short while later. Lance could see Erin was sagging with fatigue, pale with it, but she asked for more coffee anyway. Stubborn and determined, this woman. He admired it, but he was a little worried for her anyway.

He got the coffee for her and waited to see if she'd tell him why she feared sleep. Finally she said, "Nate must know this county really well."

"Better than anyone. He's an invaluable resource."

"Nice, too."

"Very."

She cocked a brow at him. "Six daughters, huh?"

"Yeah." He smiled. "There was a time when everyone around here thought he must be overwhelmed at home. He never seemed like it. But then he found out he had a son he hadn't known about. Seth."

"I was going to ask because he only mentioned his daughters. None of my business." She closed her eyes briefly, and let her head fall back to rest against the cushion behind her.

"Around here it's everyone's business," he said. "We all know the story. Nate went off to war not knowing he'd left his girlfriend pregnant. Her father didn't like Nate. Nate was known as a bit of a troublemaker, so unbeknownst to either of them, her father intercepted their letters. Marge thought Nate had forgotten her, and Nate figured he was getting Dear Johnned for some reason. Marge's family sent her away to have the baby and forced her to put it up for adoption."

Her eyes opened. "Different times." Uglier times.

"Very different. Anyway, Nate came home and married Marge and it wasn't until almost twenty years ago that Seth showed up on their doorstep. Marge had never whispered a word about the baby, figuring it was too late to mend."

"That must have been a scene."

"More than a scene. It almost killed their marriage."

"But everything's all right now?"

"Very all right." He watched her close her eyes again and thought how small and frail she looked right now. But he'd caught glimpses of the real Erin, tough, determined, strong. One beautiful woman, and he suspected she wouldn't like it if she guessed how much he wanted to wrap her up and keep her safe from the world out there.

He was responding to her need at the moment, though. He knew she didn't really want a white knight. What she wanted was to regain her strength and take care of herself the way she once had.

But pale, pained and weary though she might be, she was still a sexy package. He wondered about that, about his elemental response to her. These days he was old enough not to be chasing random skirts. Few women evoked a sexual response in him, and when they did it was usually fleeting unless he really liked them.

But this woman was creeping under his skin in unexpected ways, and he didn't know what to make of it. Was he seeing the woman she had been before all this? Or was he seeing a waif in need of help? He was sure the latter would infuriate her, and if he was honest with himself, that type had never really appealed to him. He didn't want to spend the rest of his life taking care of someone who wouldn't take care of herself.

Her eyes popped open again. "I thought you promised me two really big dogs?"

"They're in their run out back. I didn't know if you'd want to be smothered."

"I already got overwhelmed by the crew who just visited. Will they jump on me?"

"I hope I taught them better manners."

She tilted her head and smiled. "Then I'd love to meet

them. I never thought my job would allow me to keep a dog, and I adore them."

"I'll get them, but I want to get out of this uniform first."

"Go ahead." Then her head drooped backward again. As he headed for his bedroom, he wondered what it was going to take to get this woman to go to bed and sleep.

He donned his oldest pair of jeans, well-worn and soft, and a sweatshirt he'd cut the sleeves off to just above his elbows. Evenings could get cool, even in the summer. He noted the time with shock. Just past nine. Early, even though it felt like it should be much later.

His back door opened directly onto the large dog run, and his boys were waiting for him. Rufus was over two hundred pounds of brindled English mastiff, and Bernie— real original name, that—was the Saint Bernard, not all that much smaller in appearance than Rufus. They raced around him in happy circles, wagging their tales. He'd left buckets of water outside for them, and a trough full of kibble, so he wasn't worried they were hungry or thirsty.

But as soon as they'd finished greeting him and bumping against him to get their pats and scratches, he saw them raise their heads at the same instant.

They smelled something new.

In a flash they tore down the hallway, and he spared a moment to hope like hell that they didn't embarrass him. When he reached the living room, however, they were sitting politely in front of Erin, tails wagging, heads cocked curiously. She was looking back at them with a faint smile.

"They do fill a room," she said when he appeared.

"Hold your hand out and let them sniff you," he said. "They're dying to be your friend. Look at those tails."

He was delighted to hear her laugh quietly. She offered her hand and the dogs inhaled her scent, their tails still wagging. Apparently they liked her, because before he could say spit, their heads were bumping together to find a place on her lap.

He saw her wince.

"Let me…" he started, but she stopped him.

"No, it's not that bad." Then she surprised him by reaching out both hands to scratch behind their ears. And the last thing he would have expected was to hear her cooing at them. "Aren't you big, beautiful boys," she said quietly. "Gorgeous guys. You know it, don't you. Yes, you do. Your eyes are so soft. Really soft. Ooh, you like that, don't you?"

So he went to make more of the coffee she seemed so determined to use as a crutch to stay awake, and left her to enjoy his boys. When he returned ten minutes later, a huge puddle of fur surrounded her and the chair.

And she was sound asleep.

With a cockeyed smile, he watched them for awhile, finding it both interesting and amazing that the presence of his dogs had finally allowed her to sleep.

Chapter 5

The call of nature awoke Erin a couple of hours later. It took her a moment to remember where she was, but when she opened her eyes she saw Lance sitting on the couch across from her, reading by the light of a single lamp. As soon as she stirred, he looked up with a smile.

"Feel better?" he asked.

"A bit," she agreed. Then she looked down at the puddle of dogs at her feet. They'd raised their heads and were looking up at her. "Um, will they let me go to the bathroom?"

"Rufus. Bernie. Here." At once the dogs rose, an interesting process that seemed to happen by bits as they organized their large bodies, and they trotted over to him. "Sit," he said. Both obeyed immediately.

"Well trained, too," she remarked. She'd stiffened again from too much sitting, but managed to push herself to her feet. Once again the shock of pain hit her, but it subsided after a few deep breaths.

"Down the hall, just past your bedroom," Lance said. "Are you going to bed or do you want coffee?"

"Coffee, please." She feared sleeping too deeply or too long, she realized as she eased her way down the hallway. The Bureau had done that to her with their insistence she be protected. The safety she'd felt since leaving Chicago had evaporated completely.

As she finished taking care of her needs and washed her face quickly, she thought about that and decided she wanted to discuss this with Lance. Something wasn't right here, and it was bugging her. Oh, not with the protection she was receiving, but with something else. The Bureau's response didn't make real sense unless they had reason to believe this guy would hunt her. What made them think that? She wished she could call and find out.

But if she did, she'd once again reveal her whereabouts. Someone would ask a question, like whether she was satisfied with her protection.

Who, she wondered, had figured that she'd even stay here long enough to need it? Who, she wondered, was hoping she'd stay put? She'd got the read on her escape potential from the local sheriff, but who in Chicago would know this area that way? Who would understand that running wouldn't be a good option? Other than the Bureau, of course. There was little they couldn't find out if they wanted to.

Maybe if she'd been thinking more clearly she would have just bailed this morning, before anyone had a chance to catch up to her. Damn, had she been stupid again, deciding she wanted to just settle this matter? Brave words about having the showdown here.

She looked in the mirror, at the drawn shadow of herself she'd become, and said aloud, "Just give me my brain back."

Nobody knew more acutely than she just how far below par she was, and Lance was the only person she could test her thinking on. He seemed like a bright guy, and he had law enforcement experience.

She leaned against the sink for a few minutes, taking in again all that had happened to her. Apparently she had some issues to resolve that went beyond the immediate injuries. How many of them were being caused by her lingering fatigue, only time would tell. But right now she needed a sounding board.

She straightened again, ignoring tight muscles, equally tight scar tissue and a whole bunch of internal twinges. She not only had outward scars from flying debris, but she had some inside from the gunshot, from the blast wave that hadn't been entirely blocked by the tree that had probably saved her life. They'd pulled a piece of wood out of her liver, for heaven's sake.

It was a miracle she was still here. Just that simple. Thinking about that as she walked back down the hall, she decided that her decision to stay here might not have been a moment of poor judgment. Maybe she hoped to bait the guy into the open, to finally get this scum who got his jollies from ending the lives of young women.

For the first time in weeks, she felt a real fire in her belly for justice. Maybe even some vengeance.

She smelled fresh coffee and realized that Lance had anticipated her. When she reentered the living room, a steaming mug sat by the rocker. He had another beside him on the end table. The dogs lifted their heads to give her sloppy grins but remained at Lance's feet. They put their heads down as soon as she sat and closed their eyes.

"They're beautiful dogs," she told him, feeling an unexpected twinge of a wholly different kind. Man, this guy was sexy, and those blue-green eyes of his took her breath away. As if she was in any condition for that.

"I'm kinda fond of them."

She eased back into the rocker and eyed the bottle of pills that still sat beside her.

"Go ahead," he said. "If it'll make you feel better, the dogs and I will keep watch while you sleep."

She shook her head a little. "Maybe later, if you don't mind. Right now I want to talk."

He waved a large open hand. "You have the floor."

"First, I appreciate everything you're doing for me."

He tilted his head, smiling faintly. "Goes without saying."

"But…I'm not sure I'm thinking clearly about things. I've made some stupid mistakes, like leaving Chicago, like not paying attention to the possibility I could be followed. Like deciding to make a stand here as if this is a Gary Cooper movie."

At that he snorted, amused. "Gary Cooper, huh? You like the oldies?"

"Some of them," she admitted. "I guess you do, too."

"*High Noon.* Classic."

"Yeah, and purely mythical. Six-guns on main street at noon. Like that's going to happen. Reality is a whole lot uglier."

She watched his smile fade. "Yeah, it is," he agreed.

"I've put an undue burden on your department."

"Nah. Those guys you met tonight? They're not deputies. Sometimes we need 'em, and they step up. Mostly they enjoy an ordinary life with their families. If you ask me, they like a chance to be useful, or they'd say no."

"Maybe," she acknowledged. "But some of us realize the nightmares things like this could awaken in them."

"They still don't say no. But let's get back to you."

He was right. She was evading the subject. She'd told him she wanted to talk and now she was talking about everything except the concerns that had popped into her head.

"There's something wrong with this whole setup," she said finally.

"In what way?"

That was the hard part. "I wanted to call the field office earlier, to find out why they think the UNSUB would even follow me. Why he's moved out of the typical profile in their minds. Because he came after me in the first place? I wasn't in his victim profile, that's for sure. But I'm more than a thousand miles away now. Even if someone let it slip where I am, why should he make such a trip? I don't know who he is. If there's a leak, he should know that."

"Maybe that didn't leak. Or maybe he doesn't believe it. Or maybe he never really fit a familiar profile. Profiles have their limits, Erin. I think you know that."

She nodded, trying to conceal a wince as her neck protested. "But…them asking you to provide protection for me…that seems way out of line unless they know something I don't. That worries me."

"Something else is worrying you," he said, leaning forward to rest his elbows on his splayed legs. "Why don't you just spit it out?"

She hesitated, knowing how crazy it sounded. But then she decided to let it fly. If he told her she was crazy, she might feel a whole lot better. "Why," she said finally, "did they want me pinned in place?"

His head jerked a little at that. "That's how you're feeling?"

"I could have left this morning. I could have hit the

road to anywhere else. Asking you all for protection made it more likely I'd stay."

"Gary Cooper," he said.

"Exactly. They know me, probably better than I know myself. Except for them calling the sheriff, I'd have moved on this morning. They knew I'd get my back up and decide to stick it out. So why? Why do they want that? To use me as bait? Then they must have a reason to think he's still after me, because I'm even less of a threat to him now than I was before he shot me."

The silence in the room became palpable. The dogs, apparently feeling the tension, stirred and began to pace. One of them gave a quiet whine.

"Settle," Lance said, never taking his gaze from Erin. The dogs looked at him, then dropped to their bellies. Their postures remained alert, however, and their heads didn't lower to the floor between their paws.

Then Lance spoke the words she hadn't yet allowed to cross her own mind.

"Maybe," he said, "they think you're a specified target."

He watched Erin reach for the pill bottle and tip one into her hand. "Here comes la-la land," she said.

"Help yourself." He figured she needed it after what he'd just said. He couldn't believe the words had popped out of him, but they had, and reconsidering them he couldn't take them back. The question now was who on the inside wanted to put Erin out of the picture. That could be almost anyone, even less visible than this bomber. It didn't even have to be an FBI agent. Plenty of others must have been working on this task force in various capacities, including clerical workers. It opened up a whole range of possibilities. But clearly the Bureau felt someone was after Erin particularly. Either that, or they believed that if her location became known, they could find out where their leak was. Carefully parsing out information was often a good way to discover who had loose lips.

Instead of taking the pill, Erin set it on the table beside the bottle.

"Let me get you some water," he said.

"No. Not yet."

He could see her mental wheels spinning. She drained half her coffee cup without speaking a word, then sat with her eyes narrowed. After a bit, she said, "I could call Fran."

"Fran?"

"My best friend and fellow agent. Except when I thought of that earlier, I hesitated. Why, I don't know, except that by the following morning your sheriff had a call from my field office. She could have let them know where I was."

"Maybe I was the one who did that," he reminded her.

She gave a slight nod. "I trust Fran, but I don't trust her not to tell our bosses if she's worried about me. So, I didn't call. Which means I don't trust my own colleagues anymore."

"Plenty of reason for that." He waited, reaching over to pet one of his dogs. He didn't want to jump in and take over. He wanted her to work this through on her own, because he didn't think she was nearly as stupid right now as she seemed to think. She might not have considered some possibilities because of her health, but she was putting puzzle pieces together right now.

So was he, for that matter, and he didn't like the way they were fitting. Someone had leaked enough information about Erin that the bomber had not only wanted to get her, but had known her name, how to reach her by phone and where she lived. Seemingly, now that she was off the task force because she was on medical leave, she was no longer a threat. Whatever she had discovered was known to everyone working the case. Not for a while would she discover anything else. Maybe never. They might not return her to the task force at all.

So she ought to be in the clear. But the Bureau feared for her enough to call a local sheriff and ask for her protection. He hated to think that Erin might be correct, that they might have known she would decide to remain in place. Because if they had acted for that reason, then she was right: she was being used as bait.

But bait for whom? A bomber they couldn't identify? Or someone in their own ranks they wanted to draw out? He could imagine that some people didn't like her. Almost no one was universally liked. But to have the kind of enemy who wanted her dead?

Maybe her bosses believed it was a possibility. Maybe they thought that was the explanation for the leak that had almost killed her. God, as a rule, the Feds were a tight-lipped bunch. He'd worked on a couple of cases with them in Denver and had felt a gnawing frustration at how little they were willing to share even when they were on the same side.

A thought occurred to him. "You ever bring down a cop?"

Her eyes widened a shade. "You think the bomber could be a real cop?"

"I don't know. I'm just asking. You folks are the ones who investigate cops who cross certain lines. You come in to investigate rogue departments and rogue cops. So have you ever brought down any cops?"

"Yes," she said. A sigh escaped. "Oh, yes. For a while

I was on a police corruption task force. We brought down quite a few guys. That's an idea worth entertaining."

He figured it was. And this woman needed to sleep. He sought something to say that would allow her to let go until morning. "I'm getting you a glass of water," he said finally. "Take at least a half dose of those pain pills and get some sleep. We'll both be thinking better in the morning."

Then she said something that told him how alive her trauma was. "Will the dogs be on alert?"

"Believe it. And I'm going to be sleeping with one eye open. I'm not hard to wake. Besides, there's a perimeter around this house now, okay? And I seriously doubt anyone could have found you at my place so fast."

At last she nodded. He went to get her water, and when he came back he was relieved that she took one of those pills. "Pain is exhausting," he reminded her. "A good night's sleep will do you wonders."

"I hope so. I just wish recovery didn't take so long."

He watched her stand stiffly.

"You need any help unpacking? I set the cases on top of the dresser, so I hope you don't have to move them."

"I've moved them before. Good night, Lance. And thanks for everything." She picked up her pill bottle and her pistol and hobbled away. Just watching her made him wince. She'd probably sat in that rocker too long.

But there was nothing more he could do for her. Except keep watch. He slept on the couch with the dogs nearby, sure he or they would hear any untoward sound.

Throughout the night, he woke every so often and walked through the house, checking things. Pointless, but it made him feel better to do it.

Erin had left her door open, and he saw her lying on her side beneath the green comforter. In sleep she looked less drawn, less pinched. Unicorns and rainbows were exactly what she needed right now.

Nodding to himself, he returned to the couch. Sleep brought him dreams of making love to the woman who slept only a few feet away.

In the morning, gray light poured through the windows. Lance didn't expect rain because this was their dry time of year. Whatever clouds boiled up often seemed to dump their load farther along and not here.

But he didn't mind the cloudiness. After showering and shaving, he donned his favorite jeans and a fresh blue polo shirt. He let the dogs out back to run off some energy, making sure the buckets were full of water and kibble. Then he went to the kitchen to start breakfast with no idea if Erin would even wake for hours yet. One thing he knew—he'd need a grocery run soon. He wasn't stocked up for a houseguest.

How would he manage that, he wondered. He didn't feel he ought to take her into town, but he wasn't sure he should leave her alone out here. Unexpected logistical problems. His fault for not having thought of them before bringing her here.

"Good morning."

Surprised that she was awake so early, he turned and saw her. Hair still tousled from sleep, wearing a cotton nightgown that nearly reached her ankles, she looked good enough to eat. And much better than she had looked last night.

"I thought you'd sleep longer," he said.

"I always answer the call of frying bacon. Can I use the shower?"

"Help yourself. Fresh towels are in the closet just behind the bathroom door."

"Thanks."

He was sorry to see her vanish again, but turned back to his cooking. Time to make sure he prepared enough for two. She'd displayed a pretty good appetite yesterday, so he guessed she wasn't one of those women who barely nibbled at a plate of food. Good. He hated that.

Since he'd risen, he'd been rolling around the pieces of the puzzle she'd given him, trying to fit them together, sensing important pieces were still missing. He'd almost bet she didn't know what they were. She hadn't given him the feeling that she was withholding.

But it was frustrating. No real certainty that this guy would come after her, other than the concern her field office had shown. No idea when he might show up if he did. No idea who he was. Suspicions about her colleagues that he wasn't prepared to casually dismiss.

The whole situation stank, but that made no difference. He'd volunteered to join her on this journey, regardless of where it took them. Besides, he just plain couldn't see himself walking away. Not just because he was a cop either, but because he was also a man.

The woman needed someone on her side. He'd never tell her that because he suspected she considered herself well able to take care of herself, injuries notwithstanding. In fact, she'd preferred it to hiding out in a safe house.

No, she'd taken off into the great unknown all by herself, only to wind up surrounded by the protection she thought she could do without. Probably didn't make her a happy camper.

When Erin reappeared, she was wearing some khaki slacks with a red blouse that heightened her rosy appearance. He hoped that rosiness would remain. Her short black hair was still damp and curling in ringlets all over. He guessed she didn't want to bother with the effort of drying it out and combing it straighter. He liked the effect, though.

"You're looking better," he remarked, safely skirting the subject of how pretty she was.

"Feeling better, too," she said with a smile. "Oh, I'm far from healed, but when I got up this morning, the initial shock of pain wasn't as strong as it has been. Good sign."

"I'd say so. Maybe those pain meds helped you have a more relaxed sleep."

She tilted her head, thanking him as he put coffee in front of her. "Maybe you're right. I hadn't thought about what might be happening when I'm asleep. Like being tense because I didn't want to make something hurt by moving wrong."

"Exactly. Eggs?"

She looked at the platter of bacon on the table and the tower of buttered rye toast. "Actually, do you have any peanut butter?"

He did, and brought the jar to the table along with a knife for spreading. "Just be careful of my grandmother's fine china. That peanut butter jar has been in the family for generations."

She laughed, a delightful sound, as he put a plate in front of her. "Dig in. I'm going to make myself a couple of eggs. You want jam or jelly?"

"Just the peanut butter."

Soon they faced each other across the table. Erin seemed determined to direct the conversation away from her predicament, and he was fine with that.

"So how long has your family lived here?" she asked.

"The Conroes started ranching here over a hundred and twenty years ago."

She raised her gaze from her toast. "Those are some deep roots. Did everybody stay?"

"Of course not." He half smiled. "Just so much ranch to go around, and some of the family wanted a better style of life."

"And you left to become a cop."

"Well, my dad had wound down the ranch quite a bit. It was getting to be too much. Raising cattle is expensive these days and most of the price of beef isn't reaching the independent rancher. It's a hard way to make a living unless you've got a big factory farm."

"So the land lies fallow?"

"A neighbor grazes his sheep on some of it. The rest…" He shrugged. "I toy with the things I could do with it, but I'm not ready to give up law enforcement. I like my work too much. You?"

"Same here. I like what I do." She flushed faintly. "When I was a kid I wanted to grow up to be a caped crusader."

"Dang, I don't think the FBI issues capes."

She laughed again, a full, comfortable laugh. "They overlooked that part. Still, I'm proud of what I've done. Like you, I suppose."

"Any family?"

She hesitated. "My family was dysfunctional. My mother was an alcoholic. Despite our best efforts, that pretty much drove us apart and not together. So…mostly strangers. I have a sister, though, and I see her once a year."

"Where is she?"

"She's volunteering as a doctor with the World Health Organization in Africa."

He forgot his breakfast. "That's pretty impressive."

"I think so." She bit into her peanut butter toast and

he watched as she licked a bit of peanut butter off her lip. The urge to lick those lips himself nearly swamped him. Damn, he had to cut this out somehow. It was the last thing either of them needed. He really had to remember her frail state. And the fear she must be facing.

"I'm thinking I have to get some groceries soon," he remarked. "It might be wise to take care of that sooner than later, on the theory that if this perp is coming after you it'll take him at least a little time to get here. You want to come?"

She looked up, and he could see her pondering. "Preparing for a siege?"

"I hope not, for both our sakes. But I didn't shop for two this week. So?"

She looked down, then met his gaze again. "I'll go with you, if that won't cause problems."

"Good. I'll arrange it with the rest of the detail. We'll be watched in town while someone keeps an eye on the house."

He could see how much that idea relieved her. Of course it did. It would be beyond irony to go grocery shopping and come back to a house that was rigged with a bomb.

"You know, it sickens me," she said presently.

"What?"

"You're risking your family's house for me. Have you even thought about that?"

Not in depth, because his instinct was to care for her. A human life had always seemed more important to him than property. "I know," he said finally.

"It would be awful, Lance." Her face had taken on an almost pleading expression. "I'd never forgive myself."

"Forgive yourself for what? You didn't ask this guy to try to kill you. That's all on him. And frankly, in this county there's no better place to put you. In town others would be at risk. Out here, it's just you and me."

"And your house."

He shrugged. "Houses can be rebuilt."

"Not with the memories."

Nothing he could say to that. "Look, just trust those other guys out there, okay? Your UNSUB has no idea what he's going to be walking into."

Her mouth curved wryly. "A buzz saw?"

"Pretty much."

She shook her head a little and reached for another piece of toast. She spread the peanut butter thinly, then helped herself to a strip of bacon. "I need to get out, need to walk around to keep my strength up, so thanks for taking me along to the grocery."

He liked the way she was willing to let go of a conversation when it was done. No obsession in this one, unless she used it all on her job. And she granted him the right to make his own decision about the risks. Nothing quite like working with a pro.

After he finished eating, he insisted that he'd do the dishes. "No point stirring up your discomfort again," he said. That ended that.

But before he washed up, he called Gage. "We need to go to town to do some grocery shopping. I'm taking Agent Sanders with me…Thanks."

She was waiting when he hung up the phone. "He's having Nate contact the team and will call when they're ready for us to move."

She simply nodded, apparently used to this kind of thing. But of course, she'd probably worked on a variety of stakeouts and protection details in her career. She certainly seemed willing to grant that these men knew what they were doing. She didn't ask for details, or try to take control in any way.

Which brought him to something else he wanted to know about her. He hesitated while they settled in the living room with coffee. Finally he just asked. "Are you feeling as if you've given up control?"

"Well, I have, haven't I?"

He nodded. "Driving you nuts?"

"A little. But teams work together. If I have a part to play, I suspect I'll know it when the time comes."

"It's possible that nothing at all will happen."

"I can hope." She paused. "You know, Lance, I may be more worried that nothing happens. How do we know this is over, short of catching the guy? At some point I'm going to need to return to Chicago. At some point I'll be ready to go back to work. I could take advantage of your hospitality with weeks for no good reason at all."

He didn't see it that way at all, but supposed he should avoid letting her know that he was enjoying her company. "You're not taking advantage of me. I volunteered, remember?"

And once again she let it go.

But she had a valid concern, he admitted. She might never be safe until they had this guy in a cell, and when she went back to work she might be even more exposed than she was here. Right now, this creep had a huge advantage: he could simply wait her out, wait for her to return to Chicago.

But, judging by the call Gage had got, the Bureau didn't think so. That was all they had to work with right now.

Finally they got the go-ahead to visit the grocery. As Erin eased into his truck, she winced a little and seemed to have trouble settling comfortably. Unlike when he'd picked her up along the road, she wasn't likely to sleep through it. For the first time he noticed just how many jolts there were in the gravel road. She sucked a breath each time they hit one, so he slowed down.

"You were married?" she asked.

He got the feeling she wanted some distraction. "For three years. Then she met someone else. Until that point I thought it was all good."

"People change."

"Yeah, they do. And sometimes they grow apart without even realizing it until it all blows up. I guess we were growing apart and I didn't know."

"I'm sorry."

"I was back then, too," he admitted. "Not anymore. I'm long over it."

"How old are you?"

"Thirty-seven. You?"

"Thirty-three."

"I'm surprised you aren't settled."

"I thought I was for a while. That didn't work either. My job's not easy to live with. Lots of secrets and long hours."

He hadn't thought about the secrets part. That could be a problem for some people, all the things you couldn't talk about. "And he's stalking you?"

"Not exactly. Occasional calls suggesting we try again. But after the way it blew up, I'm not interested. It was ugly, and he spewed a lot of the ugliness. Nothing like the hideous things that can be said by people you've trusted and who know you well."

"Oh, I hear you." Loud and clear. May had shredded him at the end with her reasons for leaving. She knew every button to push.

He'd got past May's attack, but he wondered if Erin

had got past the scars from hers. The way she had talked about not needing another man in her life probably said it all. He'd certainly be wise to keep that in mind.

Besides, she was an agent with a job to go back to. And go she would. She'd worked hard to get into the Bureau and to stay there. Why would anyone give that up?

"So did you go to law school?" he asked, to keep on distracting her.

"Yes."

The brevity of the answer suggested the pain was starting to dominate again. He hurried to reassure her. "Paved road just ahead."

"Good." She was looking around. "So where's our protection detail?"

"You shouldn't see them, not the way they operate."

"But how else will they follow us to town?"

"Eyes in the sky."

"Really." At that she seemed to forget her discomfort and twisted to look at him. Just then they reached the smooth pavement. "A helicopter? Out here?"

"We have a few, mostly for medevacs and search and rescue."

"And they can be used for something like this?"

"Believe it. They're all equipped with long-range lenses for observation. And night gear, of course."

He glanced at her and thought she looked impressed. This little backwater sheriff's department probably didn't look quite so backwater to her now.

For some reason, that made him proud as punch. If she thought she was dealing with Mayberry, she was in for a surprise.

Chapter 6

By the time they reached the grocery store, Erin was ready to walk. Somehow that didn't seem as painful as sitting inside a moving vehicle, even one that was clearly being driven as gently as possible. Every bend or bump in the road made her move in uncomfortable ways. Not much to do about that.

She climbed out under her own steam, and tried stretching a little, stifling a few small cries as something inside her told her to cut it out. She'd been advised of the necessity of stretching to keep adhesions from forming, to keep herself loose and mobile. The last thing she wanted to do was curl into a small ball and cause all of this to take longer…or to give herself a new set of problems.

She didn't argue, however, when Lance suggested she push the cart. It steadied her the way her walker—which she had refused to use—was supposed to. And today, for once, she appreciated that.

Uneasiness crept throughout her body. For the first time in her life, being in public made her uncomfortable. Man, she hoped she wasn't developing another problem, a psychological one. She was already messed up enough, and suspected she hadn't begun to plumb the aftereffects of having been shot and having her house blown up.

People looked at her curiously, then smiled faintly when they realized she was with Lance, whom they greeted warmly. She noticed he introduced her only as his friend. She guessed the gossip was about to fly, which concerned her a bit. Someone looking for her in this town could easily find out she was staying with Lance.

But he must have thought about that? She decided to bring it up when they were back in the car.

Lance asked for her suggestions about food and meals. It was kind of embarrassing to admit that she rarely cooked for herself. It was far easier, as a single person in a big city, just to find a good meal at a restaurant. Less work, less hassle, and more variety than she was likely to make for herself.

"So you don't cook?" He smiled. "My pleasure, then. I enjoy it. I find it a good way to unwind."

She felt even more exposed as they crossed the parking lot. A warm wind had kicked up, tossing nearby trees and blowing the occasional piece of trash across the black-top. One unattended shopping cart entered its own derby, heading for a curb. No cars in the way, thank goodness.

Lance told her to wait inside the car while he loaded groceries. Much as she hated to be so helpless, the truth was she was shaking again, feeling her strength ebbing once more. She needed rest. Damn, how she hated that. Walking around a grocery shouldn't have left her feeling as if she had just climbed Everest at a jog.

"You like Danish?" he asked as he climbed in with her and started the engine.

"All kinds," she confessed.

"Then I'll swing by the bakery. Good excuse to indulge my sweet tooth."

She balked, exerting the only control she could. "Not just for me."

He was just about to release the parking break when he turned and smiled at her. "Not just for you," he said. "I think I mentioned I have a sweet tooth. I usually avoid it, but today I'm in the mood."

"But you wouldn't just get it for yourself."

"You're just the excuse."

She let it go. It was a silly thing to argue about, and there were a lot more important issues. "I want to help pay for the groceries."

"I'll bill the Bureau when we return you safely."

At that her prickliness softened and she laughed. "Good luck with that."

"Hey, I'm on *their* detail. I should be able to expense it." But he laughed, too.

She had watched intently for her group of guardians, but didn't see them anywhere. Lance had said they would be around, but even looking for them hadn't helped. That was good. Amazing, even. She had been well trained in the fine art of observation and facial identification.

"Lance?"

"Yeah?" He pulled up against a curb in front of a bakery.

"You introduced me as your friend to all those people. How likely is that to get around?"

"Everyone in town will know it soon."

She drew a sharp breath of apprehension. "That's not good."

"Well, we want the guy to find you if he comes. But honestly, Erin, the last thing these folks will do is discuss you with a stranger. Gossip may be a favorite pastime around here, but nobody shares anything personal with strangers."

She felt like a piece of cheese in a mousetrap. But maybe that was the whole point now. She'd decided to stay here and have the showdown, rather than continue running. *She* had made the choice. If she was the cheese, there was only one way the rat could find her.

"Will you be all right here?" he asked.

"Sure." Although she still felt exposed as he climbed out and walked into the bakery. She hated to give in to the fear. She wasn't used to being afraid, as a rule. In dangerous situations, adrenaline usually carried her through, and the fear never really touched her. This was different. She felt like she was wearing a target with no idea where the threat might be. No idea who might be a threat. Everyone walking these streets appeared to belong here, but since she hadn't seen the guy's face, how would she know?

The urge to keep moving was strong, but a ruthless judgment of her own physical condition reminded her that even walking to the end of the block might be a little more than she could manage after the grocery and its parking lot.

She saw Lance emerge quickly and was struck again by what an appealing man he was. He walked with easy confidence, he smiled at everyone he met and shortly climbed in beside her with a white paper bag that emitted mouthwatering aromas. The guy was mouthwatering himself.

Instead of fighting it, she allowed her attraction for him to take over. It was better than fear any day.

"Raspberry Danish," he said as they pulled away from the curb and headed back toward his home.

"Love it," she managed to say, although somehow it had become a little difficult to breathe. Thinking about this man's attractions had revved up the only motor in her that wasn't half-dead yet. She wanted him in the rawest, most primal way possible. The likelihood of that happening, given her condition, seemed remote, but the fantasy was yummier than the Danish she could smell.

Broad shoulders, flat stomach, narrow hips, eyes the color of the waters around Key West. Eyes she could cheerfully drown in.

Soon they were out of town and on their way to his home. The flare of desire eased as fatigue began to take over again. It would have been so easy to fall asleep, but her mind refused to let her. She was still exposed out here, eyes in the sky notwithstanding. Wherever her guardians were, she could detect nothing at all.

Except for being with Lance, this whole situation stank, she thought wearily. Something wasn't right, and it wasn't just the crazy bomber who was troubling her. The details weren't adding up to her satisfaction, and until they did she couldn't ignore anything. Her mind would keep tumbling the pieces around as she tried to pick the lock, waiting for the *snick* that would tell her she had hit on something.

Her cell phone rang, but she ignored it.

"It might be your friend," Lance said.

"Fran? It probably is."

"Then…"

"I don't want to talk to her right now. I don't want to talk to anyone from back there right now."

"Ah, distrust. It's such a fruitful tree."

"Fast growing, too."

"Are you wondering about Fran?"

"Not really." That much was true. She and Fran had been best buds for years now. Distrusting her would be a betrayal of their friendship. But still…

She glanced at him again, but his attention was firmly focused on the road as they once again hit gravel and all the bumps.

"I'm sorry I can't smooth this out for you," he remarked.

"I'll live." She would, too. She was more prepared for the jolts this time.

They turned up his drive, which was hardly more than a graveled, rutted track, when she saw someone riding a horse out of the distant woods. "Who's that?" she asked swiftly.

Lance looked. "Seth Hardin, one of your protectors."

"Is something wrong?"

"I hardly think he'd be trying to look like an ordinary rancher paying a call if it was."

"Do people still ride horses to visit each other?" The idea astonished her.

"Only if it's more convenient. We *have* entered the twenty-first century."

Immediately she felt that she had offended him, but wasn't quite sure how or why. When she turned her head, however, he was smiling faintly.

"In these parts," he said after a moment, "the horse would draw less attention than a Humvee."

Despite everything, she had to laugh. "True, I guess."

"I wonder what he wants."

At that she tensed inwardly. So this wasn't expected. Her fingers gripped the armrest until her hands ached. Something had happened.

"You stay in the car," he said as they neared the house. "I'll talk to Seth."

"I want to hear."

"Then roll down your window a crack but no more."

It didn't help when he climbed out and she heard the car doors lock with a *thunk*. Locking her in or locking something out? She pressed the window button and lowered it an inch.

Seth reached them a minute later.

"What's going on?" Lance demanded.

"Just letting you know no one approached the house."

"You couldn't call?"

"You left your radio behind, didn't you."

A string of cusswords emanated from Lance that caused Erin to clap her hand over her mouth to smother a laugh. He looked so angry.

"Guess you don't usually take it grocery shopping," Seth said, flashing a smile. "Anyway, the house is safe, go on inside."

"You want some coffee?"

"Well, I do have a couple of empty thermos bottles with me."

"Then come inside. I need to bring in the groceries, but I want Erin to get comfortable. Then I'll make a few pots of coffee."

All of it was suddenly amusing to Erin. She watched Seth swing out of the saddle with practiced ease and toss the horse's reins over the porch railing.

"Let me help with those groceries," Seth said.

"First, Erin gets inside."

With effort, she unlocked her door and pushed it open. "I can do it."

"You," Lance said frankly, "have overdone it and look

like hell." Without waiting for an answer, he swept her off her feet and carried her inside.

"I do not look like hell," she argued, but even to her own ears didn't sound very forceful.

"I've seen paste with more color," he retorted.

High-handed man. He put her down on the couch, and by then Seth was toting bags of groceries inside. Together the men dealt with them while she sat steaming, first at being carried around like a sack of potatoes, and then because she really couldn't have done a thing to help at that point. Making the only point she could, she dragged herself to the rocking chair.

Listening to the men laugh in the kitchen, she felt very alone and very much on the outside.

And there was nobody but herself to blame for that.

A while later, with full thermal jugs of coffee in his saddlebags, Seth entered the living room. Lance wasn't far behind. Seth put down the bags and sat on one end of the couch. Lance remained standing in the doorway, leaning against the frame with his arms folded.

"Got a minute?" Seth asked.

"Of course," she answered. This man was giving up whatever life he had to protect her. She certainly wasn't going to be rude, although crankiness seemed to be building in her.

"I just thought you'd want to know what we're doing. At all times we have two sets of eyes on the house. Frequent air sweeps are occurring but you won't notice them because they won't fly right over. When you went into town, we followed you by air. In the middle of the day, town would be an unlikely place for this guy to take action, but a number of deputies were on alert for anything out of the ordinary at the grocery."

"Thank you," she managed.

He smiled. "Our pleasure. The thing I want to know is this—how badly do you want this guy to find you? If you want this over with, we can leak your whereabouts. If you'd rather he not find out, we can ensure that he can search the town top to bottom and not learn a damned thing."

What a decision. She sat looking at a man whose competence she didn't for a moment doubt, then glanced at Lance. "It's not fair to Lance to drag this out."

"Well, we're not exactly in control of the timeline. Don't even know who we're looking for."

Then Lance spoke. "Enough of this fairness stuff. I'm a volunteer. What *I'd* like to know is what *you* want?"

She hesitated, pursing her lips, forcing her fatigued mind to address the situation. "What do I really want?" she said finally. "Another week or two of recuperation so I can help meet this guy head-on if he shows up. And once I'm a little better, I *so* want to take him down. He killed five young women for no discernable reason other than his personal jollies. I loathe him. I want him behind bars, and I want to help put him there."

"Done," said Seth, rising. "We'll keep you invisible."

She looked up. "People know I'm here."

"People can also hear that you've left. We'll take care of it for now. Just don't tell anyone back home where you are. That seemed to have seriously worried your field office."

"Noted." More than noted. It seriously worried *her*. "Who called the sheriff anyway?"

Lance shifted. "You know, I didn't ask. Do you need to know?"

"It might give me an idea who's worried and how many people might know where I am."

"I'll check into it."

Seth scooped up his saddlebags. "Thanks for the coffee. Erin? If we shift our team, I'll personally introduce you to any new guys. Don't believe anyone but me."

Erin listened to him leave, then watched through the front window as he rode away. "Why should I only believe him?"

"Because he knows who might be helping, which might at some point be more than I do. I know most of the folks around here, but apparently Seth is developing his own case of mistrust."

She pondered that, her stomach flipping. "About what?" she asked finally.

"Right now I don't think he'd trust someone who showed up with Bureau creds wanting to see you."

Erin wasn't so sure she would either. Damn, she felt sickened. Then another thought struck her and escaped her lips before she could stop it. She was usually good at concealing her thoughts, but since her brush with death... well, silence was harder. "I feel set up," she said.

Lance's attention zeroed in on her like a laser. "How so?"

Too late to recall the words. Her stomach soured. "I don't know."

"Yes, I think you do."

She glared at him. "I'm a mess. Nobody should listen to me right now."

"I wouldn't say that." Then he crossed the room, ignored her protests, and carried her to the couch. Sitting beside him made everything else want to go away. God, he smelled so good, felt so strong. It was like sitting next to a bulwark. The urge to weaken filled her, and she hated herself for it. She was no weakling.

And yet she loved being this close to him, and part of

her wished he would put his arm around her, hold her to his side, tell her everything would be okay. It would be a lie, of course, but such a sweet lie.

Then her internal spine stiffened. What kind of weak vine was she becoming? This wasn't her. This was a side of her that existed only because of a trauma and the overwhelming physical fatigue.

"Why'd you do that?" she demanded.

"Because I want you to know you're not alone."

"I figured that out," she said acidly. "And I don't like being toted around like a sack of potatoes."

"You could never resemble a sack of potatoes," he answered. Was that a laugh trembling in his voice? "Look, I wanted you closer. Sorry I took matters into my own hands."

He wanted her closer? A kernel of warmth stubbornly blossomed in her heart and between her legs. No, no, no. She was acting like a young idiot and she'd left that behind long ago.

"Now," he said, wisely changing the subject, "why do you feel set up?"

She let a sigh escape. "We went over it."

"So let's go over it again."

"You are one stubborn man."

"Back atcha."

Despite her crankiness, a small bubble of laughter escaped her.

"Better," he approved. "Now run me through it again. Maybe I'll hear something differently this time."

She sighed again, feeling like a hamster running in a wheel, but acknowledging that he might indeed pick out something he'd missed before. Or she might. "The identity of agents working on a task force is closely guarded.

The task force in this case consists of two agencies, the Bureau and ATF."

"Makes sense."

"Anyway, we have a face, the agent who addresses reporters and the public, but only when necessary. Everything else is hush-hush. Even under ordinary circumstances the Bureau doesn't like to reveal the identity or appearance of particular agents working a case. Getting my name, knowing who I was to get past the switchboard, finding my home address…those things shouldn't have been easy."

"Property records once the guy knew your name?"

She shook her head. "The deed is under my maiden name. A simple records search wouldn't link me with it."

"Layers and layers," he remarked, then fell silent.

"Anyway, as stupid as it may sound, it suddenly occurred to me that I might have been identified on purpose, not by accident."

He gave a low whistle, and stared out the window. "I don't think that was a stupid thought. Nor, I suspect, does whoever called the sheriff. Let me give him a call right now."

He rose and went to get a phone, and she sat there feeling strangely bereft. Considering she was used to being alone except at work, her reaction seemed strange. But then all her reactions seemed to be messed up right now.

Poking around inside, she tried to find the woman she had been only a month ago. She must still be in there somewhere. Or maybe she had been irrevocably changed. She hated to even think of the possibility.

Lance returned shortly. "Your ASAC called the sheriff. Tom Villiers. And he was quite definite that Gage should speak to no one else at the field office."

"That's not good," she murmured. Most definitely not

good. Tom didn't want anyone else to know what was going on. Distrust had grown there, too. A fruitful tree, as Lance had said.

He sat beside her again. "Want one of those pain pills? I can give you coffee to keep you awake."

She seriously thought about it. Every part of her seemed to be hurting since their trip to the store, and sleeping without pain last night had been restorative, at least for a while.

Then she realized that the dull aches that were so annoying her had reached the level of throbbing. The sharp spears couldn't be far behind.

She twisted her head, looking up at Lance, and realized she trusted him. "Thank you. I guess I will take some."

He nodded. "So some trust grows at last."

"I'm not a complete fool," she said a little sharply. "You didn't know me from Adam two days ago. What's more, with all that's happened with your sheriff, I think someone would have remarked that you'd been leaving town often over the past few months. So you're not my bomber, obviously."

A snort escaped him. "Finally vetted."

"Don't make fun of me."

"I'm not." For the first time he showed a spark of something besides humor and concern. The gaze he shot her was as sharp as steel. "You have every reason to be suspicious right now. Only a fool wouldn't be. How much do you trust your ASAC?"

She caught her breath. Shock seemed to ripple through her aching body. "My God." Words deserted her.

"Right. I'll get that water and your pill bottle. Don't you stir more than an inch or two."

For once she didn't argue. The new thoughts roiling

around inside her terrified her. Tom? A vague suspicion that someone on the task force might have set her up was a far cry from putting a face on that person. But Tom... She couldn't imagine it. He had fifteen years with the Bureau and a stellar record. Never a hint of trouble. By the book and a damned good investigator. He could have been the poster boy for an exceptional agent.

But the idea that anyone... Lord, would she have to start considering them all, one by one? Friends, acquaintances, coworkers? Who could be so angry with her and why?

Abruptly, she became aware that Lance was holding out her pill bottle and a glass of water. She wanted to brush it aside now, but realized that some of her injuries hurt enough that soon they'd be an utter distraction from clear thought, pill or no pill.

So she took only one instead of the recommended two. Lance had undoubtedly read the dose on the bottle, but he didn't say anything. He put them aside, then returned with fresh coffee.

"You look like you just had a really unpleasant thought," he remarked.

"I did. If I was set up, then that means that someone in the task force is in contact with the killer."

He nodded. "Obviously. What else?"

"I suddenly wondered if those first five victims were simply a cover for coming after me. And who the hell among my coworkers could actually work with a bomber? That should violate every FBI agent's code. Who could get into the Bureau with a psychological twist like that?"

"I'm not familiar with the requirements."

She sighed and let her head fall back. A shiver of pure delight ran through her as he took her hand gently in his. "You don't just take a test. You don't just finish a degree in one of a number of critical skill areas. You don't just pass a thorough background check. We're tested in real-life situations to see how we'll react. The whole time we're training, we're being watched for weaknesses, mistakes. We're watched throughout our entire careers. The Bureau doesn't want any rogue agents."

"I can sure understand why. And there have been very few over the agency's history."

"A mere handful. So fitness isn't limited to physical conditioning. It includes an ongoing and constant psychological and emotional evaluation. We tend to be boring and very stable people actually."

"Well, you're not boring."

"But I suspect I'm not very stable at the moment. When I'm physically well enough to return to duty, as you know, I'll be seeing a psychologist for evaluation."

"That's wise, don't you think?"

"Of course it is." The pill was just beginning to take effect. She could feel the faint buzz of it throughout her body and her mind. The medicine did make it possible for her to turn her head and look at him, however. Definitely a plus, she thought, looking into his amazing eyes. "No one, absolutely no one, should be involved in something like this, concealing a killer to get a fellow agent. I won't say there are no politics, but not of this kind."

"I read you. I also get that this is getting uglier by the moment, and I wouldn't have believed that was possible."

"Everything inside me is rebelling." But whether she rebelled or not, the snake had entered the garden, and with it questions and doubts were springing up like weeds.

Who the hell did she know that would be capable of such atrocity?

Chapter 7

Lance had steadily been urging her to take the pain pills. She'd slept a lot, rested a lot, and three mornings later she awoke to find that when she climbed out of bed the shock of the familiar pain that usually froze her in place had subsided to something much duller.

After showering and dressing in slacks and a black T-shirt blazoned with *FBI*, she went out to the kitchen to find him cooking breakfast.

"Good morning," she said.

He turned slightly from the stove where he seemed to be making scrambled eggs. "Morning. You look a lot better."

"I'm feeling better," she agreed, entering the kitchen. This time she got her own coffee.

"Can I say I told you so?"

"Be my guest." She smiled. "You were right. Rest works better than pushing through."

"Had a little experience of that," he agreed and turned back to the stove. "Scrambled eggs okay?"

"Fine."

"There's toast on the table."

There was also a jar of peanut butter. Silly, but it was touching that he'd been putting that out every morning since the first time she had asked for it. Even her ex hadn't bothered with that, figuring that she could get it herself if she wanted it. Which was true. But having someone think of such little things was a new experience for her.

"No more info?" she asked him.

"Nada. We're still on alert, but your field office hasn't called except once to make sure we still had eyes on you."

"Maybe I should call Fran. She must be getting really worried by now."

"Maybe," he agreed. "Tell me about Fran."

So she sat with her coffee and began spreading peanut butter in a thin layer on a slice of toast. "She's been my friend since I took my first field assignment. In a way, she was my mentor. Being women, we had our own set of problems, if you follow me."

"I do."

"So we kind of supported each other through all the hazing. We haven't always been assigned together, but we've remained friends ever since."

"Friends like that are good to have."

Maybe, she thought, keeping it to herself. The passage of time had only made her uneasier about the whole situation. Every case involved a certain amount of uncertainty and shadowboxing, at least in the initial stages. With this bomber she'd been shadowboxing for way too long. "I wonder if I should call Tom. If he's figuring out anything he wouldn't share it outside the Bureau."

"There's an idea." He brought a heaping mound of moist scrambled eggs to the table, then sat across from her with his own eggs. "You're a pretty woman, Erin Sanders. Even more so this morning. I'm not surprised your ASAC wants to date you."

His words took her aback. It wasn't that she hadn't noticed the way he looked at her sometimes, and certainly she was aware of the yearnings he awoke in her, but they'd studiously avoided such subjects. Wisely, she thought.

"I guess I shouldn't have said that," he said. "I don't want you feeling uneasy under my roof."

"I don't feel uneasy." No, what she felt was quite the opposite. She felt appreciated. Quite a contrast to feeling like a hobbled, washed-out dishrag. She summoned a smile. "You're not so bad yourself, Deputy."

He chuckled. "I guess we covered that subject as much as we ought to."

"Why?" she asked bluntly. "It's normal. If I were in better condition, you might have to look out." There, she'd said it, and it was like removing a weight from her chest. Some things were easier to deal with in the open. This was one of them.

"Oh, your condition wouldn't matter," he said, a twinkle in those aquamarine eyes. "Believe me, I could love you in a way that wouldn't cause you a single twinge."

She lost her breath. If she had been blunt, he'd just been much more so, and the images he conjured caused her heart to slam and her body to hit hyperdrive. "Just like that?" she finally managed to say.

"Just like that," he agreed. But apparently he felt they'd taken this as far as they should. "Tell me about your ex."

"Why? He doesn't have anything to do with this."

"He has plenty to do with you."

She thought it over while eating some of her toast and sipping coffee. "Okay, but then it's your turn."

One corner of his mouth twitched. "Deal."

"Paul was a great guy in many respects," she said loyally. "We were just a bad pairing. He liked regular hours, a regular life. I don't have that very often. He also started worrying about me to the point that he wanted me to quit."

"About your safety?"

She nodded. "I would venture that my job is probably safer than yours."

"Not around here," he laughed. "So he wanted you to quit. And do what, exactly?"

"That was never clear," she admitted, "but I somehow don't think he was imagining me as a police officer, period."

"What then?" But he didn't seem to expect an answer. "What did he do for a living?"

"He was a minister."

At that his head snapped up. A moment later a laugh escaped him. "Somehow I just can't see that combination."

"Apparently you're right." She was unable to repress her own smile. "I simply didn't have the inclination or time to be a good minister's wife. I thought the ground rules were clear by the time we'd dated for a while. Clearly not. It was like an elephant in the room, and the longer we ignored it, the bigger it seemed to get." Until he had finally accused her of trying to hamper his career, of preventing him from getting a position at a larger church.

He arched one eyebrow, unsuccessfully concealing a grin. "Maybe he worried that if anyone learned you were FBI it might make some in his congregation uneasy."

She was glad she had nothing in her mouth then, because a laugh burst out of her. "He'd know more about that than I would."

"Privy to all the secrets, huh? That can be an uncomfortable situation." He finished the last of his eggs and reached for a slice of toast. "So are you stir-crazy yet?"

"I've been too tired. But it'll come. I'm not used to being so inactive."

"Neither am I. Never wanted to count the cracks and stains on the ceiling."

All of sudden she felt just terrible. "I'm so sorry, Lance."

He winked. "I've built up a long list of things I need to do around here. That's not a bad thing. It's just that they're easier to ignore when I'm sweeping through in a rush."

"Well, it's my fault. I'm sure you didn't want to baby-sit someone who sleeps so much."

He shrugged one powerful shoulder. "I don't mind. You're cute when you sleep, and it's time I quit ignoring the minor details around here. When I moved in to help Mom out, there were a whole lot of major problems to deal with. Then I lost track of the small stuff."

"I haven't noticed anything," she offered. "It's a nice house." And she *did* feel just awful. She hadn't been thinking about how difficult it might be for him to be pinned in place like this.

"It could be nicer," he answered easily. "I might even take a stab at some of it when it won't bother you."

Her discomfort finally brought color to her cheeks. "You can't let me interfere with everything. That's not right."

"Like I said, I volunteered." His face darkened a shade. "I was joshing, Erin. I didn't mean to make you feel bad. Right now hanging around this house with you is probably the most important thing I could be doing. Certainly more important than patrolling the roads for speeders. Like you, I hope this guy shows up. It'd give me great satisfaction to help you put him away."

She nodded. "Thanks, Lance." Realizing she was still hungry, she reached for more toast and peanut butter. "You know, if there's a bad egg in the barrel back at the field office... Well, there must be. This is too much. When the phone call came in, we started off thinking it was a thoughtless leak. You've been in cop bars."

"Plenty."

"And conversation can get a little loose after a few drinks. Nothing intentional—one agent talking to another and someone overhears, someone who isn't on the good team. It happens."

"True."

"But now...." She paused. "Oh, well, I've been over it. Until something pops out of my subconscious, I just have to deal with not knowing."

He half smiled. "You hate that."

"Don't you?"

"Always. Most of my cases were a lot simpler. They still are. You, on the other hand..."

"I do a lot of paperwork, I spend a lot of time poring over evidence...glorified paper pushing. Wouldn't people be shocked to know?"

His smile widened. "Not like the movies, huh?"

"Rarely. Like most jobs, it's endless hours of boredom occasionally punctuated by an adrenaline surge."

"But you love it?"

"I love it. Mostly I love what we accomplish."

He finished his toast and went to get more coffee, giving her a view of a backside covered by tight denim. She dragged her gaze away quickly as he came back.

"So, back to the bar scenario," he said. "As you pointed out, it makes sense only to a certain point. Asking for you by name would have got him past the switchboard."

She nodded, chewing on her lower lip. "Absolutely. In fact, it's the only way. But my address, and what I look like?"

"Can you be sure that when he shot you he knew who you were?"

"Yes." She spoke the word slowly. "He was in uniform. He could have told me he was responding to a prowler report. An ordinary citizen would have gone back inside. He had reason to be afraid of me."

"Point taken. So somebody not only gave him your name and address, but a photo of you."

She swore quietly. Pushing back from the table, she started to pace. Bad choice. After only a few minutes she needed to sit again. She could feel Lance's sympathetic gaze on her, but right now she didn't want sympathy, she wanted *action*.

"Maybe he got a picture of you coming out of your house," Lance said.

She could tell he was trying to soothe her, but she didn't want soothing either. "Our photos," she said shortly, "are pretty much limited to our personnel files and close family. I have no close family. Haven't you noticed that when an FBI investigation becomes public, we may issue statements we feel are appropriate, but it's a US Attorney who will meet with the press? Or a designated spokesperson, whose only job is press relations. Not actively involved in the investigation side of things."

"I've noticed. Most big police departments operate the same way. Good luck flying under the radar here."

"Yeah." But she was thinking. At least her brain

seemed to be getting back into gear at last. She'd wondered if it would be permanently fogged.

"Off-topic," she said suddenly, as a memory surfaced.

"Be my guest. Want more coffee?"

She glanced at her mug. "Thanks." She also avoided watching him cross the kitchen, afraid of getting sidetracked into a totally different line of thought. She needed the popcorn cooking in her brain. At any moment a truly useful kernel might pop.

"So tell me. Off-topic," he reminded her as he returned to the table.

"Oh, when we were at Quantico, and when I've been hanging around with other agents, one of my favorite things has always been war stories from the older agents." She glanced at him and he nodded for her to continue.

"Anyway, one agent told me about a guy he met at a bar. Lots of government types hung out there from various alphabet soup agencies. CIA, NSA, Secret Service… And of course, in the mix were a certain number of spies hoping to glean information. Max—that was his name— liked to say that in the Cold War days he and the KGB attended the same parties and knew each other. Sort of. *A spy on every barstool*, he liked to say."

Lance laughed quietly. "Like a bad cartoon."

"Sort of. The letters have changed in some cases but the spies are still there in the DC area and others. We get briefed on it. Anyway, Max was in the bar, having a drink after work, and there's a guy who sits down beside him and says he's with the CIA."

"Oops."

She smiled faintly. "Not really. Some people like to pump themselves up. Max didn't announce he was FBI. He simply strung out the conversation, wondering why the guy was being so careless. Anyway, conversation goes on for a while, and this guy starts bragging about how much classified information he can access. Now Max is really interested, but pretends to dismiss it as a fish story. So the guy says he can prove it, and all he wants is twenty-five thousand dollars."

Lance whistled. "I can guess how this turns out."

"You'd be right. They meet a couple of more times, the exchange is arranged, and the idiot is arrested for espionage."

Lance leaned forward intently. "Why'd the guy do it? Seems like a paltry sum for the risk involved."

Erin shook her head. "He wanted to be a covert operative. He'd tried four times since he joined the CIA and every time failed his psychological tests. So he decided he'd prove he had the right stuff by selling to the other side."

"Seriously?" Lance looked astounded, then laughed. "I guess he kind of proved he didn't have the right stuff."

Erin nodded, but drummed her fingers briefly. "Maybe not so off-topic."

"Meaning?"

"Consider that idiot's motivation. Just to prove he could be a spy, he wound up with a twenty-year sentence. Motives can be weird, Lance. Totally unexpected. You can't possibly imagine all of them. So whoever set me up..." She shrugged and tried to prevent herself from wincing. "It's a grab bag why someone would want me gone."

He stiffened suddenly. "Someone's coming. Get out of sight."

In an instant he headed for the front of the house. As she emerged from the kitchen, she saw him pulling his gun out of the holster on the belt he kept near the front door.

Good idea, she thought, and headed back to the bedroom to strap on her shoulder holster. A quick check of her service pistol told her she was fully loaded.

Then she waited, every nerve in her body alight with wariness.

Lance watched the pickup approach, and was pretty sure who it was, but waited tensely anyway. Unannounced visits around here were rare. In town it was different, but on a ranch? Hard to know if anyone would be home without calling first, so why make a long trip?

But if this was who he thought it was, she would know.

A minute later he watched Edie Hardin climb out of the truck wearing jeans, a checkered shirt and a baseball cap. She waved as she walked up to the front porch.

"Erin? It's okay. It's Seth's wife."

Erin hurried down the hall as fast as she apparently could. "Should she know I'm here?"

"She's a helicopter pilot. She's probably been providing some of the eyes in the sky for you."

Wow. Seth was clearly of the special ops school and his wife flew helicopters? Quite a couple.

Lance threw open the door. "Hey, Edie. What brings you around?"

"Just stopping in. It occurred to me that your guest might be getting restless. I know I don't like to be out of the loop."

"Come on in. I just made a fresh pot of coffee. Erin, this is Edie Hardin, formerly a combat search-and-rescue pilot with the air force. Edie, Special Agent Erin Sanders."

The two women shook hands and exchanged smiles. "Let's hit that coffee," Edie suggested. "I was on duty overnight, and need to get home to the baby. Thank God

Marge looks after him. I don't know what Seth and I would do without her help."

"Marge?" Erin queried as they returned to the kitchen and gathered coffee to take to the living room.

"You met Nate," Lance reminded her. "Our former sheriff. His wife is Marge, Seth's her son and Edie is…"

"The absent mother, all too often," Edie laughed. "It's a good thing Ned loves his grandma."

When everyone was settled, the two women on the sofa and Lance in the rocker, Edie turned to Erin. "Sorry to say, nothing has hit our spiderweb yet. No unusual activity. Nobody skulking around in the open after dark. We *are* on high alert, Agent."

"Erin, please."

"Erin." Edie smiled. "I checked with Gage last night before I took my shift, and the locals aren't reporting any strangers hanging around. This guy, whoever he is, hasn't arrived yet."

Erin spoke. "I don't know whether to be happy or not."

Edie laughed. "You must feel like a prisoner. I, on the other hand, am thoroughly enjoying being in action again, even if it's just a high-flying stakeout."

Lance objected mildly. "You're in action quite a bit. How many people get into trouble in the mountains every year?"

Edie shrugged. "Who's counting? Besides, CSAR gave me a taste for adrenaline. I need my jolt occasionally." She winked at Erin. "What about you?"

"Right now, I'll pass. So how old is your son? Ned, you said?"

"Right. He's two. Not terrible yet, but I'm sure he'll get there."

"How do you manage it?"

"Grandma." But then Edie grew serious. "Seth and I

had a few things to work out. He'd just retired from the SEALs. I didn't want to give up my career. But in the end I made my decision based on Ned's needs. I haven't regretted it."

"I'm glad," Erin said.

"You?"

"No kids, no husband. I'm not sure how kids would fit in, the way my life goes."

"Yeah," Edie answered. "I had the same concerns. If you really want it, though, you find a way. Compromise is inevitable, a very personal decision." She rose. "Anyway, I just wanted to meet our protectee and make sure you know that we really are out there. And now I need to find my son. I'll be on night watch again tonight. Take care, Erin. Lance is a good cop, too. Don't underestimate him."

Erin glanced at him. "I definitely won't make that mistake."

"You never know with Feds," Edie remarked as she headed toward the door. "Some of you guys think local law enforcement is low on the scale. See you around, Lance."

Then she was out the door.

Erin sat staring after her, then dared to look at Lance. "Have I made you feel that way? That I look down on you?"

"Hell, no," he answered, appearing startled. "Not a bit."

"Because I know the types she means. They give us all a bad name."

"Rotten apples in every bunch," he said, dismissing it. "How is your cabin fever?"

"Pretty much through the roof. But honestly, resting these past few days has helped, so I guess I should be smart and not do anything too active. Just keep moving so I don't stiffen too much." She shook her head a little. "I'm used to being busy all the time. And not so cut off from what's happening on a case."

"That would chap me, too," he admitted. "I'm not used to sitting on my hands either. Wanna play cards or something?"

Fran called again that evening, while they were waiting for a chicken casserole to finish baking. The pain pills were wearing off, and Erin was insisting to Lance that she was going to win the next time they played Scrabble. The board lay between them on the kitchen table, and since they'd agreed to allow slang and jargon, it was filled with an awful lot of law enforcement terms and abbreviations.

Which, Erin thought, said a lot about the two of them.

She eased her phone out of her pocket and checked the caller ID. "Fran."

"Go ahead and take it," he suggested. "I'll be quiet. Maybe you can learn something."

"Maybe. Without revealing anything, I hope." Because, despite all the help she was surrounded with, she wanted some more time to heal. She wanted to face the bomber down herself, not stand by while others did it. Selfish, she supposed, but given how little they knew about the UNSUB, maybe not so selfish. The men protecting her deserved the advantage of whatever information she could glean.

"Hey, girl," said the warm voice of her best friend. "I've been worried sick. Not answering your phone?"

"Been taking a lot of pain meds. I'm sorry."

"Damn, that stinks," Fran said. "I'd hoped you'd be a lot better."

"I told you what the docs said. Maybe six months to hit full steam." Why was her heart beating nervously?

She'd talked to Fran a thousand times or more. Fran was her friend. The roots of distrust sinking deeper? God, she hated that part worst of all.

"So, where you been staying?" Fran demanded. "I hope you haven't been driving while you're taking those meds."

"Of course not. I found a little motel. Reminds me of the Bates Motel."

At that Fran laughed loudly. "Oh, girl, you're still yourself. So have you at least got a view to amuse you?"

"I suppose a truck stop could be amusing. So what's going on, Fran? You know I hate being out of the loop."

"We all feel out of the loop right now," Fran answered. "And our bad guy has apparently gone to ground. You know he was accelerating. Well, he's been quiet since you. Maybe scared the bejesus out of him because you saw him."

Erin opened her mouth to say that she couldn't remember the guy's face, but caught herself just in time. No sharing. Not now. She glanced at Lance and saw he was listening intently. She hoped he'd stop her if she revealed too much.

"If he's that scared, he's moved on," she said instead.

"Maybe so. The whole task force is quiet. Even Tom isn't saying a damn thing. Have you talked to him?"

"I haven't heard a peep from Tom," Erin lied.

"Yeah. Well, don't feel too bad. Right now there doesn't seem to be any loop at all. Everyone's poring over what little we have, but except for what happened to you, we've got nothing new. The Unabomber all over again."

"This guy doesn't strike me as the type to send a manifesto to the papers."

"Not likely," Fran agreed. "Well, enjoy your little town in Wyoming. Conard City, isn't it?"

Erin felt something crawl along her nerve endings. "What makes you think I would ever stay there?"

Fran laughed. "Pain pills? All right, you sound tired, Erin. Talk again soon?"

"You bet."

"Love you, girl. You just take care of yourself. I'll take care of Tom for you." Laughing, Fran disconnected.

Erin realized her hand was shaking as she pressed the end button and put the phone down.

"What's wrong?" Lance asked.

"Nothing, really. Just me being overly suspicious. She had no news to report, and I hope I led her to believe I'd moved on. She didn't seem intent on pinning down where I am or anything, although she asked if I was still here." She paused, thinking about it, then realized the question had sounded ordinarily casual.

"Hence a pretty good evasion," Lance remarked. "Couldn't have been easy."

Erin just gave a slight shake of her head.

"Anything else?"

"She wondered if I'd heard from Tom, which is natural because according to her he's not saying much to anyone right now. They're working my case, but…" She shrugged. "The UNSUB had been accelerating in his attacks, but since me he hasn't triggered another bomb. She thinks it's because I saw his face."

He'd just started picking up the game tiles, but now his hand paused in midmotion. "How many people know you didn't?"

"Theoretically, just Tom. He did my debrief in the hospital. He's been playing this really close to the vest, or Fran wouldn't think I'd seen the guy's face."

He nodded slowly and resumed putting tiles away. "That could be good or it could be meaningless. Definitely if the guy thinks you saw his face he might want to move on."

"Or he might want to kill me even more."

"There's that," he agreed calmly. "So what's your call on Fran? Does she think you're still in Conard City?"

"I'm not sure." She replayed the conversation in her head. "Maybe. But that's the last place they all knew where I was—Fran because I told her."

"And everyone else because I verified your ID." He sighed and gathered up more tiles. "I'm getting uneasy about your ASAC."

"Tom? Why?" She waited, every muscle in her body tightening, every wound she had protesting loudly.

"Because while it might be wise to keep your whereabouts under his vest, it remains he's the only one who knows for sure, and he's the only one the sheriff is supposed to talk to. That bothers me a bit. I can see both sides of it, of course. If he thinks he's got a leak, the only way to plug it is to keep his secrets. But if he's the leak…"

She could see his point. "But," she said after a moment's reflection, "that horse is already out of the barn. At least two people know where I am. If two do then ten do."

Sighing heavily she put her head in her hand. "How about we read some tea leaves? It'd do just as much good."

"You ever read tea leaves?" he asked, surprising her with the change of subject.

"No."

"My mother used to. She did it to amuse me when I was little. A few tea leaves always escaped the pot into the cup. When I was done drinking all but a drop or two, she'd upend the cup and turn it three times on the saucer. When she righted it, there were these leaves stuck to the bottom. She made a big deal of pretending to see things in them. As I got a little older, I'd try to read them, too. Sort of like looking at clouds and seeing animals and faces."

She waited, wondering about his point. He looked up from the Scrabble board and smiled. "Reading tea leaves is at least entertaining."

She got it then, and laughed. "Point taken."

"However," he said, then fell silent. He turned the board over, sliding the tiles onto the table, then emptying the bag of those he'd put away. "Free association can be useful. Start making words, Agent. I'll join you. We might be surprised by what pops out."

The mechanical voice, so inhuman, poured into his ear again. Sometimes he wondered what would happen if he just threw his phone into the lake, but he didn't wonder for long. The voice had found him. It must know who he was, and if he made it angry, it might turn him in.

"You need to get ready for a trip," the voice said. "Head west, straight west. Leave before dawn the day after tomorrow. I'll give you more directions."

"She'll be there?"

"Yes. You have her picture?"

Of course he did. Why would he delete it when he knew she'd survived? He wasn't a fool, despite what this voice seemed to think. "Yeah, I got it."

"Memorize it, then delete it and trash the phone. You'll find a new phone in your car. Pack up all your bombs and anything that can be traced to you. Don't leave anything behind."

Well, at least that made sense. So the voice wasn't a complete idiot, even though it had dragged him into trouble he hadn't wanted, even though it was forcing him to leave his protected place. And how the hell would it put a phone in his car?

He had been out West once, just once. He hated all the empty space. "How far west?"

"Well out of state. Near the mountains. So take cash for your journey."

"I don't have that kind of cash."

"You have the cash to make bombs and buy uniforms. Sleep in your car if you have to. You've got two days, but I'll know if you haven't started driving. I'll call tomorrow with an update."

How would the voice know that? It had told him how to turn off the tracking on his phone. An eerie feeling began to fill him. Was this voice supernatural? Psychic?

"You can't track my phone," he said, sweat breaking out on his forehead.

"No, but I can track *you*." With that the voice disconnected.

Harry sat there, shivering and sweating and wondering what the hell he was walking into. That had never bothered him before, but it bothered him now.

In fact, it terrified him.

Chapter 8

The Scrabble tiles remained on the kitchen table. For the next two days, as they sat there sharing coffee or a meal, or even as they walked by, one of them often paused to create a word. Nothing so far had seemed especially useful.

But Erin didn't mind. It amused her, especially some of the oddities that would pop up from time to time, evidently rising from Lance's subconscious or hers. The tedium of waiting without knowing if or when anything would happen needed all the relief it could get.

In one way this enforced confinement had been good for her. She noticed her pain was lessening, although she still had occasional spikes, and her endurance was growing. Lance offered no criticism over the amount of time she spent pacing. At least he could go outside and pace around his house, or into the yard to play with the dogs. He didn't seem comfortable about letting her out, though.

She stood at the window, watching him throw a stick for the dogs, and realized he was being smart, just as putting her car in his small garage had been smart. By this point, not even an eagle soaring overhead would know that anyone else was here.

Which in a way seemed stupid when she considered that she had chosen to be the bait. But she'd also asked for some time to recover, and the Conard County Sheriff's Department was certainly giving it to her. She had no doubt that when she decided she was ready to face the creep that they'd pass the word in a way that would inform half the planet of her whereabouts.

For now, though, she wouldn't even call Tom or Fran. If her field office had any information that would be useful to her, they knew how to reach her.

But man, she chafed. "I started the investigation," she told Lance when he came back inside. "Me and Tom, with the first bombing. And now I'm out of it completely."

"Well, I wouldn't say you're out of it completely," he reminded her. "They did kind of raise the red flags out here."

"You know what I mean." She walked down the hall, noticing that her stride had eased some, and turned around to come back.

"I know," he agreed. "Since we can't do anything about it, maybe we should just let it ride."

She froze in the doorway between hall and living room. "Am I obsessing?"

The smile that she liked so much and was becoming familiar with danced around his mouth. "Not any more than I would, under the circumstances. Hell, I can't even take you for a drive and show off my favorite mountains."

She looked out the window. "But we'd be safe out there."

"Unless he's already watching you here. No holes in the perimeter."

She sighed. "Okay, okay."

"I think you're getting a lot better."

"Yeah, I guess. A few more days and maybe we can unleash my location. I don't know. This is just driving me crazy." She hesitated, realizing how that might have sounded. This man had opened his house to her, was guarding her back and hadn't made her feel like any kind of imposition. She needed to quell her crankiness before she took it out on him. "I'm sorry, Lance. You're doing everything you can and then some. And I do enjoy your company. It's just that…"

"You want action," he answered simply. "I get it. Well, I could take you to bed and make you forget it all for a while."

Everything inside her lurched sharply, as if from an earthquake. She'd been trying to bury it, but with those simple words he opened wide her growing hunger for him. Purely physical, of course, and therefore downright stupid…well, it worried her that it wasn't purely physical. Other feelings stirred stubbornly, and just as stubbornly she buried them.

Irritated with herself, she snapped, "Think you're that good, huh?"

He amazed her by laughing. "I suspect we're both that desperate. You think I haven't noticed you eyeballing me?"

Oh, God. But she refused to be embarrassed. Far better to go on the attack. "You *are* a hunk," she said bluntly. "So? Does a swelled head go with that?"

"No, but another kind of swelling…"

"Stop it," she said sharply. "You can't jump my bones yet, and I don't want to jump yours."

Damn him, he caught the one word that gave her away. Arching a brow, he repeated, "Yet?"

"Oh, for the love of heaven, Lance…"

His smile widened a shade. "You're as safe with me as you want to be, Erin." Then he stepped toward her and quite boldly put his arms around her.

The urge to shove back reared in her. She didn't want to be manhandled. But then as their bodies met, it stopped feeling like manhandling. She resisted for just the barest instant, then leaned into him as if she'd been deprived of will. Dang, he felt so good, so big, so warm. He smelled good, too, of fresh air and man and even a hint of his beloved dogs.

"Now, was that so hard?" he asked quietly.

She tilted her head, part of her wanting to tell him off, but all the rest of her wanting to melt. How could anyone do that to her? Confusion spun in her head, but her body had not the least doubt. Hardly realizing it, she wound her arms around his waist.

Meeting his gaze, she discovered that fire could burn blue-green. "Lance…"

"Shh." He lifted a hand and gently tangled his fingers in her short hair. "This doesn't go anywhere you don't want. But damn, Erin, you feel so good."

She certainly did, she thought hazily. Would it be so wrong? Nothing could come of it. Safety lay in her eventual departure. No risk of things getting out of hand. Her desire for him had been growing since the instant she'd set eyes on him, and it seemed ridiculous to not enjoy it. No strings, no danger. Just a glorious romp.

She could deal with that. In fact, she wanted it so badly that she ached in a totally pleasurable way. It had been a while since passion had sidestepped her defenses so quickly.

But just as she was reaching a new level of self-realization and tipping her head to receive his kiss, the phone rang.

Lance groaned. "Under the circumstances, I can't ignore it."

"No," she agreed. She eased back, her arms falling reluctantly, hoping the phone call wouldn't last long. Inside she felt like a tornado of need, a tornado she needed to mash down quickly. This whole thing with Lance, such as it was… Was she losing her mind?

Lance went for the cordless set in the kitchen. She heard a few words, then he returned.

"That was Gage. In ten minutes your ASAC is calling back. We're going to have a conference call."

Ten minutes was long enough to get fresh coffee going. Lance swept all the letter tiles to one side and put the phone base set in the middle of the table to act as a speakerphone. He grabbed a pad and some pens from a kitchen drawer, then tore off a few sheets, keeping them for himself while he passed the pad to Erin.

"Anything else?" he asked her.

She shook her head. He could tell she was growing edgy by the stiff stillness that had overtaken her. This woman didn't have nervous habits unless you counted turning into a statue as one. He himself felt a blooming anxiety, mostly for her. Conference calls could be good or they could stink. In short, one way or another, a bomb was about to drop in their midst.

At last the phone rang. Uneasily, he sat in the chair across from her and punched the button.

"Conroe and Sanders here," he said.

The call cut in on midsentence, probably her ASAC because he didn't recognize the voice.

"...secure line," the voice was saying.

"We're patched through," he heard Gage answer. "No one can hear my end."

"All right. Deputy Conroe, this is Tom Villiers. I'm ASAC on this task force. Erin can verify."

Lance looked at Erin, who nodded. "Hi, Tom," she said.

"Good to hear your voice, Erin. How are you doing?"

"Getting better and growing a huge crop of impatience."

Villiers's laugh came over the phone. "Why does that not surprise me? But let's cut to the chase. I know Erin wants to know what's going on, and I know you *need* to know, Sheriff. By the way, nobody here is aware that I asked for protection for Agent Sanders, and nobody knows that she remained in place. Except for me. At least that's the plan. Considering the breakdown last time that put her in danger, I'm not counting on it."

"Nor are we," Gage answered. "I told you about our people and what they're doing to protect Agent Sanders. She's met my men, and I think she approves."

"I definitely approve."

Lance couldn't help smiling at her. It was the first time she'd voiced unequivocal approval of the plan the sheriff had put it place.

"Let me start by explaining something," Villiers went on. "I could have sent agents out there. I could have yanked Erin back and put her in the custody of the Marshals. But after the speed with which the bomber moved against her, using information he should not have had, I felt it best to put her under protection with an unattached agency. You follow? Erin?"

"I agree with you," she said. "The people who know

I'm still here are just a few, and quite trustworthy in my judgment."

"Good," said Villiers. "All right, we've had some developments. I'm not going to insult anyone on this call by withholding important details, but since we're still in the midst of the investigation, this must be closely guarded."

Lance watched Erin lean forward in anticipation. She'd been hungry for this. Well, so had he. Now, for the first time since she arrived here, they'd get some real information.

"It's not good news, I'm afraid," Tom said. "But let me back up a bit. The guy's been using a burner phone. Which means…"

Lance spoke. "Whoever bought it probably lied about his name and address. It's cheap and disposable."

Villiers laughed quietly. "Am I offending you? Sorry. I get pedantic at times. Okay, so he was using a burner phone. We of course logged the number from his call to Erin the day he went after her. It proved useless until just a couple of days ago. We knew the phone was making calls, but they were limited to a few times a week at odd hours and even the cell phone company couldn't localize them because they were so brief. Given the number of towers we have here, a phone might connect through a different one at times without moving, but we suspect the guy was on the move. Regardless, we couldn't pinpoint a single tower or location."

Erin nodded and Lance understood completely. It took time to trace a call back through the cell phone system, and if someone was moving… "He had his tracking turned off?"

"Absolutely. Probably removed his battery, too. And while the same number always called him, it was another burner phone and was moving around the area and most often turned off. Not even trying to make a cell tower connection. Until a week ago, we were stymied."

Erin spoke. "So he's not working alone?"

"Initially we wondered. There was always the possibility he was calling a girlfriend or someone else not involved."

"But you suspect an accomplice?" Lance asked.

"Apparently so."

Lance looked at Erin, and saw her face shadow. He knew everything inside him was congealing into ice. "So not just a random leak," she said.

"We don't know that, but I'm betting there was nothing random about the attack on you."

Erin closed her eyes briefly. "It didn't fit with what we'd seen of him to that point," she replied, her tone steely.

"No," Villiers agreed.

"So what happened?" she demanded. Lance could see the tension running through her, calm as she appeared on the outside. She damn near shimmered with it.

"We localized it. Over the past week he'd had three calls, and they all reached his phone from the same tower. By the third call, we were able to deploy StingRay to pinpoint a warehouse, got a sealed warrant and then went in last night."

For long seconds silence filled the line. "Let me guess," Gage drawled. "He wasn't there."

"No," Villiers answered. "He'd been there. No question. Bomb residue remained. His destroyed phone remained. Nothing else but a few fingerprints that aren't in our database. He'd moved on. We managed to tap into some of the calls and the lab is still working on them, in part because mechanical voice alteration was involved. But one thing is clear right now."

"Yes?" Erin asked tautly.

"He's been ordered to come after you, and his caller knows you headed west."

Lance wouldn't have blamed her if she'd erupted, screamed, blown her cool. Experienced any kind of emotional reaction to that news.

Instead she asked quite calmly, "Ordered?"

"From what we could get out of the calls we managed to capture, yes. Ordered. Someone is pulling the bomber's strings."

Silence filled the house for a few minutes after the call ended. Erin had clearly turned her thoughts inward. Finally Lance rose and went to get them some of the coffee he'd started brewing just before the call.

"StingRay?" he said presently, to draw her out of the silence that seemed to have reached inside her. "I'm not up to date on the latest tech."

Slowly her sherry-brown eyes focused on him. "Cell towers cover a wide area."

"Right."

"Not a big problem unless you're in a crowded metropolitan area. That can leave you with a whole lot of buildings to search and no probable cause for a warrant. So we have StingRay. We send in a truck with the technology, it runs around in the area covered by a particular cell tower, acting as a dummy tower itself. All cell phones in the area being searched connect with it as well as the tower, and it scoops up location information until it finds the number we're looking for. It pinpoints the phone, as much as is possible."

"Cool," said Lance. He could appreciate its usefulness. He didn't know if he liked it. "So it scoops up the info from every cell phone it passes?"

Her gaze narrowed. "Location data only. Keep in mind we're only looking for a particular phone. The rest of the scoop gets trashed. It's irrelevant."

"You don't have to get defensive," he said quietly as he sat across from her again, fresh cups of coffee on the table.

"Sorry. Anyway, we need court approval to use it. I'll admit not everyone always follows those rules, but we're supposed to."

"Fair enough." He didn't want to argue with her over this. Yeah, he had questions about how some technology was being used, but he also had enough experience to know how important it could be to the public safety. She said *court approval*. He let it go at that. Besides, people were running around with smartphones these days that they knew were broadcasting their locations, and even encouraging their friends and family to track them. Without a warrant or court order of some kind, the information would probably be inadmissible in a trial.

She sighed and lifted her mug in both hands, sipping a bit of coffee. "So someone is pulling the bomber's strings, and quite intelligently, too. Did you notice that he completely left before they could serve the warrant?"

His stomach squeezed uncomfortably. That hadn't escaped him. "Yeah."

"The evidence I found that linked the bombs? It might also have linked him to a single location. I expect they're checking into that. If they find more of exactly the same stuff, they'll be fairly sure it was him."

"He's worried about that."

"Someone sure as hell is. And how did he find out about it?"

The possibilities that were roiling now hung like oily

smoke in the room, ever shifting like some shadow beast. "Villiers sounded like a straight arrow," he offered.

."He did." She put her mug down. "He didn't have to make that call and warn us all."

But she was wondering about it all the same. He could tell. He wished he had an answer for her. Some words that could ease her mind.

But maybe the stupidest thing of all: he wanted to wrap his arms around her and protect her from all of this. As if he could. As if she'd stand for it.

She reached for the tiles and began pulling them into the middle of the table. Finally two names stared back at them: Fran and Tom.

"There must be others," he argued.

"Plenty. The whole office probably heard when I arrived here."

"When I pinged your ID."

"Yes. But only two of them know exactly where I landed. In which town. And theoretically only one of them knows that I stayed." She pushed Fran's name aside, leaving only Tom.

He ached for her, but feelings aside, he knew this would be the wrong time to become unprofessional. "Tom wouldn't have arranged protection for you."

"And Fran has been my best friend for years." With a sweep, she pushed the tiles aside.

He reached out and covered her hand with his much bigger one. "Don't narrow your focus too much. You don't need me to remind you."

She nodded. "No. At this point that could be dangerous."

He watched her close her eyes, apparently to think about this new twist. At the outset it had seemed unlikely, although not impossible, that the bomber would follow her unless he thought Erin could identify him. But now there was no question. He'd been ordered by some unknown person to take her out.

Black rage was trying to fill him, but he couldn't let it. If ever there was a time he needed a cool head, this was it.

"I didn't realize how tense I'd gotten," she said. "Everything hurts again."

He didn't suggest a pain pill, but she surprised him by getting up and going to get one herself. When she returned, she was a little bent, her lips compressed. She got a glass of water herself and downed the pill.

"Maybe," she said, "instead of unicorns and rainbows, I'll shake something loose from my subconscious."

He didn't care either way, as long as she was more comfortable than she appeared right now. "Head for the living room. I'll bring the coffee."

She nodded and limped out of sight.

He sat staring at the jumbled tiles for a minute or two, trying to sort through everything that had been said. And, maybe just as important, everything that hadn't been said.

The Bureau had got a sealed warrant to search the bomber's hidey-hole. In his experience, the Feds could get a warrant fast, so they might have had one signed the very day of the raid. It was sealed, so in theory no one knew what was in it except those in charge of the raid.

Who'd been in charge of that? Tom or someone else?

Considering how fast a warrant could be signed, how had the bomber been tipped off quickly enough to move out first? Had someone become aware they were using the StingRay thingy? Tom couldn't have kept that entirely under his vest. He'd needed not only court permission, but people to drive the truck, examine the data it collected. At least a few people must have been aware of it.

He'd destroyed his phone, so now there'd be no way

to track him. Presumably, the person pulling his strings would have tossed his own phone, too, switching to a different burner. All hope of intel was lost.

He cussed under his breath, filled a couple of mugs with fresh coffee and carried them out to the living room. Erin sat in the rocker, rocking steadily, her eyes fixed on some point beyond the room.

This woman had been through hell. Now she was facing hell again. Damned if it didn't break his heart.

She thanked him for the coffee, sipped some and kept rocking.

"Talk," he said finally. "Sometimes tossing ideas around can be useful."

"It can," she agreed. "But I'm not sure I have any ideas as much as a bunch of wisps that float by only to be dismissed."

He settled on the couch. "The puppet master is smart, altering his voice."

"Yeah." Slowly her eyes focused on him. "Does that mean he knows someone would recognize his voice if the calls were tapped? Or is it just a basic precaution?"

"Wish I knew."

"So do I. Clearly he's wired into things on the task force."

"So in your mind that means Tom Villiers?"

"Maybe." She sighed and put her coffee down, then closed her eyes, speaking slowly. "There's very little that can truly be hidden from anyone who's tied in to a task force. Sure, we have security, but those on the task force need to have access to everything."

He thought about that. "You sure can't have people compartmentalizing information. Something might get missed, something that might be meaningful to someone else. So everybody is read in on everything. At least that's how it was in Denver, and the way it usually is here."

"Exactly." She moved her head a little, as if trying to ease stiffness from her neck. "Tom stepped outside that box when he ordered protection for me, when he called today. That means he doesn't trust anyone right now. The substance of the phone calls they tapped will be available to everyone. Has to be. But what he's set up out here? The fact that he called today? That's something he can keep close to the vest. Very close."

"That's a good thing," he reminded her. "No one will know that we're ready for this guy."

She gave a slight nod and rocked some more. He wondered if the back-and-forth motion was easing her in some way or if she were self-comforting. He'd seen plenty of people under extreme duress or emotion begin rocking just that way.

"You going to be all right?" he asked her.

"I always am." But it wasn't a bold statement. Instead it sounded almost weary, halfhearted. He couldn't imagine how she felt, knowing she had been targeted like this by someone. That was the most important information right now, and it had to be shattering. She was used to being behind the protective wall of the Bureau, exposed only when she was prepared for it. Not hunted. How did anyone handle that?

From the moment he'd been told that Tom had requested protection for Erin, there'd been a sickened black spot in his heart. The need for protection had seemed extreme, but it had spoken volumes that no one could afford to ignore.

Erin had thought she'd be safe enough getting off the grid for a while until she recovered. One day after her whereabouts became known, Tom Villiers had shot holes in her sense of security, such as it was.

But even then it had seemed like a remote threat. She'd been talking about moving on, about the possibility that she was bait in the trap, but until today that had all been speculation. He doubted she had really believed it would happen.

Now this. So he asked her simply, "Want me to take you somewhere far from here? I don't want you going alone."

He thought she looked tempted, but then she shook her head. "You're a wonderful man, Lance. But look where we're at. We'll get no more information on this guy's moves. We won't know where he's going, or how much is being fed to him. Just as we almost get him, he vanishes. And now that this has happened, I don't know that I'd be safe anywhere. The minute I surface, I'll be a target again. So there's only one thing to do. I need to get my life back."

So showdown at high noon. He got it. He understood her thinking, but, man, he didn't like it.

"You know," she said presently, sounding far away, "realizing that someone wants me dead this badly is… weird."

It was more than weird, he thought. It was terrifying. He couldn't begin to imagine how it must be making her feel.

"I keep wondering," she continued, "what I could have done to make someone hate me this much. I mean, sure, I've helped put people in prison. I've caused some police departments a lot of trouble, but it wasn't ever something I did all by myself. There was always a team. No reason for me to stand out. But…Lance, I don't think this is some criminal I helped put away."

"Unlikely he'd have a hotline to the FBI."

"Exactly. So somebody involved with the task force…" She shook her head. "I don't get it."

"Maybe you don't need to look at yourself at all. Whoever is doing this, he's clearly not thinking like a regular person. This will be cold-blooded murder. Plotted and planned. Most people wouldn't take a grudge that far."

"So someone who's mentally ill."

"At least not screwed together right."

"But after all the vetting the Bureau does…" She trailed off. "Psychopaths are good at hiding their lack of feeling, their utter selfishness."

He nodded. "Makes you feel really good, doesn't it? Charming and soulless. And that could be anyone."

He rose. "Mind if I let the dogs in? It's getting warm out there."

"Be my guest. I'm crazy about them."

The dogs burst into the house, seeking the shade and relative coolness within. The day wasn't really hot, but he was aware both animals wore fur coats. While he filled a bucket with water for them in the kitchen, he heard them greeting Erin with quiet *woof*s and her answering in the soft voice, like a mother talking to a baby.

By the time he rejoined them, the dogs had collapsed happily at her feet.

Then Erin looked up at him and said one of the saddest things he'd heard in his entire life. "I have never, ever, felt so alone."

Chapter 9

Gage called back a short time later. Lance put it on speaker and Erin listened attentively.

"No more news out of the field office, but I've been talking to our protection detail. They've come up with some suggestions they're implementing. Apparently from what Villiers said, the guy could have a one-day head start on the task force. As if anyone really knows where to look. Anyway, Erin?"

"Yes?"

"I just wanted you to know we're taking additional measures. Every stranger who shows up in the area is going to be under scrutiny. Of course, I can't guarantee you he won't slip by. There's a whole lot of open space out there."

"I understand." She knotted her hands together. This situation was unique in her experience. She guessed things like this happened to others, but even in her law

enforcement career thus far, she had never pursued a
felon who was being directed like a heat-seeking missile
at one person. Never dealt with the possibility that one
of her colleagues could engage in something like this.

She understood the purpose of Witness Protection,
understood that some people remained at risk after they
finished testifying. She got it.

But she'd never been one of them, and had never expected to be. Those she knew through her work with
the Department of Justice who had needed protection
had needed it only temporarily. It wasn't like members
of a crime family testifying against each other. She'd
even known a federal prosecutor whose family had been
under protection until he finished a case against some
drug gangs.

So, yes, it happened. She wasn't a fool. But she had
never dreamed she might face it herself, and face it from
someone who most likely knew her.

"Anyway," Gage wrapped up, "I'm not going to share
the details of the changes we're making, not even with
your ASAC, Erin. You okay with that?"

"I am," she answered. Right now she couldn't afford
not to be okay with it.

After the call completed, she looked at Lance. "I don't
like myself very much right now."

"Why?" Without asking permission, he took her hand
and guided her back into the living room to sit beside
him on the couch.

"The whiniest thoughts are running around in my
head. Why me? What did I do? How do I deal with this?
I know things like this can happen."

He draped an arm carefully around her shoulders.
"But knowing they can happen to you is different. I get

it. Being essentially helpless has got to be tough on you. No one wants to be the cheese in the trap."

"No," she agreed and leaned her head back until it rested on his arm.

"And you feel completely alone."

"No words for it. I can't trust my friends, my colleagues… nobody."

He fell silent for a minute, then said almost carefully, "Erin, you can trust *us*. We weren't any part of this until you arrived here. You're not alone."

She tilted her head toward him and blinked rapidly as her eyes began to burn. Tears? It must be the pain pill she'd taken, she decided. She wasn't one to weep. "I'm alone in the truest sense of the word. Everyone I once trusted is under suspicion. I know you're here. I know the others are here, but it's not the same, Lance."

"I guess not."

She was being unfair, she realized. She might not have known this man very long, but he'd stepped up to the plate without hesitation when she'd needed someone. Even before she *knew* she needed him and the others. He'd invited her into his home, opened his life to her in amazing ways. Not many near-strangers would be so generous.

"I'm not trying to criticize you," she said. "I'm sorry. I'm just…"

"Dealing with the fact that you can't trust people you used to trust with your life. I can't imagine how hard that has to be. You're wearing a pair of shoes I've never had to try on."

She nodded, then without even thinking about it, she leaned toward him and rested her head on his shoulder. He seemed to turn a little, making her more comfortable.

"Somehow," he continued, "we'll get you through this. Then you'll know who you can trust again."

"I wonder if I'll ever trust again." Right now, it seemed almost impossible. When she'd been pushing those tiles around the table, whose names had she made? Tom and Fran. Her best friend and the boss she had long trusted. It didn't bode well for the future of trust in her life.

"Life without trust is pretty hard," he said. His hand moved a little, lightly rubbing her upper arm. "How's the pain?"

"It eased off. Too much tension, I guess."

"Well, I can see the improvement in you just since we first met. I think you're getting over the hump, Erin."

"One of them anyway." She sighed, as his embrace released something inside her. It was comforting to be held, an experience she hadn't allowed herself since Paul. The trashing of their marriage hadn't been all one-way, but the scars it had left had made her reluctant to get involved again. Nobody made bulletproof vests to protect you against someone you had loved.

Paul still felt guilty about it, too. She was sure that was why he called from time to time, suggesting they meet for dinner or something. If nothing else, he'd been a man with a huge conscience. Not being able to tolerate her job had probably been as unexpected for him as it had been for her. Oh, they'd discussed all the reasons why a minister and an FBI agent might not be a good pairing, but living it had been different from imagining it, a very common experience in life. Her lack of time to participate in his congregation's activities as his wife had evidently started to cause comments and make him uneasy. Like water dripping, it had eventually worn him down. Just as she had become increasingly worn by his growing pressure to spend more time with him and his church.

Doomed to failure.

She had no intention of ever repeating that mistake.

But, relaxed from the pain pill she had taken, she could see no reason not to accept the comfort Lance was offering. It was innocent enough, and he was a good man.

And today had certainly ripped through her like a tornado. Yes, there'd always been the suspicion that someone in the task force had leaked her identity, but she was sure she, and even Tom, hadn't considered the likelihood that someone wanted her dead. That one of their own might be an accomplice to this hideous bomber.

But now there was no escaping the fact that she'd been deliberately targeted, and the information he had provided just a short while ago certainly suggested that it was someone with access to the most confidential information. Such as the fact they'd located the bomber and were getting a warrant. Even the bit about knowing she had headed west didn't seem as huge as that.

Who the hell did she know who would set a crazed bomber on her, tell him to follow her?

"Psychopath," she murmured.

"Who? The person who's aiding the bomber?"

"Apparently. The bomber is a sick twist in a hundred ways, though I wouldn't venture to diagnose him. But someone who could work with a person and then arrange something like this? Someone who doesn't care about all the other women this guy might kill if he slips away? Soulless, like you said. A psychopath, and cunning."

"Not so cunning that Tom Villiers isn't aware of him."

"Apparently." Was it possible to physically hurt from a sense of betrayal?

His hand ran along her upper arm once more. "Why'd you pull Fran's and Tom's names out like that with the tiles?"

"I'm not sure. Maybe because I trust them most, and now I'm wondering?"

"It would certainly be a huge betrayal. The biggest of all."

Yes, it would, she thought. She hated the feeling. Hated having to wonder about all the people she had intuitively trusted. And why had she trusted most of them? Because she worked with them. Because they were agents, too. Because they supposedly shared a common goal—taking a bomber off the streets.

She'd never been a truly distrustful person. Being suspicious wasn't second nature to her, but something she had learned on the job. When they were dealing with a case, it was time to be suspicious and distrustful, but not of the people she was working with.

This fell in a whole different ballpark, and she didn't quite know how to manage it. She would never be the same again, not after this.

Then Lance startled her. "You ever date?" he asked.

"Date?" She twisted her head to look at him.

"You know, go out with a guy to a movie or for dinner."

"Occasionally. Since my divorce I keep it casual and brief."

"So do I." He flashed a sudden smile.

"Where did that question come from?"

"Hey." He half shrugged. "It's a different topic and I think we can both safely take a break from the treadmill. For a little while. But you're looking tired again. How about you let that pill do its work? I want to wander a bit outside the house, stretch my legs, give the dogs a workout before they start to bounce off walls."

"I could come," she suggested tentatively.

"I'd like that. But not until you've had a nap. Whether you know it or not, that pill is starting to hit you."

"Pupils dilated?"

"Heavy eyelids."

Dang, his grin was engaging. She hated to let him go, but she knew he was right. If she could slow her mind down for a few minutes, she had no doubt she'd fall into a deep sleep for an hour or two. She'd have liked to sleep leaning against him, but he'd probably go stir-crazy along with the dogs. "I can play fetch with them later?"

"Promise. As long as nothing changes."

So she gave up the battle. His regimen of rest had been doing wonders for her, and now that a killer was zeroing in on her again, catching whatever shut-eye she could seemed wise.

So she laid her hand on his thigh, feeling powerful muscles, and squeezed gently. Then she rose. "I *will* take a nap. But don't let me sleep too long."

She almost laughed at the look on his face. Apparently her touching his thigh had been pleasurable for him. Well, it sure had been for her, too.

A short while later, she had climbed into some comfy running shorts and a T-shirt and then into bed. Much to her relief, her mind gave up its incessant spinning almost instantly.

She was astonished to realize it was nearly dark when she awoke. Carefully she rolled over and looked at the digital clock by the bed. Good heavens, she'd slept eight hours. Shocked, she sat up slowly, expecting the return visit of aches and pains, relieved to find out they weren't too bad.

Well, it would come when she stood. Didn't it always? Sleep offered its own pain relief, one that usually wore off quickly upon awakening. She stood cautiously, awaiting the slam that usually hit her, although in all honesty it had been lessening. Still, it could be enough to freeze her in place for a second or two.

But this time all she felt were a few sharp twinges. Scar tissue didn't like stretching. Some of her internal wounds seemed to enjoy reminding her that organs and muscle had been severely insulted.

But not now. Twinges and pangs, some sharper than others, but not like she'd been experiencing upon her arrival here. Definitely Lance's recipe of resting had worked for her.

Sighing with relief, she changed into long pants that would conceal the scars from the sewn-up gashes on her legs. Even her pants irritated her waist less than usual.

No question, she was getting better at last. Lance was right. She seemed to have got past a hump. Smiling, she ran a brush through her hair and made up her mind to just enjoy the relative comfort. Thinking about the mess that was bearing down on her could wait.

She was surprised to find Lance waiting for her in the hallway, smiling.

"I thought I heard you stirring. Good nap?"

"Nap? I got a whole night's sleep."

He laughed. "You must have needed it. No playing fetch with the dogs tonight, though. Maybe in the morning."

As if to confirm the decision, two furry heads looked out of the living room, grinning at her.

"Are those dogs grinning? Can they do that?"

"You know," he said, "some folks say they can't. Others say they learn to do it from us. Me, I think they grin."

She liked that idea. Lance took her hand. "I have a surprise for you."

"Really? What?"

"Come to the kitchen and see."

She had thought the kitchen was dark, but as they approached the door to it, she saw flickering light. "What…"

But before she could ask, he drew her around the corner and she stopped. The table was set for two, and two tall tapers sat burning between the plates. "Lance! What is this?"

"Well, I can't take you out for dinner right now, so I figured we could do it right here."

The date he had mentioned. Part of her wanted to flee, fearing deeper involvement, but another part of her was incredibly touched. Even her husband hadn't arranged something like this for her. Then she saw the vase.

"Flowers?" she said, her voice barely emerging.

"There are a few wildflowers out back. Indian paintbrush, some daisies and marigolds my mother nursed for years. I thought they might set a more cheerful mood."

She looked at him. "But why?" She hadn't expected such a romantic gesture.

He just shook his head, still smiling. "Because I wanted to? Because you deserve it? Stop being an agent. Sit down and enjoy. I'll handle everything."

He drew her into his arms, holding her with utter gentleness, and bent to kiss her. The minute his lips touched her, she softened inside, everything letting go in the sheer pleasure of his touch. He didn't press it, just gave her a few butterfly kisses. When he raised his head he was smiling. "Our first date," he said.

Then he guided her to a chair, his hand trailing over her shoulder and back as if he were reluctant to lose the contact with her. She smiled up at him and was rewarded with another light kiss before he turned to the stove.

She looked out the window at the darkness that lurked.

Somewhere out there a killer was moving ever closer to her. Then she shook herself internally, and put such thoughts aside.

For a little while, instead of being Agent Sanders, it was probably perfectly safe to be just Erin. She made up her mind to enjoy herself and Lance.

On a lonely, dark road somewhere on the plains, the bomber glanced at the cell phone on the seat beside him and seriously thought about tossing it out the window. It would drive the voice mad not to be able to reach him.

At this point he no longer cared whether he killed that FBI agent who might be able to finger him. She'd run from him and she'd stay on the run. He could always deal with her when she came back.

But he did care that he was being prevented from finding himself another woman to teach a lesson to, and from using the bombs in his trunk. Occasionally he thought about stopping at one of the widely separated farmhouses and leaving a surprise for someone, but as angry as he was at being pushed around like this, he was no fool.

The bomb might give away his whereabouts. It might also kill a child. Women were one thing, but never in his life had he harmed a child, and he wasn't about to start.

Young women. Not women like that FBI agent. That bothered him. She was so into him that she'd studied his work and had managed to link all his bombs. He wasn't sure how—the voice hadn't shared that—but he was impressed, since he worked so hard to make each one different. He didn't want to leave any kind of signature, but apparently he had.

But the agent, she wouldn't ignore him the way too many women did. He'd grown utterly sick of the way they would chat with him, even flirt with him for a while in the clubs. And then all too often, they would start looking through him, start edging away. He never could understand why. He knew he was handsome; he had a mirror. He often wore a police uniform because women liked uniforms.

Some girls didn't treat him that way. Occasionally one would come home with him, or had while he'd kept his apartment. But the ones he remembered most were the ones who looked through him like he was a bug. He wanted to teach them a lesson, make an example of them. No man deserved that kind of treatment from a female.

So about a year ago, he'd decided to get even. And for his method he'd chosen something he'd always enjoyed using: explosives. He was very creative with them, making his own mixtures, fine-tuning. Just the way he had learned when working with the demolition company and then the fireworks start-up. From making a rocket, it was only a small step to making a bomb that would kill only one person.

He should have stuck with his plan despite the voice. Despite hearing they were closing in on him. They'd never have caught him, but allowing the voice to frighten him into taking action against an FBI agent? That had to be the height of stupidity.

What if the voice had lied, anyway? He'd allowed himself to be put in an extremely dangerous position, and once he'd made that mistake, he was caught like a fish on a hook.

Now there was an agent out there who might be able to identify him. He was no longer invisible. And the voice claimed to be protecting him?

He felt like banging his head on the steering wheel. How could he have been so stupid?

He looked at the phone again, longing to toss it. Except the voice had said it would know where he was. It couldn't be from the phone. Just as he had been taught, he'd turned off the tracking and removed the battery. The next call was supposed to come at ten tonight, ninety minutes from now. He would pull over, put the battery in and get his directions.

But...the voice must have put some kind of tracking device on his car. Tracing the phone calls had to be difficult and he doubted the voice had the ability, especially now that he was out on the prairie. No, his car must have a tracking device. If he could find it...

But he'd already looked once. If there was one there, he couldn't recognize it. Not that he knew all that much about what was supposed to be in a car.

He supposed he could change cars and escape the voice. But the agent he'd almost killed could identify him. If they had drawn a picture of his face from her description, it was probably already secretly circulating.

He'd have to hide out for years. No drawing was enough to get him convicted, but that agent pointing a finger at him could.

Damn!

He gripped the wheel tighter, frustrated and angry enough to explode. How nice it would be if he could get at the voice. The voice that now seeped into his dreams as he drove into the night and into unknown territory.

Sometimes he wondered if the voice knew where it was sending him. Sometimes he wondered if it knew as much as it claimed. Maybe he was on a wild-goose chase, although he had to admit it was better to be out here.

He'd heard the news on his car radio. The very night after he'd left, his warehouse had been raided. He should have blown it up, but the voice had been insistent, forbidding him to do any such thing. Why?

That questioned plagued him, and he started to think about how the voice could know so much. Was it in law enforcement? Did it know because it was part of the investigation? Had it been trying to protect people it knew when he'd suggested leaving a bomb behind?

He didn't know whether the idea tickled him or not. He kind of liked thinking a cop of some kind was on his side. But another part of him soured about what that could mean.

Yeah, he was going to have to find a way to track the voice down after this job was done. He had to pay attention to every word it said. Every single one. Because sooner or later it might well betray itself.

Then he'd have one hell of a mission. One he'd enjoy more than any other.

Because if there was one thing he hated, it was being toyed with.

Lance had pulled out all the stops he could on dinner. Considering that he hadn't shopped with a romantic meal in mind, he congratulated himself that he'd managed to turn some chicken breasts into an above-average meal with a garlic sauce. Brown rice had been keeping warm in his rice maker, and he added assorted cooked carrots as a vegetable. He even wasted a little time on arranging the food attractively.

Erin was duly appreciative and showered him with smiles and comments about how delicious everything was.

Success, he thought. He could have wiped his brow with relief. When cooking for himself he seldom tried to be fancy, and then worrying about making something that would keep until she woke up had proved another minor challenge.

But it had made her smile, and that was the best part. This woman had been getting seriously down, not that he could blame her. Never once in his life had he felt as isolated as she must be feeling now. He could only try to imagine it.

But instead of allowing the conversation to turn serious, he entertained her with the many names he had for his dogs.

"Why so many?" she asked curiously.

"Because they pop out of my mouth and somehow stick. Take Bernie for example. He loves cheesy snacks. Mine. I try not to feed them much in the way of people food, but the begging goes on anyway. Anyhow, one evening I dropped a cheese cracker on the floor. Now, he'd been begging for them earlier but when I didn't give him any he'd left the room for a while. When he came back in, that cracker was sitting right on the floor. And he walked past it. That was when I dubbed him Mr. Super Genius Wonder Dog."

She laughed so hard at that he watched her hold her sides. "I love it!"

"And when I first got Rufus, he had a drinking problem."

"What?" She looked startled.

"He was a rescue from a local puppy mill we shut down. Anyway, when I brought him home, he'd drain a huge water bowl the minute I put it down. Which had the usual result. I called him the Pee-anist, and later changed it to Mozart."

"Oh, man!" She wiped tears from her eyes as she continued to laugh. "Did he get over his problem?"

"Yeah, that was interesting. We went off to the vet because I was afraid he was sick. The vet figured he'd just been water-deprived for too long in that mill. So we came home with instructions on exactly how much water I was to give him each day according to his weight, and to parse it out. Two weeks later the problem was gone."

Her smile faded. "You know, that's sad."

"It was. But he's fit as a fiddle now. Anyway, over the three or four years I've had them, they've grown a crop of names, silly as they are. I've learned one thing, though."

"What's that?"

"Dogs will answer to almost any name." He laughed quietly and shook his head. "Which I guess means it's all in your physical signals and tone of voice. But they understand a lot of words, too."

"I've heard that." Her plate nearly clean, she pushed it to one side and leaned her forearms on the table. "For instance?"

"Never say the word *treat* when they can hear. Context doesn't matter. I could be talking to you about a treat of some kind, but they'd hear that word and be all over me. There are others, of course. They seem to be always alert for words that are meaningful to them. I got Bernie when we took him away from an abusive owner. Some cusswords, even spoken mildly in the middle of a sentence, would make him cower. I don't cuss nearly as much as I used to." Just remembering how he had felt when he had realized that could still upset him. Nobody, human or animal, deserved to be treated that way.

"Darn, Lance, this is sad."

"It often is when you adopt a mistreated animal. They sure don't hold any grudges, though. Anyway, there are other important words like *out*, *walk*, *food*. I sometimes think they understand a whole lot more of what I say than I'll ever guess. They only let me know they understand when it matters to them."

"You might be right. Where are they now?"

"In their run. I didn't want soulful eyes disturbing our romantic dinner."

He saw her head come up at his choice of words and waited for fire to rain down on his head. Her eyes occasionally expressed interest in him, but everything else about her said she was off-limits. She might settle for a fling, but he wasn't sure he could, so best just leave that alone. But romantic dinner? Why had he let that pop out?

"This *is* romantic," she said slowly. "But, Lance?"

"It's okay," he said. "I know you're leaving as soon as you can. I know you don't want another man in your life. But that doesn't mean we can't liven up your confinement with a little fun. I also need to find a way we can get you out for a while. I don't see why taking a drive in the mountains should be risky. I just know being cooped up with nobody but me must be hard on you."

She looked down a few seconds, then raised her eyes to gaze directly at him. "Being with you isn't hard at all. Do I feel a little cooped up? Well, when you come right down to it, I ought to be used to that."

"Why?"

"Because I spend most of my work hours at a desk stacked with papers, in front of a computer with a telephone glued to my ear. Then I go home, take a jog and except for sometimes having friends over..." She trailed off.

"Not much of a life?" he asked tentatively.

"Oh, it's a life, all right. Most of the shoe leather has been taken out of investigation. We bring people of interest in and question them in the office. Now, I won't say I never beat the streets or hunt someone down, but how much I get out depends on the type of investigation. Investigating a police department, for example, involves getting a warrant and then going through files, videotapes and emails."

"Glorified paper pusher?"

"Sometimes. It's like with the bombs. I spent weeks going through scene photos, studying them for a link."

"And you found one."

She smiled faintly. "I did. It was verified by forensics. But all those weeks I thought my eyes were going to fall out of my head. It just depends."

"Why are you guys involved anyway? Aren't bombs ATF territory?"

"We have a joint task force, a knitting of skills if you will." Her gaze grew distant and he almost kicked himself when he realized he'd just undone the pleasant evening he'd hoped to give her. He tried to figure out a way to turn the topic in a different direction, but it was too late. She spoke again. "We hunted the Unabomber, if you remember. ATF studies the bombs, the scenes, for all useful information. They're the technical guys on bombs. We hunt the bomber."

"So you kind of cross over into their territory?"

Her eyes narrowed. "We intersect. We were a joint task force. We always welcome fresh eyes because it's easy to get tunnel vision sometimes. Anyway, the thing I found didn't seem to be related in any way to the bombs. If I hadn't wandered through all those photographs, it might have been missed simply because it wasn't part of making an explosive device."

He nodded understanding. "So no rivalry?"

"There's always rivalry. We don't let it get in the way. Anyhow, they dissected everything they got relevant to the bombs themselves, and were tracking down suppliers of the various parts. I just noticed…something."

He let it go. Clearly she wasn't going to tell him what it was and he was getting the message. Joint task force, everyone cheerfully working together.

Except for one person, perhaps.

Then she utterly knocked the wind from him.

"Lance?"

"Yo?"

"You said you could make love with me without hurting me."

He stared at her, wondering where the devil that had come from. His body had no problem with this. It stirred immediately, the banked fires of his desire reaching blast furnace proportions. Had that pill worn off yet? Had she taken another? Was she losing her marbles?

He'd never expected her to be so bold. Oh, she was outspoken about everything else, but except for an almost-kiss and a friendly hug on the couch, she'd been keeping well clear of him. Occasionally he felt as if he might fall into the category of a hand grenade she didn't want to handle.

He probably did. He'd heard her on the phone with her friend saying that she didn't want a man in her life. But he'd never suspected she might be the type for a one-night stand either.

Yes, he'd opened his yap and said it, but it was in a heedless moment, one of those things that happened when your body was throbbing with hunger. He had some genuine concerns here. He tried to douse the blast furnace, at least a little bit.

"Lance?"

Finally he spoke guardedly. "What's going on? Are you sure you're thinking clearly? You're not the staying kind, at least not here, and you said the last thing you needed in your life was a man."

Something sparked in her gaze. "How many times are you going to remind me of that? Anyway, I didn't just make a proposal of marriage."

"That's not what I mean. And you damn well know it. This seems out of the blue."

"Out of the blue?" she repeated. If brown eyes could blaze, hers did. "You give me flowers and candles and call this a date and you're offended?"

"Did I say I was offended?" Realizing his voice had risen a bit, he lowered it. "I'm worried."

"Worried?" She blinked at him.

"Yeah, worried. You've been locked up with me for days. No fun, I agree. But I don't want to be a diversion, even if… Well, hell, you're an attractive woman but…"

"But what?"

"You're feeling better. I don't want to be your test case for whether you can enjoy sex again, and I'm sure you wouldn't like yourself very much if you used me that way."

"Use you? You were the one who first mentioned making love." Fury sparkled all over her like static electricity. If people really had auras, hers must be an angry red. "What was the point of this dinner?"

"It wasn't a seduction. It was a gift to make you a little more cheerful."

"Oh." The wind went out of her sails. She looked at her arms on the table. He thought she even sagged a bit. "You're probably right. I'm ugly anyway."

"Ugly?" This conversation was rapidly spinning out of control and he had no idea where it was heading. "You're not ugly!"

"You should see my body. It'd turn you off. It'd turn anyone off. Scars everywhere. I'm hideous!"

"I'm sure you're not." His worry was growing. What was she trying to accomplish here?

"How would you know?" she said bitterly. "I look like someone ran me through a meat grinder."

He scratched his neck impatiently. What was it she needed? Reassurance? The feeling that she wasn't so alone? That someone could be trusted to care for her in every way? Or just a fling into forgetfulness?

"I'm sorry," she said finally, her voice stiff. "I thought you wanted..."

He interrupted forcefully. "What I want isn't the issue here. Of course I want you, woman! I'd have to be dead not to want you. But I'm not young enough and stupid enough to just jump in. The question here is what *you* want and whether it would be good for you."

She surprised him with a half smile, utterly mirthless. "Really? How is anyone supposed to know that? I got married once and it turned out bad. Some things you just can't know, Lance."

"Tell me about it." He ran his fingers through his hair. He felt they were utterly at cross-purposes here. Maybe she was reacting from shock. The news earlier certainly should have shaken her more than it had seemed to.

Someone she knew had put a target on her back. Maybe a price on her head. She was sitting out here in the back of beyond with no one to trust except people she hardly knew.

She was usually a very level, contained person. Kind of what you'd expect of an FBI agent. But now she seemed to be going off the rails. He couldn't trust this, not unless she made herself clearer.

He rose, on a deep impulse he couldn't deny, and rounded the table to kneel beside her. Touching her arm where it rested on the table, he said, "Erin, I want you. Absolutely no question of that. And however many scars you have, they're badges, not the result of a meat grinder. I don't want to fight with you. But...I want you to be sure, so I'm going to ask you to let this go for just a little while. If you still feel the same in an hour or so, tell me."

Her eyes looked strange, a little swollen? And certainly pinched. Finally she murmured, "You don't trust me."

"I didn't say that."

"I mean, you don't trust me to know what I want."

Well, he couldn't deny that. Not at this moment. He wanted to kick his own butt again. How had he managed to make this about trust, the very thing that was troubling her most right now?

The urge to stride out the door and walk off frustrated passion and clear his head was in danger of winning the day. How had this turned into such a mess? What was he doing wrong? He thought he was protecting her, but apparently she didn't feel that way.

Or maybe she didn't like feeling that anyone thought she needed protecting from anything, least of all herself. Damn, there was enough of that going on right now.

Slowly, very carefully, he wrapped his arms around her and drew her gently closer until her shoulder rested against his chest. God, she felt fragile, yet he knew how strong she must really be. She made light of being mostly a paper pusher, but FBI agents carried guns for a reason. She'd probably faced very real danger more than once, and just didn't like to talk about it. Right now, however, she was recovering from serious injuries, struggling with being a hunted woman, struggling with the shredding of every bit of trust she had depended on with her colleagues.

He simply didn't want to encourage her to do something that might be just a moment of weakness she'd regret. Or a mistake that might disgust her later. How could he convey that? Apparently he was doing a terrible job of it.

Never had he felt so inept.

Chapter 10

Erin enjoyed the gentle hug Lance gave her, but no hug would paper over what had just happened. She'd let him know she wanted him, and he'd made excuses. Used *her* as an excuse. So what if he'd been gentle about it?

She let him hug her a little longer than she should have. When she was certain he believed she had accepted his reasoning, she pulled out of his arms.

"I need to go for a walk," she announced. "Certainly it has to be safe for me to take a stroll."

He remained kneeling beside her, and something in his expression suggested that she hadn't fooled him. "Let me call the guys first. Let them know. I don't want you mistaken for the UNSUB."

Through a sniperscope they could see her clearly enough, and she imagined a group like that had other, even better options for seeing a thousand yards. But she couldn't logically argue against giving them a heads-up.

"I'll get my jacket." And her pistol. She'd grown lax about wearing it indoors. That needed to stop.

She watched him rise and reach for the radio on the kitchen counter, then stood and headed down the hall herself, shaking out stiffness as she went.

She roiled inside, feeling conflicted in a way she seldom did. She mostly lived what she thought of as a "bright line" life. She knew where she was headed, she knew the rules she needed to follow and when she absolutely had to break them and pretty much everything seemed clear to her. She wasn't used to internal debates about what she felt or what she was doing.

Maybe she'd been living too simplistically. Maybe she'd become a creature of her career. Maybe she'd buried most of her feelings in the logic of investigation. FBI, through and through.

Life was certainly easier without a lot of gray areas. When she'd been younger, she'd actually fallen in love and thought she could combine her career with a marriage. How ridiculous that had turned out to be. The question, she supposed now, was had she let herself go too far in the other direction, putting her career above everything?

She guessed she had. Little more than a month ago she'd almost died. Surely a little reevaluation was the least she should expect?

Mortality didn't frighten her. Not now. When she'd finally become alert enough to realize that she'd been at death's door, there had been a period when she had wished they had just let her die.

Not because she hurt so much, but because it would have been so easy to just let go. Instead, she had returned to life, with all its messiness, and a near obsession with finding a bomber that she couldn't even act on because she wasn't fit for duty.

Now she'd made her life even messier by giving in to a craving for a man who evidently didn't want her. Not that she could blame him. Except for Tom, men had stopped expressing an interest in her a while ago. She made no attempt to be sexy or attractive, and probably froze them almost from the very first words that they exchanged.

She'd become an ice queen.

Then that monster had blown her into a whole new world where she was the prey and couldn't do damn all to take care of herself. Hence the road trip, trying to take control again of what she *could* control.

She didn't need a psychologist to tell her that.

Nor did she need all these muddled thoughts. Treat it like a stakeout, she told herself. Wait, watch and remain contained until it was time for action. Don't wander any mental or emotional byways that might distract from the business at hand.

A killer was looking for her, and she needed to be ready, not fighting internal demons.

Lance waited by the front door. "All clear," he said.

"I'll go alone."

He frowned faintly. "No."

"No? I can do whatever I choose."

"Sure. So can I. You've never walked my yard or anything else around here. Consider me your Seeing Eye dog. It's dark out there."

Anger stirred in her. "I need to be alone."

"Then pretend I'm not around. I won't say a word."

God, this situation was beginning to feel like ever-tightening bungee cords. Today's call had certainly not made it any better. She couldn't even reach out to Fran. Not now. Nobody to talk to but a hunk who'd just turned down her advances after expressing interest. She guessed she'd finally managed to freeze him, too.

Without a word, she eased into her jacket and stepped out the front door. She heard him follow, but didn't look back.

The waning crescent moon offered some light, but not much. She stood at the porch railing, waiting for her eyes to adapt, and soaking up the exotic aromas of the country. The air smelled fresher than the city, without the inevitable exhaust fumes, incinerators or baking trash receptacles. No delicious aromas issuing from restaurant kitchen exhaust fans. She might have been dropped in an alien world.

Nor could she identify the scents that filled the night here. If this went on long enough, maybe she'd ask, but for right now it was all the cue she needed to remind her that she was in unfamiliar territory. This was not the night of a large city or even a small town.

Shortly she began to realize that there were more stars in the sky than she had ever seen before. She almost asked if that was the Milky Way, then realized it must be. The beauty overhead was ineffable. Wondrous. So many stars up there that she could almost feel the immense depth of space in which a tiny Earth traveled. Enough to make her feel almost dizzy.

But for that sliver of moon, she might not have been able to see anything at all, beyond the faint glow that worked its way out of the curtained windows of the house.

It would definitely not be wise to wander far without a flashlight.

She could feel Lance standing behind her, but true to his word he didn't speak, although he was probably wondering if she was all right.

She continued to wait anyway, wanting her eyes to

fully adapt. She could have asked for a flashlight, but that would have narrowed her view and washed away the magic of the star-strewn night.

So she waited, gradually growing aware that the night was not silent. A breeze ruffled through grasses and she thought she heard the chirp and buzz of insects. A whole world hidden by shadow.

At last she felt she could see well enough to descend the steps. She gripped the rail, ignoring the protests from her legs and hip. It would all heal eventually. For now she just needed to ignore it.

She liked feeling good to feel ground beneath her feet again, even the irregular ground that was Lance's yard. Not a floor or pavement, but the crunch of gravel and grass. And so much wide-open space until her gaze reached the hulking blackness of the trees that surrounded the house at about a thousand yards. Slowly, she started walking, feeling as if she needed to get her sea legs under her. Maybe she did.

She decided it was best to walk near the house where there was more light. Maybe in the morning she could stroll down the drive to the road.

But then she remembered anew that she was hunted. Impossible to know when that guy had left Chicago, or how fast he was coming. He could be here at any moment. The magic seeped out of the night.

What the hell did she think she was doing? But she kept walking anyway, around the side to the back where she knew she'd find the dog run and the dogs. She was missing those animals.

But with each step the night changed, becoming more sinister. Shrubs ran alongside the house. They hadn't disturbed her before, but tonight they seemed to hide secrets. Her heart began to hammer and her mouth went dry.

What was happening to her? There was nothing out here. She could see that. All she had to do was round the next corner and she'd see Rufus and Bernie. She wanted to see them.

But then the shadows shifted. Something was moving in the shrubbery. She froze. A man rose up and turned toward her...

Lance, who had been quietly following about six paces behind, saw Erin freeze. Immediately on high alert, he wondered if she'd seen or heard something. To him, however, the night seemed benign. The fellows on watch had said the only things moving anywhere around them were sheep, his neighbor's cattle, some raccoons and a bear out by the creek. Sounded like a normal inventory to him.

But Erin remained frozen. So he crept up quietly, wondering what she had discovered. Just before he reached her, she emitted a keening cry, then dropped, rolling herself into a ball.

He flew across the distance between them. The dogs started barking furiously, probably because of her cry, not because someone was lurking, but he couldn't chance it. Without trying to figure out what had happened, he scooped the woman up off the ground and ran with her back around, up the front porch and into the house.

The radio on his belt started squawking as soon as he got inside.

"Lance? Lance, what the hell?"

He ignored it until he was able to put Erin on the couch. She was shaking from head to foot, curled defensively, her face utterly colorless. Shock. But what had she seen?

He pulled the radio off his belt and hit the transmit button. "I'm here."

"What the hell got you running? We didn't see anyone approach."

"Erin saw or heard something. I don't know. She seems to be in shock. I'm going to get some blankets."

"We'll be right there."

He got a comforter out of his closet, the warmest he had, and covered her with it. Somehow he had to elevate her feet, but each time he tried to loosen the knot she had formed, she resisted and he didn't want to hurt her.

He could see no injury, thank God, but something had happened to her and he began to suspect what it was.

All he could do was call her name, over and over again, and wait for her to return. The terror in her eyes seemed directed at something far away. If he had to guess, he'd bet she'd walked right back into the night when she had been nearly killed.

The dogs set up a new round of barking, which meant the men had arrived. Still bending over Erin, he rubbed her shoulder until he felt her relax slightly.

"Erin, I'm taking your pistol."

She heard that. In an instant her eyes snapped to his face and he could have shouted with relief. Not entirely back yet, still shaking, but aware. She gave an infinitesimal nod.

Gently he pulled the comforter back, unsnapped her holster and removed her service pistol, placing it on the end table. Then he pulled the comforter back up to her chin. Her gaze found him again.

"Lance?"

"I'm here. You're fine. Just keeping you warm."

Another almost imperceptible nod, then she closed her eyes.

The knock at the door was meant to be heard. No

neighborly rap, but a fist-pounding. He'd banged on enough doors himself that way to recognize it.

"I'll be right back," he told Erin.

He opened the door to see Micah Parish. Covered in black from head to toe. "Nothing out there," Micah told him. "She okay?"

"I'm betting flashback."

Micah nodded. "We're going to pull the perimeter back now, unless you need something."

"If I need anything it might be an ambulance. We'll see. She seems to be coming out of it."

"It's a bad thing, all right." With a nod of his head, Micah sifted into the shadows once more.

When Lance turned around, he saw Erin sitting up. Her trembling appeared to have eased, but her eyes looked hollow and her skin was still paper white.

"I'm getting you some warm, sweet coffee," he told her.

"I don't like it sweet." Her voice sounded thin.

"You need the sugar. Think of it as medicine." At least she was talking. And arguing. Relief almost brought a smile to his face.

The dinner coffee was still good, so he filled his biggest mug with it, added more milk than she usually liked and two teaspoons of sugar.

She had pulled her arms free of the comforter, and took the mug.

"Medicine," he reminded her, then pulled the rocker over so he could sit facing her. The milk had cooled the coffee enough that she drained the mug immediately. Just like medicine. Now he *did* smile. "More?" he asked.

She nodded. "Less sugar, please."

He searched her face, noted that some of her color

was returning. "Okay. I'll make it the way you like it this time."

"Lance?"

He had just risen and taken a step toward the kitchen. He looked back.

"I'm sorry," she said.

"No apology wanted or needed. Just sit tight."

For a long time, neither of them spoke. Gradually Erin uncurled completely, wincing a bit with every move. He watched her, wishing he could help, figuring his help would be about as welcome as fleas on a dog right then. Now she had a new problem to deal with, and they both knew it.

All he wanted was to see the old Erin, the one who still peeked out when pain wasn't lashing her. The woman who could listen to her boss that morning, absorb some tough blows and still tick over possibilities in her mind, trying to work the problem.

He knew, though, that that woman might never fully return. She was trying to, hence that strange argument over dinner. She was not only feeling alone, but she was feeling a total lack of control. Life was pushing her every which way, dealing nasty blows, and she couldn't even step out of the line of fire.

After another cup of coffee and a refill, she spoke. "I don't know what happened."

"Want to tell me?"

She started to shake her head, then stopped. "It was weird, Lance. I could feel the night changing. It went from being absolutely beautiful—I mean, I've never been anywhere I could see so many stars before, and the air here smells so different, so clean…"

She trailed off and he waited patiently. The cop in him

was exploding with questions, but he tamped them down. She didn't need a cop, she needed a friend.

"Anyway…" The word was almost a sigh. "It started feeling different. Threatening. And then… And then…" Pinched eyes lifted to his. "I was there again. Walking around my house, and seeing the guy move, seeing the muzzle flash… I was *there*."

"I thought that might be what happened. A flashback."

"Damn." Now she sounded angry. "I already had enough problems to deal with. How am I ever going to work again if I can do that?"

"You might never do it again, Erin. But tonight…"

She interrupted. "That was really a stupid idea, walking around the house. It should have occurred to me it would be just like that night."

"Why?"

She frowned at him, her soft lips pulling downward. "Why?"

"Why would it have occurred to you? You're in a different place, literally. And I take it you haven't had a flashback before."

"No," she admitted. She put her mug down next to her pistol and knit her fingers.

"Then how could you possibly know that something out there would trigger one? It may never do so again. If you want, we'll go take another walk in a little while, when you have more color and energy. We'll test it. But right now you don't know what the trigger was or if it'll ever happen again. Want some of that Danish? I froze half of it."

His abrupt change of subject served its purpose. The first smile flickered over her face. "I'd love it."

"It'll take me a minute. Thank the powers that be for microwaves."

That even drew a small laugh from her. Erin was returning.

She suggested they take their coffee and Danish onto the front porch. He didn't miss the significance of that. She wanted to take back at least a piece of the night. He agreed and they settled into the old Adirondack chairs that his father had built for his mother out of some fine hardwood that had stood up well to the years. Side by side they stared out into the dark, and he waited to see what would happen.

At first she stirred frequently, but the cool breeze kept blowing and nothing changed in the night except the moon rose higher and the stars wheeled in their courses. Gradually she grew still, and he wondered if she had dozed off, until she spoke.

"I love Adirondack chairs," she remarked. She sounded normal now.

"So did my mother. She jonesed for them for years, then my dad announced he'd make some for her. Of course, as she said, he couldn't just buy some regular old lumber and nails. No, he had to turn it into a special project. He ordered maple at the lumber yard, used dowels to hold them together instead of nails, and by the time he got done she swore he'd built heirlooms instead of the two simple chairs she had wanted. Probably cost more, too."

She laughed softly. "It sounds like he loved her."

"He did, although at the time she claimed he was doing all that just to make her feel bad for asking so often. She said it, but I don't think she believed it."

"She might have felt bad that he was working so hard on it. A little guilt?"

"Maybe."

"Well, he did a fine job."

He couldn't argue with that. His dad had always believed a job was worth doing only if you did it well. But then, at last, she addressed the problem.

"Now," she said, "I have something else to worry about."

"The flashback?"

"Yes."

His chest tightened a bit. As if this woman didn't already have enough troubles? Sometimes he wished he owned a magic wand instead of a collapsible baton. "Like I said, it might never happen again."

"Lance. I need to be able to trust my mind."

"I know." But he had no answer for that. Only time could provide an answer to this one. "After this is all over and you can head home, maybe it would be good to see someone who specializes in post-traumatic stress."

Then she startled him. "Did you leave Denver PD because of what happened?"

Ah, hell, soul-baring time? He'd been around the block a few times with himself on this, he knew the answer, but it wasn't one he wanted to give her, not when she was feeling like this. "Yes," he said finally.

"Flashbacks?"

"No. Tension that wouldn't quit. I couldn't feel comfortable on the streets anymore. I felt like there was a threat around every corner. It made me a dangerous cop."

"Did something happen?" Her voice had grown soft.

"No. But something would have sooner or later. I was living a constant adrenaline push when I was working outside the station, and not even time and therapy helped. So I changed to small-town policing."

"That helped?"

"Infinitely. I like my job. In Denver I'd begun to hate it." But for her sake he needed to point something else out. "That was just me, Erin. A lot of guys don't develop any problem."

"Or they aren't as self-aware as you," she remarked quietly.

Well, he reckoned that was a possibility. He leaned back into the welcoming embrace of the chair his father had built so many years ago. At the other end of the porch, sadly unused, was another, child-sized, built for him when he was seven. It hadn't been used since he'd outgrown it, but he kept on refinishing it because it was a treasure.

When she remained silent, he spoke again. "Don't mentally throw away your job because of a single incident, Erin. It's clear you love it. You might be just fine a little way down the road. But, dang it, you had to have some reaction to all of this. You've been so cool, taking off on your own, dealing with some pretty bad news today... You're doing great as far as I can see."

"Maybe." She stirred a little. "Curling up in a ball that tight was not my smartest move."

"Hurting?" He hardly needed the answer. He didn't see how she couldn't be.

"I'll be okay."

So he sipped his coffee and waited for whatever came next. The two of them had been doing a lot of waiting, enough to craze them both a bit, he supposed.

Staring out over the empty fields to the woods, he wondered how far away the threat lay. If the man had any idea where Erin was, or if he just knew the general vicinity? Who on the inside was feeding him information, and could he access stuff that Tom was trying so hard to keep secret?

Or was it Tom himself, the guy who knew everything

and might be doing this just to create the illusion of innocence?

She spoke. "Is your frequent use of the word *dang* for the benefit of Bernie?"

He laughed quietly, surprised by the direction of her thoughts. "Yeah. *Damn* disturbs him. *Hell* not so much. Stronger words, very much."

"So even dogs can get post-traumatic stress."

That caught him. Frankly, he'd never thought of it that way, but rather as a learned response, the way the dogs reacted to words like *treat*. "Yes. I guess so. I hadn't thought about it."

"I'm in good company, then," she said. Clearly she was trying to lighten the moment.

"The best," he agreed.

Then she surprised him. "I'm ready to try walking around the house again." Moving gingerly, she eased out of the chair.

"Are you sure?" Tendrils of panic began to wind around his heart. He absolutely dreaded seeing her like that again, but he understood her impulse. This was something she needed to do, and postponing it might only make her more afraid of herself.

He gave her huge credit for determination.

"Yes. Now."

"Okay, I'll stay out of the way, but I'm keeping eyes on you. Let me radio the guys so they know we're moving."

She turned her head toward him. "Did they see what happened to me?"

"Only that I was running with you."

"Okay." That seemed to ease her mind. "I guess they're paying attention."

They sure were, he thought. A radio call cleared the walk. Erin descended from the porch with less steadiness than earlier, but he put that down to the cramped position she'd been in such a short while ago. All that pain that had quieted down had probably resurged big-time.

He descended the steps, too, and watched her disappear around the corner of the house. Brave to a fault, he thought, but felt a deep admiration for her. Facing her devils head-on. Not everyone would do that.

Then, quietly he followed, keeping his eyes on her as she walked slowly along the side of the house, tensing as the critical position neared.

She passed it. She kept walking, and finally rounded the back corner. The dogs set up a yammering, and he heard her speak to them.

Relief punctured the balloon of tension that had swelled in him, and he hurried to catch up. He found her standing at the chain-link fence, with the dogs bouncing around and standing on their hind legs by turns, trying to lick her through the fence. She laughed.

In an instant the world was right again.

Well, sort of.

Erin clung to the fence, hurting all over, but filled with a relief that left her almost weak. The dogs' joy seemed perfect to the moment, but the big thing was that she had reached them. She had got here without any more trouble. Thank God. She leaned her forehead against the fence, felt a sloppy tongue work its way through and lap her cheek. Then she heard Lance's approach.

"You made it," he said simply.

She nodded, unable to speak. She'd made it. One small victory. Man, she needed that victory. At this point, even the smallest one would do.

When her legs steadied, she let go of the fence and

turned. Even in the night's dim light she could see he was smiling. "Let's go back now."

"Want me to stay behind again?"

"Please."

So they repeated the odd walk in the opposite direction, but when she climbed the porch steps, she amazed him by pumping her fist. He could see that had hurt, but he laughed anyway.

"Yesss!" she crowed.

He applauded. "Great job." He laughed again. Okay then. She was feeling a whole lot better.

"Go as far as Wyoming," the mechanical voice said.

Harry wanted to smash the phone. "Then what?"

"Wait for your next instruction. And don't do anything stupid, Harry."

He was so angry, so frustrated, so driven by the need to set a bomb… Take the girl who'd checked him in at the motel. She'd looked right through him, had barely glanced at his phony ID, hadn't even said *thank you* when he paid in cash. She deserved a lesson. But he couldn't take care of her now because of the voice.

The inability to act was driving him crazy. He blamed the voice for it.

"Just one bomb…"

"No!" The voice snapped the word. "If you do that you might as well put a neon light on the map and tell them where you are. Is that what you really want?"

Well, no. Of course he'd move on immediately, well before the bomb went off, but the voice's mention of a map painted a clear image in his mind. He could see a glowing line leading from Chicago to his present point. But he argued anyway, because he hated the voice. "They wouldn't know it was me."

"The whole problem," said the mechanical voice, "is that because of what Agent Sanders figured out, they'd know it was you within hours. Are you forgetting, Harry? Are you forgetting that *I* know where you are?"

He hated that threat hanging over his head. He swore yet again that when he'd taken out this damn FBI agent, who ought to be dead right now, he was going to find the voice and turn it into a red mist.

"Take a few deep breaths, Harry," said the voice. "It'll be over soon, and then you'll be free to settle somewhere else and continue your work."

That hit him like a gut punch. "Somewhere else?" He didn't want to be anywhere else. Chicago was the place he knew. A strange place…well, it would take him time to set up again.

"They already found your lab," the voice said. "You'd need to move anyway. Be grateful I warned you."

Grateful. He was supposed to be grateful?

But he took those deep breaths, and began to settle down. A kind of coldness overtook him. Yeah, he could start somewhere else. He could leave bombs all over the country, get those chippies like the one at the motel desk. Maybe it would be better.

"When will you know where I need to go next?"

"Soon," the mechanical voice said. "Soon. I need some time. But I warned you they were coming. Remember that. I saved you. I'll get the information."

Of that Harry felt not the least doubt. What he doubted was that he'd be happy about it. Already he was in the middle of nowhere, which didn't make him feel at all safe.

And now he'd been told yet again not to pursue his real mission. No, he was pursuing someone else's mission.

Anger bubbled up in him again, red as a demon's eyes.

Somebody needed a lesson even more than that woman at the front desk. Much more.

Somehow he was going to provide it.

Chapter 11

Erin didn't sleep very well. Yesterday had delivered that shocking phone call from Tom, and last night the shock of discovering she could have a disabling flashback. She felt as if someone had kicked her legs right out from under her. How could she go back to work if she couldn't trust her own mind?

That terrified her almost as much as the awareness that one of her colleagues had painted a target on her.

Finally, she gave up. Her stomach growled with hunger and sleep eluded her as determinedly as any criminal ever had. Since the house felt a bit chilly, she pulled on her crimson robe over her nightshirt, donned her matching slippers and went to get a snack and coffee.

She tried to move silently. She had no idea whether Lance had fallen asleep on the sofa or in his bed. Either way, she didn't want to disturb him. Moving as surreptitiously as a cat burglar, she got the loaf of bread out along with the jar of peanut butter. Half a sandwich, she decided. Starting the coffee made more noise, unfortunately. She had to run the water, then the glass pot clattered a bit as she put it on the warming plate. At least scooping coffee into the basket didn't betray her.

"Can't sleep?"

She froze. "Damn." She looked over her shoulder. "I didn't want to wake you."

He stood leaning against the door frame, his hair mussed, a day's growth of beard a heavy shadow on his chin. Jeans rode his hips, but he hadn't pulled on a shirt. She looked quickly away, knowing the image of his muscled chest and belly had just been seared into her brain. His arms were powerful, too, although not the overly muscled kind that came from heavy workouts at the gym.

"Been sleeping with one eye open," he said casually. "You making enough coffee for two?"

"Now I am."

"Thanks. Be right back."

She watched him disappear around the corner, sorry to see him go. He returned just a minute later wearing a chambray shirt that he hadn't bothered to button. Almost as appealing as her first view of him.

Shaking her head at herself, she pulled out a small plate and quickly made herself half a sandwich. "You want one?" she asked.

"No, thanks. I'm not big on peanut butter."

That got her attention in a new way. Plate in hand, she turned from the counter. "Then why do you have it?"

"Dogs," he said, shrugging one shoulder. Then his aquamarine eyes twinkled. "Ever had to give a pill to a big dog?"

"Can't say I have," she admitted as she eased into a chair across from him. The coffee pot still gurgled.

"Well, it's possible to do it without enticements, but ever so much more pleasant if you wrap the pill in some peanut butter or Braunschweiger. They gobble it down."

In spite of her mood, a quiet laugh escaped her. "I'd gobble it down, too."

The coffee pot hissed, announcing it was finished. Before she could move, Lance rose and went to get it for them. "You still hurting?" he asked casually.

"A bit."

"Keeping you awake?"

"No. I've got enough else to keep me awake."

"Ah." He said nothing else as he opened the fridge. She watched him pull out a wedge of cheese, then some crackers from the cupboard. "This is my poison," he remarked. "Help yourself if you want any."

She hadn't expected this to turn into a middle-of-the-night meal. Just a little to quiet her stomach. But when he started slicing that cheese on the board and it crumbled, a testimony to its aging, she started thinking it looked really good.

Two dogs wandered into the kitchen, filling it up with their big bodies. Both walked over to the table, sniffing curiously, then sat. There was no mistaking the plea in their gazes.

"All right," Lance said, pretending annoyance. "One piece. That's it."

Erin felt a smile grow on her face as he handed each dog one small piece of cheese. She was a bit astonished by how quickly they snapped it from his hand and swallowed it.

"Settle," he said. They complied with heavy sighs. Bernie gave a huff that sounded like disgust. "You know," Lance said, looking at them, "I think dogs miss one of the best parts of life."

"What's that?"

"The way they wolfed that cheese down. Do you think they even savored it?"

Her smile widened. "Maybe it was all in the aroma. And of course, in the fact that you shared with them."

"Hah." A bark of laughter escaped him. "Sharing. That's probably it. Don't ever exchange gifts without including the dogs."

That grabbed her attention, planting her firmly in the now. "Really? They understand gifts?"

"You'd better believe it. The first year I had Bernie, I had some friends over for Christmas. We'd drawn names for gag gifts, the usual kind of thing. Anyway, I realized Bernie was pushing at the paper and packages after we started handing out the gifts, and looking really sad. Every time a package was opened he was right there checking it out. If he'd been able to talk he couldn't have been any clearer. He wanted a present, too."

"Wow. So what did you do?"

"I raced into the kitchen to get a rawhide bone and wrapped it quickly. He pulled the paper off it, settled down to gnaw on it, and no more pining after that. And yes, he had a rawhide bone already. What he wanted was to be included in the pack sharing. Every Christmas since, they get some new tennis balls or chew toys."

Something inside her softened. The tough officer of the law, who had initially seemed so intimidating to her, had a really gentle side to him. She liked that about him. He'd rescued two dogs; he'd rescued her. The man had a big heart and was strong enough and secure enough to put it on display. "Aww, Lance, that's adorable."

He flashed an engaging grin. "I have my moments."

She finished her sandwich and reached for a piece of cheese. He didn't say any more, but from their positions on the floor two dogs watched intently as he put each piece of cheese or cracker into his mouth. They hadn't given up hope.

Maybe, she thought, the dogs had it right. Never give up hope. In the end, their hopes were answered. Each of them got a wheat cracker.

"So," said Lance casually, "what's eating you other than the series of shocks yesterday?"

"Isn't that enough?" As soon as she spoke, she regretted the edge in her tone. She regretted it even more when he threw up a hand.

"Fine," he said. "Bottle it all up. But the thing is, I see us as partners on this one. Now maybe you consider yourself above partnering with a sheriff's deputy. If so, okay. Have it your way."

"I don't…" She began swiftly. Oh, God, had she given him that impression? "We're equals, Lance. That's how I see it."

"Then this is how you treat your colleagues? As if they can't listen or help? That you always have to go it alone?"

All of a sudden her ex's voice rose in her mind, a complaint long buried with his other complaints. *You never let me inside!*

"Oh, God," she murmured and put her face in her hands.

At once Lance was beside her, his hand on her shoulder. "Erin? Erin, I didn't mean to upset you."

"Yes, you did, and you were right." Slowly she raised her face from her hands and looked at him, into his entrancing blue-green eyes, now looking so concerned. "You've been wonderfully patient with me. But I've got a problem."

"Wanna share?"

"I'm a control freak. And I learned when I was a kid

to keep everything to myself. I still do, unless it's information on a case. Well, here I am, with no control whatsoever, and that's driving me crazy."

"I think this situation would drive anyone crazy," he said. "Which is not to minimize what you're feeling. It's driving *me* crazy, too. I don't like knowing there's a threat out there and all I can do is wait for it to arrive."

Then he released her shoulder and resumed his seat. Apparently he wasn't going to press her. Ordinarily she'd have been grateful for that, as it meant she could avoid deflecting him, but she'd been realizing something about herself and she didn't especially like it.

"Life is cleaner when you keep it all professional," she said slowly. "Easier to manage. But it's only half a life, isn't it?"

"I guess that depends on what you want. You *did* try marriage."

Her mouth twisted. "Oh, yes, I did, and it blew up in my face. I was lousy at emotional intimacy. Or so I was told."

"I can't speak to that."

"You've seen me. It takes a pain pill to lower my walls. Sad, huh?"

"I'm not sure about that. Life teaches us to be careful who we share ourselves with. I'm not one to be blaring every feeling and thought I have to anyone who'll hold still enough to listen for a few."

The image almost made her smile. But she was looking into a deeper pit than that. Bottom line, being professional was good on the job, but it took you just so far. "You know, if I'd been honest with even one of my colleagues about how uneasy the bomber's phone call had made me, I wouldn't have been home alone that night." She faced it squarely, admitting her own deficiency.

"They weren't worried about it?"

"That's the thing. Everyone was focused on the fact we had a number to watch. Nobody thought the guy would be able to figure out where I lived."

"But you were worried?"

"Yeah. I was. He didn't threaten me in that call. He just taunted me."

"How?"

"He basically said he was smarter than all of us, and even though I'd found a link between his bombs, we'd never find him. That's not a threat."

He rested his elbows on the table and leaned forward. His shirt fell open even more. She'd vastly have preferred to admire the view he was giving her than think about all this. But as always, business first.

"Not a threat," he agreed. "Not directly anyway. But the fact he knew your name and could get past the switchboard? That was threatening all by itself. I'm not surprised it made you uneasy."

"Nobody else seemed especially worried, and I don't blame them. My face wasn't out there, my home was under my maiden name. There was no logical reason to think I was at risk."

"Also no reason to think your uneasiness should be dismissed. So if you'd told them…?"

"They'd have sent some people home with me." She sighed. "But once again I wanted to appear professional, not given to hysteria."

He nodded slowly. "*Hysteria.* Interesting word. Also sexist. So you didn't want to appear less than a man? Am I right? Only a woman would react as you did to that phone call?"

Anger sparked in her, but before she could glare at him, she acknowledged the justice of what he was saying. He was right. She'd made it into the elite boys' club and she couldn't afford to appear weak. From her very first day with the Bureau, she'd understood.

"I get it," he said when she didn't answer. "You'd think in this day and age... Well, I saw it on the job in Denver. Women on the force had to be as tough as any guy. Tougher maybe. Even though it wasn't out in the open, they needed to work harder, do better, be tougher... Oh, I get it."

She hesitated then said, "You're more perceptive than most."

"I just like to watch people. Men are just assumed to be all those things, but a woman has to prove them repeatedly."

She felt a surge of real warmth for him. Fran had understood, but Fran was a woman. Sometimes they'd joked about it, tried to make light of it, but the pressure was there anyway. "It's not that bad," she said finally. And it was something she usually preferred not to think about at all.

"I suppose," he said. "And what good would it do to talk about it? Sour you on your job? I don't want to do that."

Right then she wasn't all that sure how she felt about her job. Everything had been knocked sideways. But as an investigative agent, she hadn't been exposed to the same kinds of dangers street agents encountered very often, which meant she really hadn't had to prove the "tougher" part except a handful of times. "Would you have done what I did, leave town?" she asked.

"Me? I don't know. Gage said he understood your reluctance to go to a safe house. I'll take his word for it. But remember, you're talking to a guy who switched to small-town policing because he couldn't trust himself anymore. It's not comparable."

"It's not?" She pushed back from the table and left the kitchen. Aching, always aching, although it was getting somewhat better.

Lance followed her. "Did I say something wrong?"

"No." She gave a small shake of her head. "We have very different experiences. I never worked on the streets like you did. I told you, I mostly dealt with investigations. Records, phone calls, interviews, occasionally serving warrants and so on. Yeah, there were a few times it got dangerous, but not like what you did all the time, like the guys in our street units have to do. I was just wondering if I was ill-prepared. Not ready to deal with the violence or the aftermath."

She turned to face him and read surprise there. "Erin? Do you really think anyone is prepared the first time they're the object of violence? It's one thing to see it happen to others, or see the aftermath. It's entirely another to be the target of it. Oh, you can be aware it might happen to you, but tell me just who'd go out to police those streets if they really, truly believed it would happen to them?"

She felt a wry smile tug at the corners of her mouth. "Like who'd drive if they believed they'd get in an accident?"

"Exactly. Knowing it might happen is a whole different thing from believing it will. There's just so much you can be prepared. So you toughed out some uneasiness— justifiable uneasiness—and got the worst possible outcome. Like you said, nobody should have been able to find you. So of course you ignored your own internal warning. Most of us would have. Gage told you he did and what it cost him. You've nothing to blame yourself for."

"Maybe I do," she said quietly. "I can't seem to deal with not being in control."

"Ahh." The sound escaped him like a sigh. "Now *that* you can blame on being a cop. Everyone likes to believe they're in control, but only cops are expected to have it all the time. Wasn't that part of your training, to take control of any situation?"

She nodded. "Sure."

He moved his head and lifted his brow as if to say, *See?*

"I guess control is an illusion," she murmured. "Like getting behind the wheel of a car. The driver can do everything right and still get hit by a drunk driver, or someone swerving unexpectedly to avoid an obstacle in the road."

"Exactly." Then he took the conversation in an entirely unexpected direction, nearly knocking the wind from her. "That pass you made at me? Well, that halfhearted pass that nearly caused us to fight. Was that you trying to take control?"

She stared at him. Her outward calm was usually mirrored internally. She had long schooled herself to stay in control of her internal life as much as possible, but his question blew away all the pretense, and left her emotions bubbling out over her carefully constructed walls. Like the bomb that had almost killed her, it shredded her defenses. She felt nearly scalded by the seething cauldron of needs, desires and fears that simple question uncovered.

As a child she had learned to contain herself, and to remain blind to the ugliness around her. As an adult she had taken off the blinders but had clung to self-containment. With that one frank question, containment vanished.

But she had also schooled herself to be scrupulously truthful when it would do no harm. She had been asked a question, and felt she'd betray them both if she didn't answer it honestly. Lance certainly didn't deserve that. This wasn't just about her, it was about him, as well.

"Partly," she said bluntly. "You may have noticed I'm not in control of anything right now."

"Granted. And?"

It was the *and* that proved so hard to answer. She steeled herself and said something she had been hoping to bury in some safe repository once she left here. "I want you. The first instant I saw you, tired and hurting though I was, I felt it instantly. It's not going away. But maybe it had better."

"Maybe. But why?"

"I told you! I'm a mess physically. That bomb did a real number on me. You might as well make love to an ugly plastic doll."

She hated that a slow smile began to crease his face. He was enjoying this. Well, of course, what man didn't want to hear that he was a desirable hunk? She ought to just take a hike right now, except she doubted she'd make it very far. Just admitting her hunger for him seemed to have only made her feel weaker.

Then he blew her away again. "You ever hear of the handcuff game?"

"What?" She was sure her face had lost every bit of its impassivity.

He took a step toward her. "What's got you worried, Erin? That you still hurt too much? That you'd be a passive lover? That you couldn't take control?"

Each question hit her almost like a punch, but each one caused her heart to beat more heavily.

"Some people do that for fun," he said. "Take a totally submissive and passive role. You don't have to do a damn thing to please me. You already do enough to drive me half-crazy with wanting you. Now, if you'd feel guilty for being passive, I could restrain you. And then you wouldn't have a choice anymore."

She could barely breathe. Hot lava seemed to be bubbling in her aching core, answering each beat of her heart. "Is that your kink?" she managed to whisper.

"My only kink is that both of us should enjoy the experience." He took another step toward her. "Now, if you think you could relax and give up control freely, nothing more is needed. But if you need a little help doing that, I'll oblige. Your choice. But either way when you feel better, you can take as much control as you want."

Her eyes closed, as heated rivers of hunger began to pour through her veins.

"Shall we try?" he asked. "See how far we go?"

"I'm ugly," she said again, hating the way her voice broke.

"You haven't got a mark on you that I haven't seen somewhere. Maybe more than most, but nothing I haven't seen. Erin?"

The answer slipped out of her on a sigh. "Yes."

He took her hand and guided her slowly to the bedroom. Her eyes didn't want to open anymore, they felt heavy, unnecessary, but she opened them a bit to see the way. In the darkened bedroom she felt safer.

Then he took her gently by the shoulders. "Just remember. This isn't a test. This isn't the be-all end-all. It's supposed to be fun. Play. If it stops being fun, let me know."

On the surface it seemed like such a simple request, but Lance knew it wasn't. His need for her had become a stampede inside him, and he recognized it was dangerous. He closed his eyes and reached for every bit of self-control he had.

Erin had told him more than she realized when she had said her mother was an alcoholic. He didn't need a diagram to know she had grown up feeling as if she could control nothing, feeling as if she needed to hide someplace inside herself for the only security she could find. Her entire childhood had been out of control because alcoholics were unpredictable. Oh, some might just mope quietly, but many didn't. Some became violent. Some became abusive. Some became the life of the party. And all too often a kid never knew which of those moods would appear.

Looking at this woman, he believed much of her childhood had been lived in fear of emotional storms and attacks. Buffeted by the winds of her mother's chemically induced moods, what control could she claim, other than to lock herself away inside? He'd almost bet that her father had been an enabler, preferring peace to confrontation, refusing to face his wife's alcoholism. Leaving his kids without an ally.

Now she was here, with no control again. Acute awareness of the pitfalls caused him to move slowly. He'd tried to relax her with his light remarks about cuff play, but he had no intention of removing her autonomy unless she outright asked for it. She'd already lost all control, and he wasn't going to take another bit from her now.

He paused just long enough to pull a condom from the beside table and toss the packet where he could reach it.

Standing close, he pushed the robe from her shoulders to puddle on the floor and caressed her face lightly with his fingertips. She'd put on a tiny bit of weight since she'd arrived, making her face softer, but she was still classically beautiful. Her skin felt like satin beneath his fingers, but as he traced around behind her ears, he felt a scar. He kept his fingers from pausing there, knowing

this moment would be repeated many times as he dis-
robed her.

A sigh escaped her, and along with it the last of her
tension.

"You're so pretty," he murmured. "Even worn as you
were when I first saw you I thought so, and you're getting prettier with each day. How do you do it, Erin?"

Her eyes fluttered open a bit as she looked at him. "Do
what?" she whispered.

"Remain so reserved and drive me so crazy at the
same time. I'm crazy with wanting you."

The smallest of smiles appeared on her lips, and now
he traced them with his fingertip. She spoke. "Careful.
My ex thought I was the ice queen."

"Maybe your ex should have looked in the mirror.
You still okay?"

"If any pain is left, it's lost, Lance. You're driving everything away."

His turn to smile. Bending, he found her mouth with
his and tried a gentle, tentative kiss. "Better than a pain
pill," he remarked as he lifted his mouth just a bit.

At that she laughed quietly, a surprising sound, then
delighted him by lifting her arms and wrapping one
around his waist. With the other she found his head and
drew him in for a full kiss. Taking control. He let her.

Her mouth was warm, moist, welcoming, and her
tongue played with his readily, at first teasing with little strokes, then driving against his in an unmistakable
mating rhythm. His blood pounded through him in time
with her tongue.

But even as he let his arms slide down her back, reality sent him a summons. He could feel a few ridges of
scars on her back, and in a moment of needed clarity he

recalled that this woman was far from healed. She would wear out fast unless he protected her.

Another force rose in him, every bit as strong as his passion, the desire to protect her, to make this experience good, not to have it come crashing down on her as everything else in her life had lately, reminding her of things that these moments demanded be forgotten for just this little while.

It was hard, but he tore his mouth from hers. "Easy," he murmured roughly. "No rush."

She was already panting. She hardly opened her eyes, just gave a small nod. Tremors began to ripple through her, and he couldn't tell if they were from fatigue or need.

He just knew he had to make her comfortable as quickly as he could. Moving as gently as possible, he eased her nightshirt over her head and discovered her small, rounded breasts. Scars, visible even in the dim light, made the reason for gentleness apparent. One side in particular showed red stripes. Her arm must have been over her head. But now was not the time to look at them. Gently he urged her to sit, then lie on the bed. He bent with her, bending over her to kiss her, to keep her from getting nervous. He knew a moment of fear, huge fear, that he might inadvertently do something to ruin this tenuous trust she was giving him.

Dropping kisses all over her face, he lightly brushed his hands over her breasts. Then she surprised him.

"I won't break."

He lifted his head a bit and found her smiling sleepily. "I don't want to hurt you."

She lifted her hand to cup his cheek. "Lance, I'm not that fragile. Pain is inevitable right now, no matter how hard you try to avoid it."

"I promised you…"

"You promised something that would have me lying here like a dummy. I believe you could do it, but is that what we both want?" Then she gave a surprising little laugh. "Count on me to ruin the mood."

Well, he was certainly losing it, he realized. It was trickling away rapidly.

She gave his shoulder a small shove. Immediately he straightened to stand beside the bed. Then, without a word, she stood up. Wincing a little, she removed her undies and slippers.

Helplessly, he drank her in with his eyes. Exquisite in every line, a body that had been built by keeping in shape, at least until recently. Long legs, perfectly shaped, a narrow waist and delightful breasts that seemed to go with the rest of her package, as if she had been honed in every respect. The thatch of dark curls at the apex of her legs drew him like honey.

"Like I said, I look like I've been through a meat grinder."

He shook his head. "I've seen what meat grinders do. You don't come close."

The passion that had leached away began to fill him again as he scented hers. Muskiness emanated from her, speaking her excitement as clear as anything could. She hadn't lost the mood. She had just taken charge.

He might have laughed except the pounding had begun within him again.

"Now you," she said, sitting gingerly on the edge of the bed.

He obliged readily enough. Over the years he'd got used to the bullet scars on his arms and thighs, and time had faded them somewhat. He knew what she'd see, although he didn't think about it often. A reasonably fit man in his midthirties who right now had a raging erection.

She watched with a faint smile, as if he were unwrapping a package, but impatience made him less than graceful. His shirt went without a problem, but when he shoved down his jeans and underwear, everything got tangled up.

He cussed and she laughed as he plopped beside her to work off his boots. This wasn't going the way he had anticipated at all.

But none of that mattered when she jolted him by laying a hand on his scarred thigh, right over one of the bullet scars.

"It was bad," she said.

Her touch nearly sucked the last of the air from him but he managed to shuck the rest of his clothes. When he looked at her, everything else in the world went away.

Her sherry-brown eyes seemed to penetrate to his innermost being, and the fire he saw there echoed the fire in his own body. Hot, hammering need resurged and ran along his nerve endings until he was little more than a heat-seaking missile headed straight for her center.

"Erin," he whispered.

"I know," she answered just as quietly. Her hand slid up his thigh and captured his erection. He sucked air between his teeth. She stroked him lightly and squeezed until he groaned. Then she reached for the condom, opened the package and rolled it on him, the sexiest thing any woman had ever done for him.

"Take me," she whispered. "Please, just take me."

He was only too eager to oblige her, but even in the midst of the inferno, he managed to remember her delicate state.

Gently he pushed her back, then slid to the floor to kneel between her parted thighs.

"Lance…"

"Shh…" He wasn't going to put his weight on her. He

feared the burden of it might cause her pain and shatter this incredible experience. "Close your eyes...."

Reaching out, he traced her contours lightly, as if his hands were feathers. Brushing, never grabbing. Over and over he traced her face, neck, breasts and belly, his hardness cradled in the moist heat between her legs.

Her soft sighs began to turn into moans of delight. Leaning forward, propping himself on his elbows, he followed the path his hands had taken with his tongue, licking lightly at her nipples until they grew large and hard for him. Only then did he suck gently. When he felt her hands grab his head, trying to draw him closer, he knew sheer male triumph.

She wanted more. Harder. Faster. But he didn't dare give it to her, so he continued teasing as her moans grew louder.

Then, slowly, he trailed his mouth downward, feeling her abdominal muscles quiver beneath each touch of his tongue. She cried his name finally, and her hips heaved, reaching for him.

But not yet. Straightening, he looked down at the patch between her thighs and with the gentlest of touches, parted her petals, exposing her. She groaned as his fingers ran along her, finding moist satin, finding at last the hardening nub of nerves. When he touched that knot, a keening sound passed her lips and her hands gripped the bed almost desperately.

Ice queen? No way.

Taking pleasure in the torment he gave her, he continued a little longer, then when he feared she might rear up and hurt herself, he bowed his head and tasted her.

A deep groan escaped her at the touch. Her taste was sweet, good, her response pushing him to the edge of his own endurance.

"Lance, now…please…"

Straightening a little more, he guided himself into her, filling her slowly, feeling passion tighten his body as if he were a winding spring. Her hands let go of the bed, reaching for him, but he ignored the gesture. He knew what she needed, and feared what he might do if he went too far.

So using one hand for balance, he began to rock in and out of her while using his other hand to caress that knot of nerves, determined to launch her into space.

The last conscious thought began to escape him as need pushed him into rhythms older than time. In and out, feeling her tighten around him, amazed when somehow her legs found their way around his hips, as if to lock him to her.

He forgot everything else. He heard her cry out, felt her buck with completion, felt the shudders rip through her. He exploded into her, the inside of his head turning as white as a blazing sun.

Chapter 12

When she climbed out of the shower, Erin wanted nothing more than a luxurious day spent enjoying the wonders that Lance had shown her. She hurt all over, but the pain was not all bad. Some of it was a beautiful reminder of the loving they had shared.

But as she was toweling off, she felt a chill trickle down her spine. The bathroom was still warm and steamy; the rest of her didn't feel cold. It was as if an icy stream ran down her back.

She froze, closing her eyes, gripping the towel rack. It was coming. With some instinct that went beyond her five senses, she knew the hour approached. The bomber. He was near.

She tried to shake it off as she dressed, but ignoring the discomfort of still-fresh scars she donned clothing more suited to operations: heavy black pants with multiple pockets, her black T-shirt, her shoulder holster. And where the hell was her vest?

In her car's trunk still. Or maybe Lance had moved it. She grabbed the towel, rubbing her hair impatiently to get the last of the moisture from it, then finger-combed it into some semblance of order.

As she left the bedroom, she heard Lance in the kitchen. The morning's light was beginning to arrive. After a night with almost no sleep, it seemed too bright even though the day was far from fully born.

She rounded the corner and saw him at the stove. He'd pulled on jeans and an unbuttoned blue shirt.

"Where's my vest?" she asked.

He pivoted sharply. "Did something happen?"

"No. I just…" How could she even say such a thing out loud? It sounded crazy.

He pulled the pan off the burner and turned off the gas flame. "Okay."

She hesitated. "Okay, what?"

"Your instincts are goading you. I'd hoped we'd get a few minutes this morning just to indulge ourselves, but I guess it'll have to wait."

She felt her heart and stomach plummet. "Lance, it isn't… It was wonderful. I wanted that, too, but…"

He crossed the space and took her gently by the shoulders. "Good morning, Erin." He brushed a kiss on her lips and she felt her insides start to melt all over again. "It was the most beautiful night of my life. Clear?"

She nodded.

"But far be it from me to ignore another cop's instincts. Grab some coffee. I'll get your vest. Then we can try to eat breakfast."

He returned in just a couple of minutes with both of their vests and hung them over the chair backs. Grateful, she eased into one of the chairs with her coffee.

"Let's see if I can salvage this bacon. Want some?"

"Yes, please."

He turned the flame on again and soon the bacon was sizzling, filling the room with enticing aromas. He surprised her by grabbing for his radio then. "Hey, Nate," he said. "We've got some intuition going on here. Put everyone on high alert."

Nate's voice crackled back. "Will do. Are you calling Gage or should I?"

"I will."

He placed the radio on the table. She could hear Nate's voice as he talked with the team. Then he reached for the phone, cradling it between ear and shoulder as he flipped the bacon onto a paper towel and started a few more slices.

"Hey, Gage," he said. "Heard anything from the folks back in Chicago?…Okay…No, Erin's got a feeling… Right…Okay, thanks."

When he hung up, he eyed Erin. "What triggered it?"

"I don't know. It was like…a weird feeling. Icy. Stupid."

"Don't ever say that. Something triggered that feeling. Something's working on you. Just because you can't pinpoint it doesn't mean it isn't valid."

He checked the bacon, then leaned back against the counter, folding his arms. "Street smarts," he said.

She lifted an eyebrow. "I don't work the streets very often."

"Doesn't mean you don't have them. You know your team. You know one of them is probably involved in this. Some little ticker inside you is going, and it's registering that something isn't right, and that it's been wrong for long enough now that the guy might almost be here. Hell, he might be here already."

He unfolded his arms and turned the bacon. "Eggs?"

"This morning, yes. Just one."

"Done." Then he got her the peanut butter and put a couple of slices of toast on the table for her. "I told you we got good guys out there. We do. But we couldn't ring this place with enough men to be sure nobody would penetrate the perimeter. Nate'll probably put the chopper up, but it can't see through trees. So look out there and you see the woods only a thousand yards away. That's our safety zone. It's not huge."

She nodded. Her stomach knotted so tightly that she wondered if she could eat at all. "It's nothing specific," she tried again. Getting weird feelings wasn't common for her. Instinct? Intuition? Or something goading her because it didn't feel right? Impossible to tell.

She pulled out her cell phone and looked at it. No messages. Not even Fran. Fran, who had visited her daily in the hospital. Fran, who had called every single day since she'd left on her road trip.

The letter tiles still sat at the edge of the table against the wall. Reaching for them, she spelled out Fran's and Tom's names again. Then she shoved Tom's to one side.

"Fran?" Lance said as he brought plates of food to the table. "Why Fran?"

"Something's not right," she said slowly. So Fran hadn't called. Why would she? She was probably busy with trying to track this creep and… She looked up, her head almost jerking. "She asked if I was still here."

Moving slowly, as if his mind were on something else, Lance sat facing her. Slowly he nodded. "But Tom *knows* you are."

"True." But she stared at the tiles anyway, ignoring her breakfast. "Fran," she said, almost tasting the name. "Why?"

"I don't know." Nor did she. Her best friend? Or was she?

"You said she's been your friend and mentor since your first assignment." Unlike her, his appetite didn't appear to be disturbed. He heaped his plate with scrambled eggs and bacon, and reached for a couple of pieces of buttered toast.

"She has been."

"But?"

"That's just it. I don't know."

"Okay." He let it drop, but she didn't think he was going to leave it there. "Eat. If we get involved in any action, we'll need our energy."

Obediently, she began to move food to her own plate. A small helping of eggs. One strip of bacon. A slice of toast. She skipped the peanut butter.

"When this is over," he remarked, "I want to schedule some time for just the two of us. How about you?"

That sounded so good to her that she briefly forgot the sense of approaching menace that was disturbing her. "Let's just see how this goes." She was still afraid to commit, and hated herself for it. But last night hadn't settled anything, it had only made her want more. More time with this man, time to find out what it was like when no shadow hovered over them. For just a little while, they'd moved apart from the world, stolen time together, and it had been more than memorable. It had left her shaken with awareness that she was not the person she had always thought. She was capable of giving herself fully to another person, despite what Paul had believed. She had shared things about herself with Lance that she had never shared with anyone. And last night, she had felt safe enough to ultimately relinquish control. She wanted more of that. She wanted more of this man who had proved he didn't mind it when she *did* take control.

He was a pretty special guy, and she wished she could

just savor that discovery, their mutual discovery. Instead she was sitting here worrying about a killer who might not be anywhere near.

Except she believed he was. She couldn't say why, but the certainty had crept into her bones. The murderous thug was near, and getting nearer. The perimeter around them was necessarily porous. Lance was right. They could put a thousand men out there and this guy could still slip by them.

She was going to wind up facing her demon again.

The bomber sat looking at a road sign in the early morning light. Mornings were not his favorite time of day, but this was when the voice had said it would call.

Welcome. Conard County, Wyoming. Population 9,432.

He couldn't imagine a county with so few people, despite the miles he'd put in since leaving Chicago. The empty spaces out here gave him the willies. How could people stand it? Even the mountains didn't alleviate the sense of barrenness, emptiness. The ends of the earth.

He spread out the map again, studying it as if it might answer why any human being on earth would choose to live here. He'd already discovered most of the side roads weren't very good, a lot of gravel and dirt, some pavement, but most of them looked as if they didn't get used a whole lot. The state highway was okay, but nothing like the wide roads he was used to in Chicago. Trucks blew by him in both directions from time to time, but only occasional cars. This was probably a place most people passed through, not a destination.

The biggest mark on the map was Conard City. A few other little towns were scattered around the county, but when he flipped over the map he was appalled to read the numbers. Haleyville, population 276? Ben's Inn, population 9? Nine? Really? That sounded like a family, two trailers and something they called an inn. Did anyone even stop there?

Damn, he'd fallen down the rabbit hole. These folks probably thought three buildings and a courthouse made a town.

And there was a courthouse in Conard City. The map mentioned it. He wondered what else he'd find there, if he had to go that far. For some reason, the movie *Deliverance* sprang to his mind, and Conard City became a place filled with toothpick-chewing, slack-jawed, glassy-eyed, Western-dressed zombies. He wanted to crumple the map. The voice was crazy. No big-deal FBI agent would be out here in these sticks. No, she'd moved on, he was sure.

The phone rang, and for once he was eager to reach for it. Surprised he was even getting a call out here. In more than one place his phone had registered no signal at all.

But it was ringing now, and he hoped it was with the news that the voice had been wrong, his target wasn't out here in the middle of nowhere after all, and that he should come back to the comforts of city life, pavement, bars, buildings…all the things that made him feel safe.

Snatching the phone from the seat, he answered it. The voice was less clear than usual, crackling with the lousy signal. "You're there?"

"At the county line."

"They're waiting for you."

Waiting for him? He froze and felt his skin begin to crawl. "I'm leaving."

"No! They don't know who you are. They just know you're coming. They're ready, but not ready enough for you."

Despite everything, despite hating that voice, he felt his chest swell a little with pride. How many cops and agents had he successfully evaded for months? The voice finally acknowledged his brilliance. It was about damn time.

"You can slip past…" The voice faded in static.

"What?" he said. "You're breaking up."

"Get closer to town. Drive through it. Stop about 15… out."

"Which town?"

"The biggest one. I'll call…six hours."

Then the voice was gone, and he was left listening to a crackling line and the ceaseless wind that pummeled him through his open side window.

He could run now, he was sure. If the voice couldn't call him, it couldn't track him. Except he wasn't sure he was far enough away from it. For all he knew it had been following him since Chicago.

He looked quickly into the rearview mirror, but saw nothing. No one. Miles and miles of empty space. No, the voice wasn't out there. At least not close.

But the voice knew who he was. Once again the iron tendrils closed around him. He should never have been scared enough to try to kill that agent. He should have run right then.

But now it was too late. The agent could identify him. The voice knew his name.

The web was slowly strangling him.

"We should take you out of here," Lance said. "Move you." They'd shifted to the living room. Breakfast dishes remained behind, forgotten for now.

"What good will that do?" Erin asked. "He may know I'm in the vicinity, but he won't know where unless some-one tells him. Are we getting ready to spread the word?"

He hesitated. He'd been pacing restlessly because he couldn't escape the feeling that her gut instinct was right. The guy had been pointed in her direction like a missile. Someone had to know where she was. No one in the Bureau knew exactly where, but Tom, at a minimum, knew she was being guarded by the sheriff here.

How long would it take this creep to figure out where? And while he had the greatest respect for the men keeping an eye on him, he was quite sure there wasn't a defensive line in existence that wasn't as porous as a sieve in places.

His insides were churning in an unfamiliar way. Never had he been this scared for someone before, not to this degree, not even during that hostage situation. Of course, this time he was personally involved. Reaching for his cool, level head had grown increasingly difficult.

"We need some kind of plan," he insisted. "You may be the cheese in the trap for this guy, but we have to find a way to keep him from blowing us up before we can do anything about it. Seriously, this is a far cry from a gunfight."

"No kidding," she said quietly. "Stealthy, surreptitious. If he slips past those guys, we won't even know it."

"Exactly."

"There's another thing."

"What's that?"

She sighed, rocking gently in the chair. "He needs to do more than be found with a bomb. The bomb will cause him trouble, no question. But to tie it to attempted murder would send him away for a long time. What I found links the bombs. It doesn't link this one guy to them."

He froze. "And if this bomb doesn't have whatever you found…"

"Then all we have is a guy carrying a bomb that he

might intend to use for a whole lot of things besides murder."

Lance swore quietly and resumed his pacing. "I've been too distracted."

"By what?"

"By you," he said bluntly. When he glanced at her, he knew a spurt of pleasure that her cheeks colored. "Been sitting here on my duff, sure those guys would catch him, all without thinking about the bigger picture."

"I haven't exactly been at my best either," she said quietly. "You're a bit of a distraction yourself. But no, I was sitting here thinking, too. He's got to get that bomb here. To this house. Then we've got him."

"Then what? What if it goes off too quickly? I don't know about you, but I don't want to wind up as photo evidence in a double homicide trial."

He watched her grimace, and it was clearly not from pain. "Pretty picture," she remarked.

"Well?" It was the truth.

"You're right." She rocked a little more quickly, then slowed down again. Reaching up, she rubbed her neck as if tension was building in her. "Okay. We've got to get the bomb to the house. Get him. In that order."

"You skipped a step. Get us out of here before the bomb explodes. What's his usual delay time?"

"Sadly, we don't know. It couldn't have been a very long delay after he shot me or I'd be dead. But we don't know if that's his usual procedure. His other victims were found at home, hours after they'd last been seen. Sometimes he used a timer, sometimes a remote trigger."

He turned that around in his mind. "It's conceivable, then, that at least some of his bombs were placed days before he detonated them."

"Yes."

"Great." His frustration reached a new level.

"Lance," Erin said.

"What?" He looked at her, surprised by the almost-humor of her tone.

"If the guy weren't so devious we'd already have him."

He caught himself, sighed and tried to settle. Or at least make an effort to. "Sorry."

"No, I get it. We're both sick of waiting. We want action. I asked for some time to get stronger, and I got it. Now I'm ready to deal. You're probably more than ready. I couldn't have asked for a better person to share house arrest with, but I've had it. I want this guy, and I want this whole damn thing over."

He finally sat on the couch facing her. He hoped she didn't want to shed him, too, but brushed the selfish thought away. More important things faced them right now. "Okay, we still need a plan."

She nodded. "Would your guys consider letting him through? Watching him?"

"I'm sure they would if it sounds like a feasible plan. Presuming they catch sight of him, if they warn us, I can get you out of here quickly."

"Then he might do nothing."

Lance felt an extraordinary urge to growl. "Don't tell me you're planning to stay here while he blows up the house?"

"I was hoping he wouldn't blow up your house at all. The question is, can your team get to him while he's placing the bomb?"

"Probably. I think we need a conference on this. It's no good, us making plans if we leave important people out of it."

"I know." She ran her fingers through her hair, tousling it and apparently not caring. "Okay, let's talk to all the guys, if that can be arranged. We need a meeting of minds."

They agreed to sleep in shifts until some of the others arrived in the late afternoon. They were told only Seth and Nate would come, while the others would remain on patrol.

Watching Erin doze on the couch, Lance for the first time in his life truly hated being a cop. A civilian wouldn't have recognized that intent needed to be proved against the bomber in order to get the maximum conviction. As she had said, he could be carrying a bomb for a lot of reasons. He'd get into trouble for it, but not the kind of trouble he'd get for attempted murder. And if it didn't have the thing in it that had caused Erin to link his bombs, then they'd have trouble making a case for the other murders unless for some reason the guy decided to spew his guts.

The cop in him got all of that. The man in him just wanted to pack that woman up and get her away from here. What had he been thinking at the outset? That this would just be for a few days? That the Bureau would swoop in and remove her, given some time? Oh, he'd talked bravely about it, but some obstinate part of his brain had believed this would all be resolved before they got to this point.

Well, it hadn't been. And crawling through his mind was an inky, icy awareness that the bomber had had enough time to get here, that he'd been told by whomever was working with him that he was to head west to get Erin.

Real, but not real. Some eternal optimism of the human mind and soul, believing it would never come to pass.

Well, they were out of time. He agreed with Erin about

that. He didn't know what had triggered her, but he always listened to a cop's gut instinct. Those instincts were honed by an experience that could never be expressed, never written in a manual. Erin was an investigator and something had clanged her alarm bells. No way would he dismiss that.

So the guy was out there, probably close, and Erin was his target. She might have wanted a showdown at high noon, but while her attitude had initially impressed him, she was no longer a stranger. And last night she had become something far more.

He smothered a sigh and looked out the window at the passing day. Shadows had begun to lengthen with the deepening afternoon. Once those mountains swallowed the sun, that would be gone. Bright enough to see, but without the depth that could reveal so much. As a cop, he hated the way flat light sucked perspective away.

He knew something dangerous lived inside him. It had jostled at him uncomfortably after he was shot until he had wisely headed back here to a place where he didn't feel there was a threat in every shadow. But that feeling was coming back, driven by his concern for Erin.

After what she'd been through, she'd probably need to make some changes, too. Life could never feel quite the same after someone tried to kill you. But first they needed to take care of this issue.

Rising, he wandered back to the kitchen and looked at the breakfast clutter and the name Fran formed by the letter tiles. Why had she done that? She had a long friendship with the woman. Was the simple question about where she was staying enough to override all of that? Or was Erin simply responding to the changes within herself?

Or was she responding to something she had sensed

for a long time about her best friend, that the woman wasn't a completely straight arrow?

But what could Fran possibly have against her to cause this? It didn't make sense. Most of the time, people had a good reason for murder. Or at least what they believed to be a good reason. Had Fran wanted Tom's interest and become angry when Tom wanted to date Erin instead?

It didn't strike him as a reason for killing someone, but then he'd never wanted to kill anyone.

Why would Fran want Erin dead anyway? Erin clearly wasn't interested in Tom and had said so. No, if it was Fran—and he wasn't at all convinced of that—there had to be another reason.

He heard movement and turned to see Erin in the doorway, rubbing her eyes. "Your turn," she said.

"I'm not sleepy."

One corner of her mouth lifted. "You're going to regret that later."

"Maybe." But he was too wired. Too deep into problem-solving mode to be able to let go. He knew how much he hated to have things dangling in the wind, unfixable by any means of his own. It made him something of a bulldog even when the response wasn't useful.

He reached for dirty dishes and carried some of them to the sink. "I'll make coffee. Seth and Nate should be here in a little while."

She started to help him clear the table, but he waved her to a seat. "Save what you've got, Agent. We might be needing it soon."

She gave a little nod and slid into one of the chairs. The vests still hung over the backs of them, ready for duty. Her pistol, which she'd put on the end table while she napped, once again sat securely in her holster.

Once he'd put all the dishes to soak in the sink, he

pulled out some cheese, crackers and peanut butter. Breakfast had been hours ago and neither of them had eaten much. "Want some toast?" he asked.

"Crackers are fine."

He noted the way she had fixated on the tiles in front of her.

"Tell me about Fran," he said as he joined her.

She raised her gaze. "In what way?"

"Well, you seem to keep landing on her. Does something about her disturb you? Do you think she's interested in Tom and bothered that he's interested in you?"

She shook her head a little and lifted a wheat cracker, holding it but doing nothing with it. "Not Tom."

"So sure?"

"It's not like he's been coming on hot and heavy. Meeting for lunch is hardly that. What's more, I turned him down and told Fran I just wasn't interested. You heard me. What do I need that for?"

Her reaction disturbed him at a purely male level. How the hell could he have forgotten her saying to Fran that she had enough problems without adding a man to the mix?

"Okay," he said slowly, putting his inner caveman back in place. "So it's not jealousy."

"Not that kind."

Her choice of words struck him. He waited a moment but when she said nothing more he asked, "What kind of jealousy, then?"

"Nothing really." She shrugged and nibbled at the cracker.

"Erin." His tone pressed her.

"Like I said, nothing. There was some watercooler gossip that I might get a promotion because of the link I found between the bombs, but that's all it was. Gossip.

She's been an agent longer than I have. Based on seniority alone I'm not likely to get promoted before her."

Logical, he thought, but not necessarily true.

"Not everyone gets a promotion anyway," she continued. He was glad when she reached for some cheese and popped it into her mouth. He rose and went to get them some coffee. "Pay increases with time, yes, but there aren't a whole lot of promotions to go around. We aren't the biggest organization by any means. Almost half of us aren't even special agents."

"So what's the distinction?" He thought he knew, but he wanted her to keep talking because something might pop out.

"Oh, we have all kinds of people involved in labs, cybercrime investigations, a lot of things. They're agents, too. But a special agent has a gun and arrest authority. We don't make up the entire FBI."

He rejoined her with the coffee. "You said you're mostly a paper pusher. How did you wind up a special agent, then?"

"I was selected at Quantico, and my first assignment involved a crime task force." She looked down. "We were all special agents of necessity. And some are always needed in the field. So…me."

"So you *have* done some street work."

She blew air. Shook her head a little. Finally said, "Yeah. It's been a while, but yeah. After this I might move to cybercrimes or something equally unadventurous."

He almost laughed. He didn't quite see it, but he could understand it. "So why did you act like you never were in the dangerous part?"

"Because Paul hated it. Because for the past four years I *have* been mostly an investigator and paper pusher. I like the brain work. I don't like the other part that much.

I can do it. I *will* do it when it's needed. Take when they went to the bomber's lab—if I'd still been on duty, I'd have been one of the people busting into the place, weapon drawn. Wouldn't have hesitated. But finding him is a bigger challenge. I like the game."

He nodded, wondering if she had any idea how much she had revealed when she said *Paul hated it*. How much of her feeling about it came from that? Certainly enough to make her try to conceal it. Sad. "Are you still hearing Paul in your head?"

"Too often, probably." Her smile lacked humor. "Nothing like love to leave you open to a real smackdown."

Another sad commentary. He wished he could deny it, but he'd received a bit of a smackdown when May left him. Everyone needed a reason for bailing on a long relationship, but there were excuses that didn't have to leave huge scars. "Too bad we can't learn to break up without wounding someone."

She gave a short laugh. "Ruptures always hurt. Try to make one without a reason."

It was true, he thought. The statement *I'm leaving you* always raised the inevitable questions: *Why? What did I do?* And with that, the gladiators entered the arena.

"You ever hear that old cop joke?" he asked. "The one about the wife leaving?"

"Loads. Which one in particular?"

"Cop comes home and finds a note on the refrigerator. It says, *I'm leaving you for anyone else*."

Her eyes widened, then a laugh escaped her. "Good one. And probably true much of the time."

"I don't doubt it. Okay, so you did some time on the streets, basically, as part of a crime task force. That had to be dangerous."

"More dangerous for our informants and undercover

operatives. But yes, it was dangerous sooner or later for all of us."

"Which left you packing that lovely Glock 23. And your ex left you not very proud of that fact."

Her gaze dropped. "We weren't very well suited. The odd thing is that I didn't realize that at the beginning, before we got married."

He reached across the table and took her hand. "I don't think that's odd at all. We fall in love. What else is there?"

"And then reality hits."

"Not always." He squeezed her hand, then let go, wishing that he could instead just sweep her away to bed. But the clock was marching forward, they didn't know when the threat would arrive, or from where, and Nate and Seth would probably be here soon.

Even as he thought about it, he heard the sound of an approaching vehicle. He rose at once and went to the front window. "Nate," he announced. "I'd recognize that truck anywhere."

She had followed him. "It looks like it's been through a war."

"I don't know how he keeps it together, but he bought it from the department ages ago when we moved to newer vehicles. His wife, Marge, on the other hand, drives a sporty little red thing. She says it's making up for all the years she drove a full-size van to cart six daughters around."

Erin made a sound of amusement. "Go, Marge. But Nate has his favorite old nag."

"You got it. For all I know it's the same SUV he drove for a while when he was sheriff."

She laughed softly. "Thank you for introducing me to your county. You make me feel like I'm part of things."

You can be. He caught the words before they popped

out. He wasn't ready to be making suggestions like that, and anyway, looming over them was the inescapable fact that she had to return eventually to her job in Chicago. Unlike her ex, he had no desire to change her. She was remarkable just the way she was.

Unfortunately, that meant he was eventually going to lose big-time.

Chapter 13

Nate parked in front and climbed out, stretching comfortably while turning slowly as if taking in his surroundings. Only then did he climb the porch. Lance let him in before he knocked.

He greeted Erin with a warm smile. "You're looking a whole lot better than the first time I saw you."

It was true, Lance thought. Her eyes no longer looked hollow, and the circles beneath them were gone.

"I'm much better," Erin said. "But it's time to get going."

Nate nodded. "Instinct kicking in. I hear you. Seth will be here soon. In the meantime, point me toward the coffee. The one thing I haven't missed since I retired is Velma's coffee. Used to have to drink the stuff so as not to offend that woman. She's a fire-breathing dragon."

Erin laughed, even though she'd met the dispatcher only once. "Perfect description."

"Just don't quote me," Nate replied with a wink.

"Actually," Lance said, "she'd probably love it. She has a death grip on that desk."

"Reckon Velma thinks retirement is for other folks." Nate shook his head as they moved into the kitchen for the coffee. "I've depended on that woman for a lot of years. The whole department has. Nobody will replace her."

When Seth arrived a short while later, the four of them gathered in the living room. Seth had once again arrived on horseback, and Erin thought the front of the house looked like a casual late afternoon gathering of ranchers, not official at all. A battered SUV and a horse seemed like good cover.

But her rest had simply given her the energy to grow uneasier. She wondered how she could possibly explain to these men the feelings that plagued her, the sense that the threat was imminent. She had nothing to base it on. In fact, under other circumstances she would have been inclined to dismiss that chill that had run through her after her shower. So many things could have caused it, and her health was still questionable.

Greetings had been exchanged, a few words of casual conversation, but then the room fell silent. Erin wondered if she was expected to speak, but she honestly didn't know where to begin. It wasn't as if she had some kind of information to impart. In fact, with the ticking of each passing minute she had begun to wonder why Lance had even listened to her. A feeling? As an agent, she knew how unhelpful many feelings were. Logic. Facts. Some kind of cause-and-effect relationship. Some kind of theory that hung on something substantial. She had none of that.

It was Lance who spoke. "All right. I gave Nate the gist. Erin's got a gut feeling that this guy is close."

Erin felt compelled to speak. "I have nothing to base it on."

Lance looked at her. "How many months have you spent pursuing this guy?"

"Eight," she admitted.

"Then whether you know it or not, you've got some kind of sense of him. An accumulation of data, however sparse, that you're operating on. Then we have the problem of your whereabouts being revealed and your ASAC thinking you need protection. That means he doesn't think the leak that got you nearly killed was a simple slipup. What's more, he called to say the killer has been ordered to come west because of you. So the bottom line is not just some feeling. The bottom line is you know this guy to some extent, and you may well know the person who set him on you, and that's working on you. You might not be able to express it in so many words, but that's all I need to add up to an instinct that shouldn't be ignored."

The two other men nodded. Nate was the first to respond. "Years ago when I was in Nam with the Green Berets, one of the first things I came to understand was how little things, cues I didn't recognize consciously, could tell me when trouble was coming. I'm sure Seth here will back me up."

"I certainly will," Seth answered. "So let's just put that part on hold. You think he's got to be near by now. We work with that."

"But the other thing," Erin began, looking at Lance and Nate, "is that we have to catch him in the act. You know that."

The silence that answered her wasn't unexpected. Of course they knew.

"Thing is," Lance admitted slowly, "I've been so busy thinking about protecting Erin, that I haven't thought about what else we have to do. We need to put this guy away for good. Stopping him on the way here, even with a bomb, isn't necessarily going to make him pay for what he's done to her and to his other victims. We need to be able to link him at least to trying to kill Erin. Whatever it was that connected his other bombs might be missing from this one."

Nate waved a hand. "I'm outta the loop on something. What do you mean about connecting the bombs?"

Erin answered. "For a while we weren't sure they were all made by the same bomber. He varies his designs every time, almost as if it's some kind of game or challenge for him. So we wondered if we were looking at copycats. It wouldn't be the first time." Statement of the obvious, she thought. No, she definitely still wasn't up to speed. "Anyway, I was the one who found the link. And considering it had nothing to do with the bomb, that it was contamination, if he builds his next bomb somewhere else we'll lose that link. So we've got to get him for at least one attempted murder—mine."

Once again silence filled the room. Seth eventually spoke. "Well, that makes this even peachier. You all are law enforcement, so I'll take your word for it. We've been focused on keeping the guy away, not letting him get to the house or Erin. This is a very different deal."

"I think we all let that one slip," Nate said. "I assumed they had enough to get the guy once we had him."

"We don't," Erin said flatly. "They found a few fingerprints at the bomb lab, but they aren't necessarily his, and they certainly aren't enough to prove that he's the bomber. Anyone could have left them there."

Lance nodded. "If we want to be able to build a legal case here, we've got to catch him in the act of trying to hurt someone."

"I guess," Nate said, his voice gravelly, "I get why they don't have agents already in place here." He eyed Erin. "I knew they thought you might be at risk. I knew they didn't want word getting out that you were here, but I didn't know they were hoping to draw the guy out."

"That wasn't explicitly stated," Erin admitted. "I'm almost certain that at the outset Tom's only thought was protecting me." But she had known. She had said as much. Thanks to her diminished health, she hadn't been operating at top form either. Sure, just pull the guy out here, maybe, and then what? It was the rest of it that was finally coming home to her.

"We had a conference call with Erin's ASAC," Lance said. "They tapped a call in which someone loosely pointed the bomber in this direction. He's coming. But no one said anything about the rest of it. Apparently we were just supposed to understand."

"No." Erin shook her head. "I honestly think Tom is just concerned that I be safe. But I'm looking at the bigger picture, and by now he probably is, too. Except that he's hampered by not knowing who he can trust. I think he was expecting me to understand all this once he knew the bomber had been directed to me. We can get the UNSUB for possession of an explosive device. That's not exactly minor but it's only a ten-year sentence under federal law. We'd like to get him for attempting to kill me. And if possible for killing those other women. So…he's got to get close. He's got to set the bomb. And somehow we've got to keep him from blowing up Lance's house."

She paused. "And it would be really helpful if we could find out who's been pulling his strings."

"Strings?" Nate sat forward. "Someone clue me in here."

"You explain it," Erin said to Lance. Her mind was already skipping ahead of what Tom had told them on that conference call and trying to figure out how they could accomplish the entire mission, not just a small part of it.

"That is downright butt-ugly," Nate said when Lance had explained it all, from the tapped calls, to the bomber being gone, to the fact that the bad guy clearly wasn't working alone.

From beneath gray, bushy brows, he regarded Erin. "Maybe they should have just staked you out like a Judas goat."

She shook her head quickly. "All of this was designed to protect me, and you've been doing a great job of it. If that's where you want to leave it, then we won't change anything."

Nate frowned.

"And what would you do then?" Lance asked. "You'd put yourself out there, wouldn't you? Like I haven't already figured that out. No, we catch the guy in the act and nail him to the wall."

"What about his bombs?" Seth asked. "How big are they?"

"They've generally been pretty small in terms of yield. Like antipersonnel devices. The one he used on my house was bigger. I understand it was set right outside my bedroom. It should have taken me out, and the subsequent fire would have pretty much erased the evidence. Well, my house burned to the ground, so he succeeded in most of that."

A tremor ran through her again. No matter how hard

she tried to stay detached and professional, every so often awareness struck her anew: someone had tried to kill her and he was still hunting her.

"So," said Seth slowly, "we have to presume a bigger bomb. Once he learns you're here, he'll probably try the same approach he used at your house. Hell, he's probably driving the Wyoming roads right now with a number of bombs."

"We could warn law enforcement in the state to watch for Illinois plates," Nate remarked.

"How many cars would we have to pull over?" Lance asked. "It's summer. Everyone's driving across this state to somewhere else. And who's to say he hasn't changed vehicles? He's certainly changed phones."

Nate chuckled. "You're right. Even so, it wouldn't get the guy to the doorstep here. I'm just dreaming. Largely because my son over there is lost in thought."

"Calculating," Seth answered. "So this guy really knows his stuff?"

"Yes," Erin answered. "We get the feeling he has some experience with explosives from before. Demolition? Fireworks? But definitely he knows his stuff. He's not just using off-the-shelf explosives either. We had one that appeared to be liquid based."

Seth cussed quietly. "That's dangerous as hell."

"Once the liquids are mixed," she agreed. "He still needs detonators, though, assuming he wants to be away from the explosion. He's also used a variety of detonation methods."

"Getting his jollies for sure," Seth remarked, falling into thought once again.

"All of which," Lance remarked, "makes it a lot more difficult to pin any or all of these crimes on him. Hence the need for catching him in the act. I don't like it, but

I get it. And we need to make a plan that will draw him in here."

"It could be some other place," Erin argued.

"Anyplace else would involve more people. No, the worst he can do here is my house and the two of us. I refuse to put anyone else at risk."

"I wasn't thinking of moving into town." She nearly snapped and regretted it instantly. He merely eyed her in response but he didn't look disturbed. Maybe he figured she was walking an emotional tightrope at the moment. And she was.

Then he addressed something she hadn't even thought of. "I'll need to get the dogs out of here in the morning. When we were just guarding Erin they were helpful. Now they might get in the way."

Other heads nodded. "Where will they go?" she asked. She'd grown fond of them, too.

"The vet has a kennel. I'll take them in the morning."

Face it, she thought, a stupid decision on her part, and she was ripping Lance's life apart, piece by piece. Part of her still wished she had just taken to the road the morning after she arrived here. But in fairness, at the time Tom had asked the sheriff to protect her, they'd had no idea how close he might be or even that he might actually come after her. As the sheriff had said, he'd already had twenty-four hours to track her since she let Fran and Tom know exactly where she was. If he had wanted to follow her, he could have hopped a plane and already been driving up to the outskirts of this town with everything he needed to make a bomb safely secured in his checked luggage.

No, the decision had been wise in light of what they had known then. Nor could she escape the fact that Tom had probably been hoping this outcome might happen, for her to draw the bomber out.

But if she'd guessed how much time she was going to have, she'd have driven to the nearest town with an airport and made tracks for the West Coast, hoping to disappear in the much larger cities there. That had been the whole point of leaving Chicago to begin with.

Instead she had got her back up. If she was the bait, let him come. Brave words that didn't feel so brave right now. Now they had no idea where this guy might be, and if she were to be utterly honest with herself, fear or no fear, she wanted him caught. Nailed. Imprisoned for life. This risk was honestly no greater than some others she'd taken in this job. Lance was correct. She might talk about being a paper pusher, but there had been times when she'd been right in the line of fire. She hadn't hesitated then.

"Okay." Seth stood. "Try this out. We let the guy reach you. We'll notify you on the radio as soon as we see him coming. The minute he starts to pull back, you two get the hell out of here. We'll take him down and disarm the bomb."

"Beautifully simple," Lance said. "Why do I think it won't be that easy?"

Seth smiled crookedly. "Because nothing ever is. But the point I'm making is you two clear the area immediately. A house can be rebuilt, two people can't. So you don't try to be brave, either of you. Don't try to take him, just clear out."

Lance nodded and looked at Erin. "What do you think?"

"I think if he sees us leave right after he's set the bomb, he won't explode it unless it's on a timer. That's a critical question. Is he going to be watching?"

Lance rubbed his chin.

"We can work that out," Seth said. "*We*'ll be watching. We won't let him leave the area while we take care of the bomb. Timer or not, he *has* to leave himself time to get away. That's long enough for us to both get him and disarm the thing."

"You're that sure?" Erin asked. "How many bombs have you disarmed?"

"A few," Seth said. "Part of my training over the years. I also have a couple of blast blankets that I picked up after the bomb scare at Jess McGregor's place. If it goes off, between body armor and those blankets, we can minimize the damage." He gave Lance a wry look. "Can't guarantee your paint won't get scorched."

"Like I care."

"And we still haven't answered another important question," Erin remarked. "How is he going to know exactly where I am?"

"Simple," said Lance. "Your ASAC is about to let the cat out of the bag for us."

Erin looked at each of them in turn, nodding slowly. "Just remember, this guy shot me. You'll have more to worry about than a bomb."

Ten minutes later, Erin called Tom's private number from Lance's phone. He promised to call back on a secure line in fifteen.

"He's leaving the office," Erin said. "He really *is* worried about a mole."

"Maybe this will help catch him," offered Nate.

"Or her," Lance said, remembering Fran's name on the table. Whether Erin wanted to acknowledge it or not, for some reason she kept lighting on the woman who was her best friend. For her sake, he hoped she was wrong. A break in that kind of trust, with her life on the line, would be hard to get over. Would she ever be able to trust again?

Nate was not one to let such a thing pass. He never had been. He'd been bullying and cajoling the people of this county as needed for over forty years. Not much had ever escaped him. "Her? You have a suspicion."

Lance glanced at Erin and saw her face shutter completely. "Maybe," he answered for her. "Just a maybe."

"Does your ASAC share your suspicion?"

Erin shook her head. "I don't know why he would. And it's not really a suspicion."

"No," Lance said. "Her name just keeps popping up. I think it's high time you mentioned it to Tom."

"I'm not sure about it!"

"No one is. And if it's not her, Tom will leave her alone. But damn it, Erin, don't you think he'd be grateful to at least have some idea who to be watching?"

"Better if he watches everyone."

"He will," Lance argued. "The man doesn't strike me as a fool. But sometimes if you're looking in the right direction the simplest thing can be the important one, one you might otherwise miss."

He watched her sit stonily, refusing to answer, but he knew her well enough now that he could tell she was thinking about it.

After a minute, he spoke again. "It's not like you're accusing her. Just say you're uneasy."

She nodded slowly, but he was unsure whether she was agreeing. Well, she might hate him forever for it, but he was going to make sure this got mentioned to Tom when he called back.

The situation was already bad enough, he thought. A bomber, and a woman he had increasingly come to care for—a woman who, if she survived this mess, was going to leave anyway. There sure wasn't much in these parts for an FBI agent to do. Even if she didn't want to go back to Chicago after this, the closest she could work would be Denver.

So he was facing loss one way or the other, but he'd vastly prefer losing her to her job.

The phone rang, dragging Lance out of his thoughts. He put it on speaker for the four of them and identified himself. Gage, it turned out, was already on the line.

"This is Tom Villiers," came the response. "We've seen the situation shift. What do you have on your end, Sheriff?"

"I'm going to let Deputy Conroe and Agent Sanders answer that. I gather from radio chatter there's been a meeting?"

"Yes," said Lance. "Because as Erin rightly pointed out, it won't be enough just to catch this guy with a bomb in his possession."

For a moment, Villiers was silent. "She's right. We're still working on all the forensics from the bomb lab. And, Erin, we found the source of that fiber. It's unfortunately common enough that it's circumstantial. It's great evidence, and not likely it would happen in more than one place, but I can already hear the defense arguing it. We have fingerprints that may or may not put our guy in the lab, but he did a pretty good cleanup. A couple of prints don't prove he built the bombs either, just that he was there probably within the last thirty days or so. Unless we can connect him in some way…well, Erin's right. We'd like to get him on five counts of murder and one count of attempted murder as well as felony possession of explosive devices, but some really hard evidence would be helpful. Right now everything is circumstantial and while we might accumulate enough for a conviction, you know we prefer a tighter case."

"We've been talking about that," Lance said. "So far we've agreed that we need to let him get to this house and set his bomb. Our team members feel that they can disarm it before he detonates it, and that they can keep him in the area while they do so. It would prove, at the very least, that he was attempting to kill Erin and me."

"It would," Villiers agreed, "especially if you all see him place the bomb. But now I've got two additional lives to worry about. Erin? How do you feel about this? You're barely recovering from your last encounter with this guy."

"I want him," she answered, her voice steely. "And I want him to spend more than ten years in prison after all he's done."

"Still can't recall his face?"

Lance didn't like her expression of near shame. For the love of heaven, the guy had shot her in the dark. Why would she remember much more than the muzzle blast? It was amazing that she remembered he was dressed in a cop's uniform.

"No," Erin answered.

Villiers spoke again. "Sheriff? Are you on board with this?"

"If my team says they can do it, they can do it. As I told Agent Sanders, these are men who have operated overseas at undisclosed locations, if you get my drift."

"I do." Once again Villiers fell silent. Distantly, through the phone, it sounded as if he were drumming his fingers. "He's probably already nearby," he said presently. "You know that. But in theory you kept Erin's location a secret."

"Yes," said Lance. No qualifications. "If anyone remembers seeing her the first day after she arrived, they'd assume she already left. And they wouldn't talk about it anyway. People pass through all the time, and most folks here don't talk to strangers."

"That's a fact," Nate said roughly. "Hell, sometimes they wouldn't even talk to me, and I was the sheriff. Strangers around here find it hard to get past *Howdy, how are ya*."

"Well, I've been silent on her whereabouts. Other than one phone call to the bomber which told him to head west, we've lost all track of him and his accomplice. Evidently they switched to different phones. So in theory he has no idea if she even stayed in your town."

"We need to change that," Erin said. "Put it out there, Tom. And put it out exactly."

"You could do that," Tom said. "Give Fran a call."

Lance watched Erin stiffen as if she'd just been tased. "Tom?" Her voice hushed. "Are you suspicious of her?"

"Right now I'm suspicious of everyone, which is why I drove to a coffee shop ten minutes away and am talking on a secure phone. Nobody has this number." Another pause then, "Erin? Are you?"

Lance waited impatiently, watching her compress her lips. If she didn't say it, he would.

Erin drew a deep breath. "Yes. I don't know why, but yes. And if I call her, you think she'll tell everyone?"

"Actually, if there's any reason to be suspicious of her, she won't tell anyone. Including me. Because I've been acting like I have no idea in hell where you went to after the first contact. That's why I asked Sheriff Dalton to step up and provide security for you. As far as anyone here knows, I believe you continued your trip. And that's significant, Erin. When you were first pinged as being in Wyoming, by an ID check, it didn't fan around this room like fire. It didn't even whisper. Nobody cared because you'd left, you should be safe. I knew, obviously, but the only other person who knew for sure was Fran. We didn't even enter it into the computers. Did you talk to anyone else?"

It lay there then in the middle of the room, the most corrosive acid in the world: distrust. Lance could imagine it creeping into Erin's heart. Not just a colleague, but a friend. Her best friend.

She was going to call Fran. He was sure of it now. It was the only way to get an answer. Expose Fran or exonerate her.

"Erin?" Villiers said, "Is this what you want to do? I know you don't often get a choice, but then we aren't often talking about your life in such an immediate way. We all know the risks that go with the job. This is bigger than the usual."

"It's what we have to do," she answered tautly. "We've got to stop this guy and put him away for good. That's not likely now that he's in the wind unless we draw him out. I know it as well as you, Tom."

"And to think you avoided the safe house." He sounded almost ironic. "Although, under the circumstances, you were right about it. For all we try to keep things under wraps, there's enough talk going around a task force that your whereabouts would have become known if you'd hunkered down here. Marshals, other agents…"

"I know."

"One thing… Whoever his accomplice is? This person told the bomber that you saw his face."

"But…" She cut herself off. "No wonder he's coming."

"Exactly. Keep that in mind before you let friendship trump sense here. This man has been told a lie so that he'll come kill you. If he'd been told you never saw his face, he wouldn't have the least interest in you."

Lance's stomach turned over and his chest tightened with rage. A fury so strong it felt as if all the air had been sucked out of the universe. He wanted to reach for Erin, to pull her into his arms as if they could hold the world at bay. He resisted the impulse, because she was a strong woman, a law officer who had the right to make her own decisions. Then, of course, they weren't alone.

He watched Erin absorb yet another blow, and wished he could take it for her.

Seth spoke, identifying himself and his background as a retired SEAL for Tom Villiers. "So we're planning to get Lance and Erin out of here as soon as the bomber has placed the bomb. He needs time to get away, and that'll give them time to get away. Once they're gone and he's retreating, we'll pick him up."

"I hope you're right," Villiers said. "I'm counting on you men to protect my agent. Erin, you're calling Fran?"

"Yes."

"Give me time to get back to the office. I want to see this go down. Sheriff, ping me as soon as the call is made."

"Will do," Gage said, speaking for the first time.

"And if you all are praying types," Tom added, "start praying now."

Chapter 14

Everyone had left, promising to be in touch later. In theory, since the bomber didn't know exactly where Erin was, they had maybe another day. In theory.

Erin still needed to call Fran, and it was amazing how reluctant she was to pull out her cell phone and do just that. She wasn't typically one to avoid things that were part of her job, although she'd apparently developed plenty of interpersonal avoidance problems over the years.

But Fran... Fran had been the first real friend she'd had, the woman she had been able to be open with about nearly everything. Fran knew the story of her childhood, had maybe even figured out how Erin had become so closed up, which was more than Paul had done.

Now this.

She had to face it. If it was Fran, they needed to know. The bomber clearly had an accomplice, someone who had found him yet failed to report his identity. That person needed to be brought to justice every bit as much as the bomber.

"It's my job, damn it."

She only realized she had spoken the words out loud when Lance replied. "Be fair to yourself. It's also your friend."

"That shouldn't matter."

"That's the theory."

She looked at him and realized his face had become dear to her. For the first time since she had started thinking about Fran as a suspect, she thought about the danger into which she had shoved Lance. Sure, he'd volunteered to protect her, but he hadn't volunteered to become a target, to potentially lose everything that mattered to him, even his life. Bold words had been spoken that day at the sheriff's, and she had done most of the bold speaking. *Showdown at high noon*? Easy words to speak when you didn't quite believe them.

But it was also too late to recall the words or the decisions she had made then. Too late. Now she just had to move forward with this.

The phone rang, startling them both. "Gage," Lance said, evidently recognizing the number on caller ID. He punched the speaker button.

"Tom called me again," Gage said shortly. "He has eyes on the suspect. He wants Erin to call now."

"Got it," Lance answered. He disconnected.

Erin could feel his gaze on her. Time to stiffen her spine and get on with it. She lifted her phone, feeling as if it weighed a ton, and drew a deep, steadying breath. Somehow she had to make this sound like a normal conversation. Then she hit the speed dial and put the phone to her ear.

Fran answered immediately. "My God, girl, I've been so worried about you. Why didn't you return my call?"

"I haven't been feeling well," Erin answered. "This is taking longer than I thought it would."

"Recovery always does," Fran said sympathetically. "Maybe you should come back here. We can all look after you."

Well, that sounded like her old friend. The fist gripping her heart eased a bit. "Actually," she said carefully, "I've met a really nice guy. I think I'm going to hang around and see what develops."

Fran let out a quiet whoop. "I thought you didn't want a man."

"That was before I met this one. I'm staying at his place."

"Oooh," Fran said, her tone conveying excitement and pleasure. "You move fast. So did you make it to the West Coast?"

"No. I'm still just outside Conard City."

"That's Wyoming, right? So dish. Tell me all about the guy. So you're staying with him? As in living with?"

Erin managed a little laugh. "He's a deputy. Lance Conroe. The guy who checked on me the very first day."

"A knight in shining armor?"

"You could say that. Anyway, he's really great, Fran. I want to give it a little more time."

"Must be dicey with you feeling so bad. I hope these feelings aren't the result of the pain pills."

Erin laughed again. "No way. He's nice, really nice."

"Sexy, too, I hope."

"Very sexy."

"Mmm-hmm," Fran said. "Just tell me he rides a horse."

"I don't know yet. I haven't been getting around much. Too busy with…other things."

Fran laughed. "I can imagine. Well, just don't worry me like this again. Okay?"

A few more words and they disconnected. Only when Erin slipped the phone back into her pocket did she realize how fast her heart was racing.

"So I'm sexy?" Lance asked.

Erin tried to let go of her anxiety. "You know it. Very. Don't forget that part." But she couldn't really bring herself to banter with him. Fran had sounded the way Fran always did. Surely it couldn't be her. "Now we have to let Tom know I called."

Lance reached for the phone and called Gage. When he hung up, all they could do was wait. Lance rose from the sofa and came to stand beside the rocking chair she had claimed for her own. "Let me get you something. We haven't been eating today. We need to keep our energy up. How about a peanut butter sandwich?"

She managed to smile at him and nod. She'd found heaven in his arms last night, only to wake to hell today. She stared at the house phone still sitting there as if it were a living and ugly thing. No, she argued, Tom will say Fran told him where she was. They still wouldn't know who was working with the bomber, but her heart insisted not knowing would be better than finding out it was Fran. Her head knew better. Whatever the price, they had to round up these killers.

She felt like a war zone internally.

Lance had just returned with a tray full of sandwiches and coffee when the phone rang. He swiftly set the tray on the small coffee table and reached for it. "You want to hear?" he asked her.

"Everything." She closed her eyes and waited, torn between hope and fear.

It was Gage. "I just talked to Tom. The suspect didn't

tell him your whereabouts. In fact, he said that after you called she left the office in a hurry. He said if this guy finds you, it couldn't be anyone else because nobody else knows. I'm sorry, Erin."

"Unless it's Tom," Erin said, clutching one final straw. "We haven't really learned anything at all."

"Sure we have," Gage said grimly. "You called your friend and told her where you were. She didn't tell anyone else but left the office. No one outside our small group knows you're staying with Lance, not even Tom. We've been talking about how no one knew where you were stashed, remember? Only this Fran knows, now. If that bomber shows up out there, you've all got your answer."

It was a long while before Erin felt she could try to swallow a bite of peanut butter sandwich. Lance was sitting cross-legged on the floor at her feet, plate and cup in front of him on the braided rug.

"Well," he said presently, "now that the bread is going stale, you want me to make fresh?"

"I'll pretend it's toast, and it's not that bad."

"Erin."

She looked at him and felt the worst urge to just grab him and run away with him from all this. Beg him to take her away to some place where they could find last night's heaven again, some place where they wouldn't have to sit watching a clock tick toward doomsday. "This feels like a countdown."

"It is." Using his arms, he swung himself around a bit so he could look straight at her. Meal forgotten, he raised one knee and draped his arm over it. "But it's the same countdown we've been on since you got here. If we're lucky, it'll be over in a day or two."

"Are you always so positive?"

He smiled slightly, the creases at the corners of his eyes deepening just a bit. "No. Not always. But watching you sit there as if you're carved out of stone and filled with the ice of misery makes me want to cheer you up."

"I'm lousy company right now."

"Understandably. It's okay. But we don't know how long this is going to go on before we get alerted, so how about we try to think about anything else? Pick a subject. Sports? Politics? What you'd like to be doing a week from now?"

Determinedly, Erin took another bite of her sandwich and washed it down with coffee that was growing cold.

"Freshen that for you?" he asked.

"Please."

He rose in one smooth movement, grabbed both mugs and disappeared into the kitchen. The minute he left the room she missed him. Now she was going totally over the top. Really?

He was right, however. She'd been involved in enough operations to know that sitting around brooding about this was not the way to go. She had learned a long time ago that the best way to handle the waiting was to talk about anything else. She'd spent hours on stakeouts or listening in on microphones while the other agents with her talked about their personal lives, or discussed the latest sports match or even what their dogs had been up to.

She needed to get over her shock about Fran and while the time in some better way than wondering, hoping and fearing the ball that was now in motion. All worrying could do was wear her out mentally and emotionally.

When Lance returned with fresh coffee, she summoned a smile. "Thanks. And you're right, I need to stop brooding."

"Kinda hard not to do. I get it. But it's not going to change a damn thing. You ever been on a stakeout?"

"I was just thinking about that. Yes, I have, and we always talked about anything else to pass the time."

"Trust me." He winked. "That second hand will move faster if we're not watching it."

She tried to laugh. "Like boiling water?"

"Same general principle." He put his mug on the floor and resumed sitting beside her.

"Wouldn't you be more comfortable on the sofa?"

"Too far away from you," he said bluntly.

She caught her breath. With those simple words he made the darkness spin away and reminded her of the light and good in life. "Oh, Lance…"

"Just promise me you'll hang around when this is over, take some more recovery time. I'd like to show you around my world a bit."

"I'd love to see more of your world," she admitted. "Fran asked if you rode a horse."

That drew a belly laugh from him. "Oh, yeah. Don't have any of my own right now, but I have plenty of friends who'll lend them to me."

He pushed himself up, picked up his plate and coffee to put them on the table, then reached out a hand. "Can you sit on the couch or are you too uncomfortable?"

She could sit on the couch, especially if he'd be right beside her. Compared to the way she'd been feeling the day he'd found her beside the road, she'd come a long way. Pain no longer overwhelmed her, and her fatigue had lessened, too.

Which didn't mean she was fit yet, but certainly a whole lot better.

She took his hand and walked the few feet to the couch. He collected her coffee, putting it and her sandwich in easy reach. "I should make us a decent meal," he remarked.

"No. Thanks, but I couldn't eat it." Instead she took another bite of peanut butter sandwich.

"So tell me, Erin. You said you eat out a lot. What are your favorite kinds of foods?"

"Mmm. Most everything. It mainly depends on my mood."

"Exotic cuisine? You won't find much of that in this town."

"When I'm in the mood for spicy food I like Thai or Vietnamese. Or sometimes Korean."

"I guess I need to brush up my cooking skills." He rested his hand on her thigh. It felt like a burning brand. "I used to go to a Korean restaurant all the time in Denver. Periodically I head down that way and stock up on kimchi."

"I love kimchi," she agreed. "Plain, in soup, mixed in my bibimbap. But I love other Korean vegetables, too. I tried making them once. On the one hand it took me an entire afternoon to prep all those vegetables. On the other I ate them for a week."

"We need to try that."

She nodded agreeably, wondering if the future would even allow it. There might be almost no future at all left anymore.

"Erin…" His arm wrapped around her and drew her closer. She tilted her head toward his face and melted inside when he kissed her lightly. "Don't sink back into the hole. We'll deal with all of this as it unfolds. You know that. No way to plan, nothing to do but wait. So back to food. Okay?"

"I could eat you up," she whispered. "But I don't dare right now."

"I know. Me either. Sure as I drag you off to my lair that damn phone will ring or the radio will squawk. My shining armor could get a little tarnished if I'm stumbling around trying to find my boots and my gun."

The image restored the smile to her face. "That might be one way to move the clock faster."

"And one way to get us into some real trouble." He dropped another kiss on her lips. "I'm going to make this up to you, Erin. But we have another problem to deal with first."

Which came right back around to the subject they were trying to avoid. She touched his cheek, winced a little as her shoulder protested. "I need to move around. Sorry."

"Go for it," he said, snagging another quick kiss. "Work the kinks out. If we can manage it, I might join you in pacing."

The voice called on time, while the long summer twilight still brightened the world. "I've got the address and directions, Harry. She's staying with a cop, so you're going to have to be extra careful. No police uniform this time."

"Tell me." He wrote down the directions on the notebook that was mostly filled with his calculations for his bombs. He supposed he'd need to hide that someplace for now. He hated the thought of losing it, though. Everything he knew and everything he'd discovered from the time he made his very first bomb was in that book. Prime evidence against him and irreplaceable for continuing his work. He had to hide it somewhere.

"How'd you find all this out?" he asked.

"The internet is a wonderful thing," was the obscure answer.

Harry wished he could access it, but out here there

were no hot spots. He supposed it was good he was getting a phone connection. Of course, that assumed the voice could find him if he ditched the damn thing. Maybe he should ditch the car as well, because if it was tracking him...

"Just remember," the voice said. "She can identify you."

That yanked him firmly back into line. He couldn't fathom the motives of the voice, or why it wanted to help him, but he guessed that didn't matter for now. He had to erase a witness. Later he could figure out a way to deal with the voice.

But it had set him a task. No police uniform to ease his approach to the house where she was staying. In fact, she was staying with a cop.

He turned that around in his head, considering the possible ramifications. Had the woman simply met up with an old friend? Or was this some kind of rural hick safe house?

The voice hadn't bothered to give him that information. Maybe it didn't know. And unfortunately, it had its number blocked so it was impossible to call back and demand answers.

He wasted a few more minutes thinking about how much he hated the voice. More than he'd ever hated the agent he'd tried to kill. Now that he wasn't quite so scared, he started thinking about that. Bombing the agent's house had exposed him. She could identify him. Before that all they had to go on was some unspecified means of determining that he'd made all the bombs.

He stared at the phone and felt loathing rise in him. So what if they knew the bombs were all made by one person? They couldn't prove it was him. They had to find him first, and he'd been safer from that before he tried to take out the agent.

Now he was in dung up to his neck and he couldn't figure a way out. What next, after he took out this agent? Was he going to spend the rest of his life dancing to the tune of an altered voice on his phone?

He swore savagely, and just barely stopped himself from smashing the phone. The voice had found him. The voice knew his name. The voice knew where he was. The voice had said it could track him.

Even if he stole another car and trashed the phone, how could he be sure it wouldn't find him again? It had found him the first time. What the hell was he caught up in?

The papers called him insane? They should only know about the voice.

Hidden in the trees, the road just far enough away that he couldn't be seen, he listened to traffic rumble past. It was slowing down as night approached, and the number of big trucks that rumbled by was growing.

He had to find a way to approach that house that sat all by itself in the middle of a clearing, from what the voice had said. He had to reach it and plant a bomb, then get away.

This was different from anything he'd done before, ever. Well, it wasn't going to happen tonight. He needed to make a plan. He needed to drive by the place and see what it looked like, not go by what the voice had told him. He didn't really trust the voice. Sure, it had got him out of the lab in time, but that didn't mean it gave a damn about what happened to Harry. No, the only thing the voice seemed to care about was killing one FBI agent.

Harry thought about that for a while. This voice must have a real problem with the agent. Maybe the Sanders woman had put the voice away for a while. Maybe this was vengeance.

Now that was something Harry could enjoy thinking about. He understood vengeance and savored it. He ripped the wrapper off a candy bar and opened another bottle of water. Roughing it wasn't his style. He decided he'd better take care of the call of nature before it got much darker.

There were worse places to spend the night than inside his car, though. Like out there under the trees with the bears and wolves he was sure must be around. In the morning he was going to take a drive. By tomorrow night, he figured he'd have a plan of some kind.

Mainly because he had to.

But no cop uniform? He started to think of other innocuous ways to make an approach. One would come to him. It always did.

By the time night began to settle and Lance moved through the house drawing all the curtains closed, Erin felt she had worked out her kinks. The pacing had been good for her, having a calming effect, and she began to feel the familiar coolness whisper through her mind, upset and despair being replaced by objectivity and determination.

The agent in her was waking again at long last, scenting the quarry, eager for the job ahead. She wouldn't exactly say that she wasn't upset about Fran or any of this, but it had receded to the part of her where she could place things on hold until she needed to deal with them.

She sensed Lance was doing the same thing. Occasionally he talked casually about nothing at all, as if they were nearly strangers. He browned some pork chops, then baked them in the oven with diced tomatoes, green peppers and cheese. A few herbs got sprinkled over the whole.

He also baked three small potatoes to go with it. Despite her lack of desire for food, as the casserole began to fill the house with its aromas, she felt her stomach growl. It amused her that in the midst of all this she could still get hungry.

It amused her less that she had to keep quashing an urge to talk Lance into running. She knew it was because of Lance, the man himself, and the way he had caused dangerous feelings to awaken in her. She wanted him, she wanted a chance to spend time with him afterward, to share in his life and find out if her own could be any better.

But first and foremost, she was an agent and she had an important job to do. If they ran from this killer, if he didn't show up…what innocent young woman would he kill next? She wouldn't be able to live with herself if she felt she had done the least thing that allowed him to continue his killing spree.

As they ate, she complimented him on the meal. "This is wonderful!"

"My own recipe. Although I've long since figured out that anything I think is original is probably in a cookbook somewhere."

She gave a stifled laugh as she spooned more tomatoes and green peppers onto her baked potato. "I can't even claim that much."

"Is it just lack of time that keeps you from cooking?"

She paused, considering it. In some ways her life had grown so routine that she didn't think much about the simple things. "Same way I use a dry cleaner," she said presently. "Anyway, nobody sane would have wanted to be in the kitchen with my mother when she cooked. She started lubricating early, and she didn't like anyone in her domain."

He paused before answering. "I'm sorry, Erin."

She managed a slight shrug. "Long time ago. She was an alcoholic, my dad was an enabler and hiding was the safest thing to do." Then she paused. "She hated me."

"What?" His tone evinced astonishment.

"She hated me. She tried not to show it, but I saw. I wasn't just a blind wall that everything bounced off. Anyway, it doesn't matter anymore. I survived."

Erin glanced up and saw Lance frowning. He swore quietly, then said, "Somehow I don't think the passage of years makes those wounds any less fresh."

"I don't know. I don't think about it a lot, but when you asked me about cooking… I think she's the reason I avoid it. The kitchen was her domain. God forbid anyone should set foot in there without permission. But, like I said, that was a long time ago."

He ate some more of his chop, then asked, "That have anything to do with your desire to become a caped crusader?"

Erin felt the mood lighten a bit and she was grateful for it. She'd survived her childhood and escaped at the first opportunity. She'd made something of herself. "I really don't know. I mean, wouldn't it have made more sense if I'd wanted to be a counselor of some kind?"

"I'm not talking about sense here. You became the biggest, toughest person you could, am I right?"

She almost squirmed. "Maybe."

He reached out to touch the back of her hand, then continued eating. "Not my place to analyze you. Let's just say that after an upbringing like that, I wouldn't have been surprised if you'd joined a gang."

She had to laugh. "No, Lance, you don't get it. I had to be perfect to please. I just wasn't quite perfect enough."

"Man. Okay, I walked into some thorns here. I'll back out. But later…later when this is over, I want to hear all about it."

"Several million people could probably tell the same story."

"Maybe. I don't know. I'm not interested in them, just you. Dismissing your experience because it could have happened to others isn't fair to yourself, is all."

Maybe he was right, she thought as she sliced another bite of pork.

He spoke. "I once heard a guy talk about burdens."

"Yes?"

"It was kind of interesting. He said when you're carrying a gigantic fifty-pound rock on your back, you don't hesitate to ask for help. But when it's fifty pounds of sand, you feel kind of guilty for making such a big deal out of some little grains of sand."

"So little problems add up?" She tilted her head. "I actually like that."

"I know I did." But he left it there, for her to think through however she chose.

After dinner she helped with the cleanup, glad to be doing something genuinely productive. It had been too long now that she'd been focused inward on her body, on her anger and even her fear. She'd been mentally and emotionally hunkered down, and next to useless. She hated being useless.

Time to pick up that bag of sand again, she thought wryly.

Later they played pinochle at the kitchen table with the dogs lying at their feet. She for one didn't think she'd be able to sleep at all, although she was concerned about Lance. Finally she called him on it.

"You hardly got any sleep at all last night," she pointed out. "I got a nap earlier. Your turn. You won't do anyone any good if you're woozy with fatigue."

"Okay," he said with surprising ease. "We'll go settle in my bed, ready to go, with the radio between us. Fair enough? Besides, the dogs will set up a racket if anything moves outside."

"Fair enough," she agreed. Even though it would be difficult to lie beside him and not make love again, she figured that inflamed fantasies would help pass the time. She had no doubt that if all they did was hold hands, she wouldn't be able to think about much else.

They took turns in the same bathroom, then changed into something that was both comfortable and serviceable. Not the way she usually dressed for work, but more like she would dress for field training. They both placed their holsters and weapons beside them on the table, and the radio was right beside Lance's head next to his gun. He made a point of turning up the volume, and the crackle filled the room with a pleasant white noise. The dogs wandered around for a few minutes before settling at the foot of the bed.

"We don't want to be able to hear anything?" she asked. Instinctively she wanted silence.

"I trust those guys and the dogs. If anything on two legs moves out there, they'll know."

"But…" She cut herself off.

He patted the bed and she lowered herself carefully beside him.

"But?" he pressed.

"There's only four of them. They've been watching for

a long time. A slip would be easy. They can't see every-thing...." She fell silent as he laid a finger across her lips.

"You only met four of them," he said quietly. "There are probably others out there, especially after today. What's more, they've done more operations like this than they can probably remember. They'll know how to spell each other, how not to get lax. Okay?"

The image of a large squad of men slinking silently through the forest, completely blacked out and ready, filled her head. Or maybe they weren't slinking. Maybe they'd picked their vantage points high in the trees. Maybe they could see everything. Maybe. But she also trusted his dogs. He'd said they'd let an intruder rob him blind, but that didn't mean they wouldn't create a fuss over one.

Lance shifted and drew her into the circle of his arms. "Let me know if I'm hurting you."

"You're driving me crazy. That's a whole different thing."

He laughed quietly. "Good. You drive me crazy, too. I'm glad I won't be the only one here suffering in silence."

She smiled into his shoulder, feeling the hum of de-sire throughout her body, but willing to just enjoy it as it was. Too many threats lurked in the night to risk be-coming inattentive.

But for now, she was happy just to be close to Lance. The bad things would come, creeping out of the dark most likely, but until they did, she made up her mind just to be a woman in a wonderful man's arms.

Chapter 15

Driving past the Conroe house on the gravel road in the morning gave Harry a full-on case of the willies. God, the place was in the middle of nowhere, at least by his reckoning. Once he had to cross that ground or go up that driveway, he'd be as exposed as a snake in the middle of the highway.

He drove by slowly, hoping this was a reasonable morning hour for someone to be on this road, and scanned the mailbox. Yeah, Conroe. That was it. A neat little house in quite a few acres of mostly bare ground. At least he thought the land was measured in acres. Worse, he could hear dogs barking. Damn! He wasn't even close and they were alerting.

Gritting his teeth, he stopped on the grassy shoulder and climbed out of his car, pretending to check a tire while scanning the setup. His nightmares couldn't have given him a worse target. He considered telling the voice to just forget it.

He made as good a mental map as he could, then climbed back in and drove away, wondering what the hell he was going to do now. Damn dogs...

He decided to hang out down the road a way and think about this whole setup. He prided himself on being able to solve problems, and even as his skin crawled now that he had seen his target, he tried to focus on the challenge. Yeah, he liked challenges. There had to be a way to get to that house without setting those dogs off.

"The dogs need to go," Lance remarked after breakfast, repeating what he'd said yesterday. "I won't risk them, and they might scare this guy off even though they're penned up. If he hears them alerting like they just did when that car drove by..."

Erin nodded. "You're right. I'm going with you," she announced.

"I'm not letting you out of my sight."

This time it was she who stole a kiss.

"Promise me," he said huskily. "Promise me you'll give me some time when this is over."

She looked up into his amazing blue-green eyes and answered that demand firmly for the first time. "I promise." It felt almost like a vow.

The dogs were eager to jump into the backseat of his SUV. They swarmed around a bit, so big that they had to make an effort to accommodate each other, but apparently eager for a drive. Lance threw a big bag of kibble in the back, then they were off, headed toward town.

Right about the time they hit the paved road, they passed a guy sitting in a car studying a map that was spread over his steering wheel. Instinctively, Lance looked. Wyoming plates. Nothing to worry about.

* * *

Harry watched them pass him and saw the dogs in the backseat. This might be his best time. No one at home, no dogs to create a problem…despite the daylight, he might draw less attention if he acted now.

It was tempting, but he continued to hesitate. He didn't want to have to wonder if his target was in the house when the bomb went off. Drumming on the steering wheel, listening to a heavy metal song in his head, he pondered his options.

No dogs now, maybe dogs later. He needed a distraction, he needed a way to draw all attention away from the Conroe house, and then he could waltz in and place his bombs. Not knowing how much time he might have made him uneasy. Ideally he'd walk in there at night, under cover of darkness…but there were the dogs. He needed to do something now, while the house was empty, while the dogs were gone. Then he'd have to make sure the woman returned. Well, if he had time, he could escape and watch from the woods. If he didn't have time, he could get inside and just wait for her.

He didn't have to blow Sanders up, although he preferred to because it left so little evidence. But he could shoot her and the guy she was with, and then he could leave a bomb behind for cleanup. By the time anyone showed up out there, the house would be cinders.

Yeah, a distraction. Something to keep everyone looking elsewhere, maybe even delay the return of the man, the woman and the dogs, because he needed some unimpeded time.

All of a sudden he noticed how dry the range was. It seemed almost to glow in invitation. Climbing out of the car he checked the wind direction. Then he began to smile.

* * *

Erin liked Mike Windwalker, the veterinarian, almost immediately. The dogs clearly agreed. They were all over him, tails wagging and tongues scraping his face. "I guess they forgot their last shots." Windwalker laughed. "So how long do you want me to keep them?"

"I honestly don't know, Mike. A few days maybe. Or I could want them back tomorrow."

Windwalker's smile faded. "Is there a problem?"

"Could be. I'll let you know."

The vet let it pass and took control of the dogs' leashes. "If you need anything, call. Want me to do a checkup?"

"Might as well."

When they were driving away, Erin asked, "Do the boys mind the kennel?"

"I guess I'm going to find out. Never needed to leave them there overnight."

Erin felt a twinge. "Lance, I'm so sorry. It's my fault..."

He shook his head impatiently. "Nothing's your fault. You tried to catch a killer. Everything that happens because of him is on his head. The dogs will be fine with Mike, and what I'm going to miss about them more than anything right now is having them on sentry duty."

She hadn't really thought of them in that context, but he was right. The idea that the dogs would bark had kept her feeling as safe last night as the presence of the radio beside the bed. She had slept, thanks to that, and she suspected Lance had, as well.

But if they were to draw the bomber to the house, the dogs would be an impediment. Still, she felt badly. She'd upended this man's life, had exposed him to a huge threat and she'd seen his relationship with those dogs. He loved them and they were his shadows.

Well, what the hell, she thought grimly. She'd messed up more than one life on her way to this point. Like Paul's, and who knew how many others apart from the criminals she helped apprehend.

She shook herself out of that train of thought, forcing her attention to the job at hand.

Lance spoke. "Since the bomber's unlikely to walk into the diner and draw a gun—he'd be pulped inside thirty seconds by Maude's frying pan and my neighbors—do you want to stop and get something to eat?"

"Still trying to keep things normal?" she asked. Her heart had begun skittering with nerves the moment they had left the dogs behind. This time, however, it was a familiar nervousness, the kind that preceded most operations for her. She could handle this.

"As normal as I can. The second hand moves faster, remember? Anyway, we're out, eyes are watching us everywhere, I'm sure, so let's take some small advantage of it."

It actually sounded good to her. He was right about one thing: while they were in town, in daylight, she seriously doubted the UNSUB would attempt anything. For a little while she could push the dark aside and try to enjoy some normalcy. Once they got back to his house, the shadows would close in again.

The diner was filled with a late breakfast crowd, many looking like retired ranchers. A group of older women had taken over a corner near the back. She and Lance chose not to sit near the window this time but she noticed he chose a seat that would give him a clear view of the door and sidewalk outside. Since it was at a table, she sat catty-corner and watched in the other direction. Some habits just wouldn't quit.

Lance was apparently determined to talk about anything except the problem they faced. "I like you," he said by way of nothing in particular.

She raised her gaze from the heaped plate of eggs, bacon and hash browns that had just slammed down in front of her accompanied by a huge stack of toast. Her heart accelerated in a different way. "I like you, too," she said forthrightly.

His smile was crooked. "That's good, since you're stuck with me until we get past this. So…are you planning to head back to Chicago once we snag this creep?"

Something about the way he asked warned her that a casual answer might be taken wrong. "I'll have to," she said slowly, honestly. "To wind up the case." She hoped that hadn't been interpreted as *get lost*.

He nodded and went back to eating.

For the first time it truly struck her that she might have become more than a protectee to Lance, that he might actually be hoping for something more than a one-night stand. Or even a fling over a few weeks.

Which brought a whole other set of demons raging up from buried places inside her. She had nothing to offer a man. Paul had made that clear. She lived inside a protective shell that apparently felt like thorns to those who cared about her. She was job obsessed…although since her wounding the thought of returning to work as an agent had grown less attractive.

Remembering some of the things she had thought about and Lance's description of her becoming the toughest person she could to compensate… She shook her head a little and reached for a slice of buttered toast.

Caped crusader? Who was she kidding? FBI agents performed an important service, but it wasn't the only service that needed doing.

But if she gave up her job, what would be left of her?

The question scared her because of how much it revealed about her. Because she didn't have an answer.

With all the months of recovery, therapy and retraining ahead of her, she had reason to fear that the Bureau might put her permanently behind a desk. Yes, that was her job most of the time, but would it be as tolerable if it became her permanent boundary?

But what other life was she fit for? Marriage certainly hadn't worked. Could she ever be remotely normal?

"Erin?"

She yanked herself out of thought and looked at Lance. "Yes?"

"Whatever you're thinking, it can't be that bad. Nothing's happened yet."

She gave him a weak smile even as she thought, *Oh yes it could be that bad*. She'd just discovered she was an empty husk filled to the brim with Special Agent. What if she were faced with the question of what else she could do with her life? Had she even given a thought to that except once, when she'd married Paul and discovered she wasn't cut out for that kind of intimacy?

But her gaze drifted back to Lance. He was different. He seemed neither intimidated by what she did, nor critical of the way she was. Of course, he wasn't trying to make a long-term investment in a future with her.

But what if he did? What if that should come to pass? It was unlikely and she knew it, but she asked herself anyway. Maybe she needed to stop being so focused on one thing and discover other things that could fulfill her.

Then a thought struck her so hard she lost her breath. Had she become a different version of her mother, wedded to a job rather than a bottle? A stunted personality, an addict with only one answer to everything?

"Erin? Do you need to get out of here?"

His perception astonished her. She was quite sure she hadn't made a sound. A forkful of hash browns was moving toward her mouth. Her plate was nearly empty.

"Erin?"

She looked at him and announced it baldly. "I'm an addict. My mother was addicted to alcohol. I seem to be addicted to the FBI."

She struggled to get her wallet, but Lance stopped her. "I've got it. Let's go."

Outside he opened the car door for her, but as she climbed in she noted the way he lifted his head. "Smoke?" he muttered.

"Smoke?"

"It's faint. God, I hope we're not having a range fire. It's a little early in the summer for that." He closed the door, then walked around to climb inside with her.

"Are range fires bad?" she asked.

"Very." As he answered, two fire trucks went roaring by, sirens screaming as they headed west down the main street.

At the edge of town they saw it: two large plumes of smoke rising to the sky. They appeared to be far away, but Erin was well aware that distances could be deceiving, and her perception of those plumes was based on guessing their size.

"Bad," Lance said. Just then the radio crackled and a voice spoke his name. He grabbed the unit and lifted it, pressing the talk button. "Go for Conroe."

"Lance," said Seth's now familiar voice. "We've got a range fire out here. It's miles from your house, and there's no reason it should jump the road anyway. But…we've got zero visibility out here. The wind is pushing a lot of that smoke our way. Stay in town while we reorganize. Right now we don't even have eyes in the sky."

"Copy, Seth."

"Just give us an hour or so. We'll figure it out."

"I read."

When he put the radio down, he pulled over to the side of the road. They watched the smoke plumes, which appeared to mash into some invisible barrier in the sky and flatten out before spreading. More cars with sirens passed them.

"You get a vote," Lance said.

She tore her gaze from the distant fires and looked at him. She felt certainty settle over her even as her heart quickened. It was time to be the agent engraved on her being. "We go in," she said. "No eyes gives him an opportunity. We can check around the house ourselves, and we can take him if necessary."

He hesitated infinitesimally. "You feeling up to it?"

She had one final score to settle, and the sooner she settled it, the sooner she could figure out her personal mess. "Right now I could take on anything." Anything except her own personal mess, that was.

He had gear in the back of his truck. Before they headed for the house, he pulled out some particulate masks and even two pairs of goggles.

She looked at them. "What the heck do you guys do out here?"

"Everything," he answered as he steered them back onto the road. "Chemical spills, fires, you name it. We don't have anyone else right around the corner."

Well, that made sense to her. They could probably call on help from elsewhere, but given the vast distances, how long might it take to arrive?

"All the local resources are going to be focused on that

fire," he warned her. "Until our team gets themselves placed in a good position, we're on our own."

"I get it. I also get that a range fire could provide an opportunity if the bomber is here."

"You think he'd start one?"

In her heart of hearts, she knew the answer. "This guy is capable of just about anything."

The smoke was beautiful. Choking but beautiful. Harry waited until it covered the ground in the direction of the Conroe house, then wrapped his face with a scarf and began moving through the woods. As the smoke thickened, even the tallest treetops began to disappear in the haze. All he had to do now was keep making his steady way under its cloak of invisibility and hope that the breeze didn't change direction.

The backpack he carried was heavy, containing two bombs plus his Glock semiautomatic. The Glock was another thing that baffled him. Shortly after the voice had first contacted him, it had turned up in his car. No license, no permit, nothing to trace it to him. But it sure felt better in the holster the last time he'd worn a police uniform than the modified toy pistol he'd worn before.

Of course, without that Glock he'd never have shot the agent. Looking back, he realized that what he should have done was offer a cover story about the report of a prowler. Sanders probably would have gone back inside. Why the hell would she think he'd just planted a bomb? Just a cop doing his job.

But no, he'd been startled, startled enough to set this whole insane mess rolling down to this moment where he was stumbling through a smoke-fogged forest, half choking, and trying to do yet again what he'd failed to achieve last time.

Something's wrong with this picture, he thought with grim humor. He'd had a good gig going until the voice. Oh, man, he wanted to get that guy. Once he misted the voice, there'd be no further threat to him. One agent gone, the one who could identify him, and then the only other person on the planet who actually knew who he was.

The longer this went on, the more he hated that voice. The more he wanted it gone forever. It was starting to creep into his dreams at night, evil and vicious and determined to use him toward its own ends.

Harry didn't like being used. He hated it almost as much as he hated being invisible to snobby young women. And he sure as hell hated being out in the woods, away from the city's sleepless protection.

He had to find out who was behind that voice. Somehow he had to draw this unwanted master out. He was willing to grant himself some small excuse for having been frightened by its first phone call. Of course he'd been wrecked by the knowledge that someone knew who he was and what he was doing. But he didn't want to keep playing the voice's games forever. He needed to regain his freedom to act and choose his own victims. All the fun of building bombs had gone away now that he was doing it for purposes other than his own.

When he reached the edge of the trees, he looked out at a bare area that was so full of smoke the Conroe house wasn't even visible. It looked like the worst pea-soup fog he'd ever seen roll in off the lake.

Perfect. The whole world had disappeared, and he could barely see the ground a few feet ahead of him. Like a Klingon warship, he had a cloak of invisibility. As long as the dogs weren't there again, he was certain to be safe. And even if they were, they'd be inside out of the smoke and probably agitated enough that an entire army could approach without their barking being taken seriously.

Besides, with the fire, it was unlikely Sanders and her boyfriend would even come back.

The fire had been a brilliant idea. Even better than he'd hoped. He had been listening to all the resources roar by him on the nearby road. Everyone's attention would be on leaping flames well behind him now. No one would be around here.

He would set two bombs in case one didn't work. He figured he could set them off during the night tonight, when the woman was tucked in a bed. And these bombs were big enough to erase the entire house. He just needed to make sure she was there.

Then he'd be done with one part of this misery. Finally. Glee began to fill him.

Erin couldn't remember ever having seen smoke this thick. Even though Lance had turned off the outside air intake, some of it made its way into the car. They were still more than a mile from the house when they both put on their goggles and masks. Creeping along became essential.

That creeping concerned her. It was taking too long. But it had another advantage. Just supposing the bomber had got to the house under cover of the smoke, he'd have to decide how to detonate his bombs. Most likely he'd use a timer, because there was no guarantee this smoke would clear soon enough for him to see the house from anywhere.

Maybe the guy had miscalculated. Of course, he might not have anything to do with the fire. Either way, this could put a halt to all his plans. How would he know if she was in the house now?

"This fire may screw everything up," she told Lance.

"Yeah, it might."

"If he wants me dead, he's got to be sure I'm there."

"I know."

She glanced toward him. "When did you become a sphinx?"

"Since I started thinking real hard. Listen, Erin, we could just get you out of here."

She almost sighed. "You know why we can't."

"I get it and I don't like it. I just had to make one more appeal to sanity."

"Sanity? More like this guy getting away with murder, and committing more of them."

He removed one hand from the wheel and held it out to her. She took it and held on to it. Amazing how comforting his grip had become. Nor did she usually roll into a potentially dangerous situation holding someone's hand. A new experience. She wondered if it was a new weakness, then decided it didn't matter.

Warm strength surrounded her fingers and she allowed herself to simply enjoy it. Little enough in her life to be enjoyed of late. At least she had found a good friend in her flight from nightmares.

Maybe she had also found something more, such as parts of herself she'd truncated so they wouldn't get in the way. She had some thinking to do.

But not right now. The house was growing closer, and perhaps they were being foolhardy to go against the wishes of her protection team. But the fire seemed just too damn convenient, especially when it had forced the team to reorganize and possibly withdraw for a while.

Nobody was watching Lance's house. And someone might have intended exactly that.

* * *

Lance should have been firmly focused on what might be awaiting them at the house, but he had been rocked to the core by Erin's comparison of her career to her mother's alcoholism. Did she really think she was an addict?

He didn't even begin to sense that in her, and was appalled by what it revealed about her poor self-image. Here she was, at the highest peak most people aspired to, a successful FBI agent, and she was considering that a failure? Oh, this woman had surely missed love in her life.

She had a right to think highly of herself and her accomplishments. Or at least to believe she was engaged in an important task. To compare it to alcoholism…well, it made his heart hurt. Once this was over…

Once this was over. It hung there in his mind as they got closer to the house. *Sure, what then*? he asked himself. Had he even managed to wedge himself just a little into her heart and life? Or would she go home to a life that she thought highlighted her failings rather than her strengths?

God, he needed to get through to her somehow. Or someone did. But now she'd been burned by her best friend. Corrosive indeed. He hated to think of the depths she was going to plumb if it turned out that Fran was working with the bomber to get her killed. Nobody could just brush that off.

"Erin?"

"Yes?"

"I know you promised me some time after this is over. Keep that promise. Please."

He could feel her gaze on him. "It's important to you?"

"Hell, yes. And don't forget it."

Then he turned into the driveway and somehow he knew, just knew, that hell was waiting for them.

* * *

The bomber heard the car approach. He cussed and hurried. The back door had been unlocked—fools, these rubes—and he'd decided to place a bomb under each of the two beds.

He had the second one almost ready, but time was against him. Working feverishly, he tried to hook the receiver to the detonator as he heard the car stop, heard car doors open and slam.

No dogs. Not that he cared right now. He was sweating fiercely all of a sudden and it was dripping on his hands, making them wet and slippery. There, at last the mechanism was in place.

Now to slip out the back door into the smoke…except then he heard the front door open, heard voices.

"We should check around outside," a woman said.

"In a minute. If he's already been here, he may have slipped away into the smoke. If so, he's using a timer, right?"

"Maybe. Or he could just be using a wireless detonator."

Harry's heart stuck in his throat. How did they know so much? How did they know he was even coming?

But then it struck him. The voice. It had warned him to run, and it had sent him here. Maybe it had betrayed him.

Rage turned his vision red as he lay beside the bed, with it between him and the door.

He heard a radio crackle. Heard a man speak. Couldn't quite make out the words.

Then the man said, "Ten minutes. Seth says they'll be here in ten."

"I heard," the woman answered drily. "Not very pleased with us, is he?"

"Can't say I blame him."

More were coming? Panic began to replace rage in Harry. He had to act and act fast, and if he didn't want to just end it all by blowing himself up with both of them, he needed to take them out now.

Moving carefully, he pulled the Glock out of the bag and released the safety. He could do this. Maybe he could even slip out the back.

Something wasn't right. Erin felt it, and looking at Lance she saw that he felt it, too. Maybe it seemed like there was a little too much smoke inside. She touched her fingers to her eyes and pointed back toward the bedrooms. He nodded and put a finger over his lips before saying, "I guess I need to make coffee for the guys."

As he spoke, he was pulling his pistol out of his holster. Erin did the same, taking hers in both hands, keeping it pointed downward.

Lance walked with heavy feet into the kitchen and turned on the water, clattering the coffeepot. Thirty seconds. Then he passed her her vest from the back of the chair.

Her fingers almost fumbled with her hurry, but then steadied. She'd done this before, and the familiarity drove away the momentary shakiness. She felt the Velcro grab, looked at him and saw him smoothing the last tape in place on his.

Now they were ready.

The weight of the Kevlar reminded her of her injuries, but they seemed far away right now, held at bay like a hungry animal by the adrenaline now rushing through her. Later there'd be time to notice, but not now.

Lance gave her a slight nod and began to move down the hallway toward the back of the house.

All of a sudden he swore. Erin, right behind him, asked, "What?"

"He must have just slipped out. See that smoke?"

Looking over his shoulder, she saw it. It was thick right by the door, a cloud.

"Clear the bedrooms," she barked.

He slipped into his room, pistol at ready, and she into the guest room. No one was there, but she caught sight of something that made her heart stop.

"The bombs are inside," she called out.

"Get to the door!"

She obeyed instantly with him right behind her. The radio started squawking. "He was just in here," Lance said. "Bombs are inside. He went out my back door."

"We're closing in," came the answer.

Then, with them standing to either side of the back door, Lance turned the knob and pulled it open.

A smudgy, smoky world greeted them. Erin stared into it, trying to see something. Anything. Then her eye picked out a swirl in the haze. Something had just passed.

She pointed. Lance nodded. Together they went out into the dog run in that direction.

Now they could hear their quarry. He'd come up against the fence. Metal clanged.

Lance keyed the radio. "He's here, dog fence."

"You need a smaller run," Erin remarked. Fencing half an acre meant that in this smoke they couldn't see the fence.

"There," Lance said quietly, pointing.

Again she saw the smoke stir. Raising her pistol, she aimed in that direction and began to hurry forward. Something inside her snapped. This was the end. Enough. One way or another, she was bringing this guy down now.

Forgetting everything, she began to run. He wasn't

getting away this time. No way. As she got closer, a hole seemed to open in the fog. She saw a figure trying to climb the eight-foot chain link. He was almost at the top.

"Freeze or I shoot," she shouted.

He froze, then started scrambling again. Spreading her legs, she took aim, gripping her pistol in both hands. Just like on the target range.

But before she could pull the trigger, Lance's gun barked beside her. The guy froze, a guttural scream escaping him. He tried to keep climbing, but as he moved again, she shot. Double tap to center mass.

Then he slid down the fence.

She had just enough time to see that the guy was holding a pistol before Lance rushed past her and dived onto him. The pistol went flying.

Then the cavalry arrived.

Epilogue

Erin emerged from the federal courthouse to a brisk, sunny Chicago day. Her testimony before the grand jury was now behind her, leaving only the trial which might be a year or more down the road. She paused on the steps and breathed in air filled with city smells, and realized she was still missing the fresher, fragrant air of Conard County.

She still had to walk carefully. Not everything had finished healing, and she was looking at probably another three months of recovery, and soon some physical therapy, before she might again be considered fit. She could live with it, especially since the psychologist had cleared her.

The inevitable wind caught at her jacket and tossed her hair, which she had allowed to grow out a little. It was a beautiful day, and it filled her with the happiness of being alive, something she suddenly realized she hadn't felt in a long, long time.

"Agent Sanders."

The familiar but unexpected voice caused her to freeze. Slowly she turned and saw Lance Conroe walking down the steps toward her. He appeared so different, wearing a business suit, that she almost didn't recognize him. He looked so good, strong and straight, and her heart fluttered with sheer happiness at seeing him, and not just a little anxiety. There was so much she hadn't told him when they talked on the phone.

"Where did you come from?" she asked, astonished. They'd been talking on the phone ever since she'd left Conard City, but he hadn't said anything about visiting.

"About four steps behind you," he joked, his aquamarine eyes reflecting sunlight. "You look wonderful." Without further ado, he slipped her arm through his and leaned over to snag a quick kiss. "Actually, I was waiting for you."

"But…" She stopped and let a smile spread across her face. "It's so good to see you!"

"It's so good to see you, too. Can I buy you a coffee or do you need to get to work?"

"I'm done for now. Let's get coffee. But why didn't you tell me you were coming?"

"Because I wanted to tell you some good news in person, if you're interested."

They began to descend the steps. "Good news?"

"I've been offered a job with Chicago PD."

She almost missed her step. He steadied her. "Lance…"

He was still smiling, but shook his head a little. "Let's get someplace inside where we can talk. My hotel okay?"

It was fine. She'd been obliged a rent a small apartment on the city's outskirts for the interim, and she was sure his hotel must be closer. A cab took them only a few blocks and soon they were walking into the elegant lobby.

A silence had fallen between them, but it felt pregnant with things that hadn't been said, that needed saying. They slipped into the hotel's quiet bar and ordered Irish coffees as they sat in a round booth.

Then they simply stared. Erin felt her eyes eating him up, soaking him in. She had missed him, but only in seeing him again had she realized just how much. It was as if an empty space in her had suddenly been filled.

"You look a far sight better," he finally said after their glass coffee mugs sat in front of them. "How do you feel?"

"Much better," she admitted. "Moving easier, sleeping better, an occasional ibuprofen but that's all."

"When will you go back to duty?"

"They want me to take another three months of convalescence." But she wasn't going to take it. She'd made up her mind about something, but was suddenly afraid to tell him. He was interviewing for a job here? Why?

She felt they were fencing, trying not to get to the heart of something, and she knew she was certainly guilty of it. But what about him? "Lance? I thought you were done with big city policing."

"I was."

"So why a job here? Did you take it?"

He shook his head slowly, his eyes dancing a little as if he were enjoying a secret. What secret? "Not yet. I need to talk to you first."

"Me? I don't have anything to say about it." Which was true, but then another thought struck her. "But, Lance, you have such a nice home in Conard County, and so many friends."

Then he dropped the bomb. "My home is wherever you are, unless you don't want me."

All the years of schooling her expression to remain

impassive didn't help now. She gaped. Her heart thundered with hope. "Lance?"

He shifted a little, revealing his discomfort. "I can't read your mind," he said. "So I'm taking a chance. Before, when you were at my place, we were mostly overwhelmed with this bomber coming after you. Speaking of which, how is that going?"

Another delay. She looked down, smothering a smile. At least she wasn't the only one who had difficulty with some subjects. "Well. We've got him. The bombs he left at your house contained the same contaminant, so we were able to hook them up circumstantially. But better yet, this Harry Wills has an outsize ego. He's been talking up a storm, enjoying an appreciative and sympathetic audience. Or maybe he just knows he's screwed regardless."

"Could be. It always amazes me when they don't lawyer up."

"Me, too. We got him one, but he won't shut up. He wants everyone to know that he was just teaching a lesson to some careless women."

"And you? Were you a lesson?"

Now it was her turn to shift uneasily. "No, he was ordered to come after me, the very first time, by someone who knew his name and said I could identify him."

Lance stiffened. "Would that be Fran?"

She nodded, her joy in the day completely dissipating. "Yeah. At first we thought the case against her was too circumstantial…until we found the receipt for the burner phone we'd been trying to track. Either way she was going to lose her job, but once we nailed her on the phone…" She shook her head. "Accomplice to attempted murder, obstructing a federal investigation… I'm sure there are other charges."

Lance asked the most important question. "But why?"

Erin lifted her gaze, feeling hollow. "I don't know. She was smart enough to listen to her lawyer. She'll probably never say. All Tom can figure is that it was some kind of twisted ambition, and she thought I was in the way because my star was rising and she wasn't. He said he wondered about it a couple of times when he overheard her telling some other agents she taught me everything I know. The amazing irony is that she located the bomber before anyone else. If she'd just turned him in..."

"She certainly went around the bend. Crazy."

"At this point who can say anything else?" She shook herself, trying to push the shadow of Fran into the background. She'd been dealing with this for weeks now, and somehow she needed to get past the betrayal. She couldn't allow it to ruin her life and living with unanswered questions was something every cop had to do. "Back to you," she said pointedly, hoping against hope that she hadn't misunderstood him.

Lance sighed, then smiled. "Well, this isn't easy."

"Why not?"

"Because I made a lot of decisions without consulting you, without knowing how you'd feel about them, and now I'm going to ask. Do you want me here in Chicago with you? If so, I'll accept that offer and be here in a month. If not, I'll go home."

Her heart was galloping now. He was giving her plenty of ways out, but she knew she didn't want them. Somehow she had changed during the time she had spent with him. Priorities had reordered. She'd faced some of her personal demons and was working on them. She was getting ready to make major changes of one kind or another. And she had hardly dared hope he might be part of them.

"Erin?"

She tilted her head. "You want that time I promised to spend with you? You don't have to come here for that."

"I want more," he said flatly. "I want an entire future with you."

The answer settled in her heart, as light as a feather, and she felt herself soar. "Then don't take a job here."

His face tightened. "Okay. Sorry."

"No," she said swiftly. "Look, I told you how bad I am at intimacy. Be patient."

"Then what are you trying to say?"

"I'm...I'm transferring to the Denver field office when I return to duty. If I return to duty."

He reached out and took her hand. She was glad of it, tired of this invisible wall that always seemed to be between them, knowing she was the cause of most of it. "If?" he repeated.

"I'm not sure I want to. Two near-death experiences make things look a bit different. I don't know what I'll do, but I have time to think about it. Your community college is talking about starting a criminal justice program, for example. The dean said I could chair the department."

He stared at her, then laughed. "My God, Erin, we've been coming at this from different sides of the same problem."

At last she was able to smile. "So it seems."

His hand tightened around hers. "I want you to be sure."

"I have three months, at least, to make up my mind. If you want me in Conard County. If it isn't important to you that I continue with the FBI."

"I swear the only thing that matters is that we're together. I love you, Erin. I think I loved you almost from the very beginning."

She gazed into his amazing eyes, feeling that love all

the way to her very core. He'd left big city policing for good reason, but was willing to take it on again just to be near her. The magnitude of that offer stole her breath. "You're wonderful," she said, her voice thickening a bit. Then she spoke words she had never expected to speak again. "I love you, too, you know."

His smile widened until it couldn't grow any broader. "I promised you another night together when this was over. I know there's a room waiting for us upstairs."

Her heart skipped, then began to dance. "Oh, yes," she breathed.

"Just one more thing," he said, pulling her a little closer. "Will you marry me?"

Joy drove the last shadows from her heart. She tugged her hand free and threw her arms around his neck, burying her face in his neck, inhaling the scent of her true home. "Absolutely," she answered, feeling more certain than she had ever felt in her life. "Don't you remember? The FBI always gets her man."

* * * * *

Don't forget previous titles in the
CONARD COUNTY:
THE NEXT GENERATION *series:*

CONARD COUNTY WITNESS
PLAYING WITH FIRE
UNDERCOVER HUNTER
SNOWSTORM CONFESSIONS
DEFENDING THE EYEWITNESS

Available now from Romantic Suspense!

MILLS & BOON®

Let us take you back in time with our Medieval Brides...

The Novice Bride – Carol Townend

The Dumont Bride – Terri Brisbin

The Lord's Forced Bride – Anne Herries

The Warrior's Princess Bride – Meriel Fuller

The Overlord's Bride – Margaret Moore

Templar Knight, Forbidden Bride – Lynna Banning

Order yours at
www.millsandboon.co.uk/medievalbrides

MILLS & BOON®

Why shop at millsandboon.co.uk?

Each year, thousands of romance readers find their perfect read at millsandboon.co.uk. That's because we're passionate about bringing you the very best romantic fiction. Here are some of the advantages of shopping at www.millsandboon.co.uk:

* **Get new books first**—you'll be able to buy your favourite books one month before they hit the shops

* **Get exclusive discounts**—you'll also be able to buy our specially created monthly collections, with up to 50% off the RRP

* **Find your favourite authors**—latest news, interviews and new releases for all your favourite authors and series on our website, plus ideas for what to try next

* **Join in**—once you've bought your favourite books, don't forget to register with us to rate, review and join in the discussions

Visit **www.millsandboon.co.uk**
for all this and more today!